To Mary
Happy Reading!

EDEN RISING

Andrew Cunningham

Copyright © 2013 Andrew Cunningham

All rights reserved.

ISBN-13: 978-1490463650

EDEN RISING

DEDICATION

To Charlotte and to Mom: Thank you for your love and support. You both made the writing of this so much easier.

PART ONE: COLLAPSE

CHAPTER 1

The Earth died in less than a minute. Maybe that's an exaggeration. It's not like the planet ceased to exist altogether. It just seemed like it. Cities were reduced to rubble. Millions of people died that day. I've since been told that 95% of the Earth's human population was wiped out. I don't know if that's true—I mean, who can know that for sure? It's not like we still have any of the technology that we once used to determine such things. But I do know that it was almost empty of people—live ones, that is—and that my life changed in an instant. Everything I had known was gone and my world would never even remotely be the same.

Ben tried to open his eyes. He could hear his name being called and felt a hand touch his neck. Looking for a pulse, maybe? The hand was soft, but cold. So cold. But then, so was he. He was disoriented and his head was pounding. His eyes flickered open, but it didn't make much difference. It was dark. After a moment his eyes adjusted to the blackness and he could just make out Lila looking down at him. She was only inches from his face and he could smell the faint scent of her shampoo. She was talking to him and the worry in her voice was apparent, but there was more. There was fear. No, it was more like panic. What had happened?

Lila was asking him if he was okay, but he couldn't answer. He realized he was shivering badly. Where was he?

And then it came back in an instant.

It all started with Richie...

*****

"Ben, I need you to do an inventory of ice cream in the freezer."

Ben looked at Richie, trying to read his face. Was this something real, or was his manager once again giving him a crap job in retaliation? He knew he was going to pay for it the moment he stood up to the creep for making jokes to the guys about Lila's small breasts. He just should have let it go. Every time in his life that he had the courage to speak out about something, he paid dearly for it. Sometimes it was just easier to shut up.

Maybe it was because he had a crush on Lila, or maybe because he was just tired of that pig making comments about the girls who worked there. It's why the girls only lasted a couple of months on average. They could sense the slime emanating from him. Ben had worked at Maiden Farms Dairy for five months, serving ice cream, washing dishes, sweeping up, all the while being told that he'd get on the grill "soon."

That was a joke. Ben knew he'd never advance to actually doing any cooking, but the economy was so bad, he was lucky to have any job. People were spooked. With rampant terrorism and the United States being in the crosshairs of just about every major nation these days, employers were scared to expand. "Keep everything at a minimum" seemed to be the rallying cry.

"Lila, you go with him."

Okay, maybe it wouldn't be so bad after all. Ben knew he finally had his chance to muster up the nerve to ask Lila out. He was seventeen. He was only about five years behind the whole world when it came to a first date. It was now or never.

Lila was sixteen, and a junior, a year behind Ben. Her shiny, black shoulder-length hair framed a somewhat average face, with the exception being a smile that revealed slight dimples and crinkly, playful eyes. Ben felt that, unlike many of the other girls, who were shallow and phony, Lila displayed awareness and intelligence.

Ben shrugged on his coat, opened the freezer door and walked in, with Lila right behind.

"Whoa, it's cold in here," he said.

"That's why they call it a freezer, you dumb schmuck," responded Richie with a mean smile, as he slammed the door behind them.

"What a jerk," said Lila.

Ben didn't say anything. He was still smarting from Richie's words. At a time when Ben needed all of his confidence, the timing of that comment sucked.

Lila sensed Ben's embarrassment. "Hey, ignore him. He's an idiot."

"Yeah, I know," mumbled Ben.

"I'm glad we're alone for a few minutes," said Lila. "I wanted to thank you."

"For what?" He finally looked at her and felt his heart skip a half-dozen beats.

"For standing up for me. Melissa heard Richie make those comments about me to the guys. She said you called him on it. That was brave to do with a sleaze like Richie. You're paying for it now, aren't you?"

Ben got a momentary burst of courage and mustered up a smile. "Well he thinks so, but I'm in here alone with you, so I'm not complaining."

He looked down, expecting some laughter from her, but all he heard was a quiet, "I'm glad."

*****

An ear-splitting screech pierced the moment. The lights surged in brightness, then flickered, before dying altogether. Ben fell to his knees clutching his head. The pain was unbearable and he couldn't breathe. The screeching disappeared, but was followed by a hissing and crackling. He tried to call out to Lila, but nothing would come. He lost consciousness.

*****

"Ben, are you okay? C'mon, wake up."

He finally found his voice, but his head was still pounding. "I'm okay...I think. Are you?"

"I think so," replied Lila. "I'm scared. Really scared. What happened? I passed out and I don't know how long we've been in here. I'm really cold!"

"Nobody checked on us," said Ben. "Richie probably lit out of here. Of course he'd forget us."

Lila helped Ben up.

"I'm afraid to open the door," she said. "What's going to be out there?"

"I don't know, but we'll freeze to death in here."

Ben was shivering so badly, he could barely walk. He pushed on the inner handle and the door opened.

How could anyone be prepared for the world we were entering? We were kids. Acne was our biggest concern. Okay, I checked out CNN sometimes when I was online. I knew that we were pissing everybody off. It had something to do with bringing democracy to the rest of the world—forcing it down their throats is what I heard. It was our way or the highway. Things had become ugly even within this country. Everything was "us" vs. "them," and everyone was a "them" if they didn't agree with "us." I didn't even know who "us" was! Like every other kid, I was doing my best to ignore it all. It really didn't concern me. Maybe I should've paid more attention. But then again, would it have mattered? I would still be walking into hell.

Everything was quiet. Ben pushed the door open further. All the lights were off, even the emergency lights, but it was daytime, so light shone through the windows. Then he saw the people. Everyone was asleep. Customers were slumped over the tables, in some cases with their head in their food. Richie was lying on the floor directly in front of the freezer. Ben spied two waitresses lying nearby.

"Omigod!" exclaimed Lila in a whisper.

"They're all unconscious," said Ben.

They couldn't bring themselves to talk loudly in the tomb-like atmosphere.

Ben leaned over Richie to feel the pulse in his neck. There was none. He fumbled for his wrist and did the same. Richie was dead. Ben jumped back in panic.

Lila was looking at Melissa's body. She bent down and checked for signs of life. When she turned toward Ben, tears were running down her face.

"They're dead. They're just dead. There's no blood or anything. They're just dead. Why?"

"I ... I don't know," answered Ben. "Maybe there was a gas leak or something and we were saved by the freezer. But where are the cops or the fire department?"

They looked at each other and had the same thought. They had to get out of there. Ben grabbed Lila's hand and they made their way to the front door, each dreading what was on the other side of it.

It was far worse.

Cars were stopped in the middle of the street, drivers slumped over in their seats. People were lying on the sidewalks. Ben didn't have to check them. He knew they were dead. It was one thing to see the adults, but seeing little kids dead was something else altogether.

Then they smelled the smoke. Ben looked down the block and saw buildings on fire. There was a single car on fire as well, and he could see the form of the driver engulfed in flames. They pulled out their cell phones at the exact same moment. Both phones were dead. Traffic lights were out. There were no alarms, nothing. Just total silence. No, not total. Ben heard a dog barking.

He felt a cold wave of panic growing inside him, but Lila's presence forced him to suppress it. "I'm not going to lose it in front of her," he told himself. Still, his stomach felt like it was about to erupt.

"The cars," he said suddenly. "The cars didn't crash when the people died. The cars died too. See how they're just stopped in the middle of the road? The cars died at the same time as the people … at the same time all the other electricity stopped."

"I don't understand." Lila's voice was cracking. "They're all dead. People, cars, lights, phones." A bird flew by. "But not the animals." She started to shake uncontrollably and seemed to lose the ability to stand. Ben helped her into a sitting position on the sidewalk, where she broke down and sobbed. As Ben held her, he felt his own tears washing down his face. She suddenly rolled away from him and, on her hands and knees, began to throw up. That was enough for Ben. He did the same, uncontrollably heaving until there was nothing left to come up. When they were done, they sat holding each other, saying nothing, wondering what had just happened to their world. Then they realized that their families were probably dead as well, and the sobs began again.

It didn't occur to us at the time that if there was no bomb and all the electricity was dead, what caused the fires? I learned later that it was cigarettes. Most of the cities in the world burned out of control, and it was simply people dying with lit cigarettes. What may have started as a couch fire, consumed a whole house. The breeze took it to the next house. Whole blocks went up in a matter of minutes. Cities burned for days. In some ways, it was good, as the fire took many of the corpses with it.

"I know the answer, but I've got to check on my parents," said Lila, when they had cried themselves out.

"I know. Me too. But I don't want to. I'm just having trouble believing that any of this is really happening," replied Ben. "And to think that I was so excited just a little while ago, because I was just getting up the courage to ask you out."

Lila looked up at him with a sad smile. "I was hoping you would. You know, I'd give anything just to hear Richie call you a dumb schmuck again. It would mean none of this is real."

Ben squeezed her harder. "Yeah, Richie doesn't seem so bad now." He got up and helped Lila to her feet. The pain in his head was subsiding. "Let's go check on our parents. Then we can figure out what to do from there."

It was a couple of miles to Lila's house, and another mile beyond that to Ben's, but they just walked it slowly, not talking, trying to take in the devastation around them. This part of town had no fires, but the dead were everywhere. By the end of the two miles, they were almost immune to the sights. Almost.

They arrived at Lila's house. Everything looked normal from the outside.

"You ready?" asked Ben.

"No," Lila answered in a tiny voice. But she moved robotically toward the front door anyway.

Her mother had been making the bed, and seemed peacefully at rest, spread across the mattress, sheets still clutched in her hands. They found Lila's father lying on the back lawn where he had been cutting the grass. Lila never said a word.

"Do you want to bury them or something?" Ben finally asked.

Lila shook her head. She looked at Ben.

"Is it bad that I don't want to bury them? I just want to leave and never come back. Is that wrong?

"I don't know what's right and what's wrong," replied Ben. "I don't know what I'm going to think when I see my family. Let's leave, and you don't ever have to come back. Is there anything you want to take?"

Lila went to her room while Ben waited in the living room. When she came down, she had changed out of her waitressing outfit and into jeans and a t-shirt. She carried a small backpack with some more clothes and some personal items. They walked out of the house silently.

Halfway to Ben's she asked, "What does it say about my life that—other than a couple changes of clothes, a toothbrush and toothpaste, and some other things from my bathroom—all I could think to take was a picture of me with my parents? Nothing else."

"That we're already in survival mode?"

"Maybe. Do you think anyone else is alive?

"God, I hope so," said Ben. "Whatever happened, the freezer must have protected us. There's gotta be other things that offered protection. Someone's got to be out there."

"Is that a good thing or a bad thing?" asked Lila. "I've seen all those apocalypse movies. The end of the world seems to bring out the worst in people."

There was something funny about that comment and Ben

found himself suddenly laughing. "Sorry," he said. "I can't believe I just laughed with all this around me."

"Laughing might keep us alive," answered Lila.

They were at Ben's house. No one was home. His parents were probably running errands—now dead. There would be no way to track them down.

Lila reached out and took his hand in hers. "Maybe it's better this way. You don't have to see them."

"Maybe. But at least you got to say goodbye to your family. I don't know which is worse."

"They're both worse."

"Yeah, I guess."

"The sun will be going down soon," said Lila. "How do you feel about staying here tonight?"

Ben nodded his head. "I don't know how I feel, but it makes sense. And we can figure out what to do and where to go from here."

Neither one knew where to begin. They knew they had to prepare for the night ahead, so Ben hunted down candles and matches, while Lila searched through the lukewarm refrigerator and the kitchen cabinets for something to eat. It was all done mechanically—they had no more emotions to vent. They discovered that the water wasn't working, so they couldn't wash up. They took turns going outside to relieve themselves. As the sun went down, they closed all the curtains and locked the doors, Lila's "apocalypse" comments still hanging in the air.

Lila found some leftover spaghetti and meatballs in the now dead fridge, as well as bread and butter. They sat at the kitchen table with a single candle to see by, neither of them overly hungry, as they stared at their cold spaghetti.

"I can't eat," Ben finally whispered. "Seeing as how my mom made this spaghetti and she's now dead, it's just creepy." He was trying desperately to hold back the tears.

"Did you have a good relationship with your parents?" asked Lila.

"Yeah. My mom was great. My dad was okay. He was always afraid I wasn't going to be enough of a man, so he tried to get me to do 'manly' things. He took me to the rifle range once—That was a joke. I really sucked at it—and signed me up for boxing, which again, I sucked at, and hated too. My mom knew I hated boxing, so she signed me up for karate. I still do that ... well ... did. I'm not any good, but at least I like it. I have ... had, I guess ... a brother in the Marines. We liked each other."

Ben broke off, shards of memories of his brother filling his head. He could no longer hold back the tears.

"Where was ... is he stationed?" asked Lila, trying to divert his attention from the past.

"Camp Pendleton in San Diego."

"Well you don't know that he's dead. It's a long way from Massachusetts to California."

"Maybe," said Ben, "But have you noticed that we haven't heard any jets? Don't you think if there was life in another part of the country, they would be checking up on this area? Sorry, I don't mean to be negative."

"Look around us. I think you have that right."

"How about you?" asked Ben. "You like your parents?"

"Kind of. I think I'm a good person, but they had a way of making me feel worthless. I never got to do anything. It's like they didn't want to let me out of their sight. I had a sister who was a lot older than me who got into drugs and died of an overdose. It was a long time ago and I was young, but I think it changed my parents."

"I'm sorry."

Lila changed the subject. "So what do we do?"

"I was thinking about that. We can't stay here. It would be too hard. We don't know where people might be who are alive, so it doesn't make sense to search for them. I think we should make a decision to go someplace and if we run across people, that will be a bonus."

"All these dead bodies will be smelling soon, and there might be disease," said Lila, "so I think we have to stay away from cities and towns for a while."

"Yeah," answered Ben. "It's also September. It's going to get really cold soon. With no power, we'll freeze here. It doesn't make sense to go west—that'll be just as cold as here. I'm thinking Florida. It'll be warm year round."

"That makes sense. We'll probably have to walk the whole way. Or maybe we can find some bikes. Are you sure all the cars are dead?"

Ben nodded his head. "From what we've seen, but we can try them."

Lila moved over to Ben and put her arms around him. "A few hours ago I barely knew you. Now all we've got is each other. That's about as weird as it gets. We're both going to have to be so strong, and I don't know how, because I'm really, really scared. We have no idea what's ahead."

She was quiet for a few moments, then sat up and said, "What's that?"

Ben saw it too. There was an bright orange glow peeking through a break in the curtains. They headed to Ben's room for a better look and were left speechless at the scene before them. The Boston skyline a few miles to the east was an inferno. Although much of what they saw was just a brilliant glow illuminating thick black clouds of smoke, Ben could actually spot flames coming from the Prudential and John Hancock towers, the two tallest landmarks in the city. It left them feeling totally defeated—just one more incomprehensible moment in an already incomprehensible day.

They spent the evening in a numbed silence, glued to the window, not moving, not talking, holding hands in a desperate attempt to hang on to something familiar. Finally, exhaustion overcame them. They slept that night fully clothed, lying on Ben's bed. As he was drifting off, it hit Ben just how radically their lives had been altered. They were surrounded by dead people. People who, just a few hours earlier, were going about their lives without a clue that they were on the verge of ceasing to exist. Fear of what lay ahead produced fitful sleeps and a lot of tears. He and Lila were just teenagers—and somewhat repressed teenagers at that. How would they survive?

CHAPTER 2

For the first time in my life, I was lying next to a girl. And yet, even though we spent much of the night holding each other, it was out of fear, not passion. It would be easy to think that this was an isolated incident, that it was only this area of the country that was hit by ... well, whatever hit us. But I knew differently. I knew the whole country was dead. What I wouldn't know for a long time was that the whole world had suffered the same fate. I spent the night thinking of all the things I'd never do again — the list was mind-boggling. I thought again and again of my family. I thought of my father, and his unsuccessful attempts to make a man out of me. I had no choice now. But the fact was, I had never been so scared in my life. Part of me felt that I had to be strong for Lila, but I secretly wanted her to be strong for me. I needed her. We needed each other. I thought of Richie's last minute decision to put Lila in the freezer with me. That split-second moment of randomness changed my life. I now know that I wouldn't have survived without her.

They got up with the sun, thankful to be done with the demons that had caused so much sleeplessness during the long night. Neither one was hungry, and they sat at the kitchen table looking at each other.

"We've got to do this," said Lila, breaking the awkward silence. "We've somehow got to find the strength to make a move or we may as well just sit here and die. But I'm so scared."

"So am I," agreed Ben. "I knew I should have taken 'End of the World 101' when they offered it last year." He looked down, embarrassed. "Sorry, lame attempt at a joke."

Lila gave a wan smile. "I like them. Like I said yesterday, we need some humor. There sure isn't any of it out there."

She continued. "So where do we start?"

"Well, if we're really going to make this trip—and I really don't see any other choice—we have to stock up on supplies," said Ben.

"If there aren't a lot of people out there, finding replacement supplies as we go shouldn't be too much of a problem," reasoned Lila. "But we have to find some basics. Let's make a list."

Ben found some paper and they began their survival list. It included freeze-dried and/or canned food, maps, backpacks, propane stove and fuel, cooking utensils, tent and sleeping bags, survival books, weapons, and first-aid supplies, including antibiotics.

"How about we spend today gathering the stuff and tomorrow packing it, then be off the next day?" suggested Ben.

"I guess that's realistic," said Lila. "I think we should leave as soon as we can. I'm really afraid of the smell and disease."

"I am too," agreed Ben. "Maybe if we're lucky, we can get out of here by tomorrow. The highway would be the most direct route, I suppose."

Lila didn't say anything, which prompted Ben to ask if anything was wrong, "besides the obvious," he added.

"I know the highway would be the fastest route," began Lila, "but I ... I don't think I could live with the concrete and the car after car after car filled with dead bodies. I need trees. I need to hear animals and see birds. I know we'll see bodies wherever we go and avoiding the highway will slow us down a lot, but I just don't think I can do it."

"I'm okay with that," said Ben. He suddenly realized that Lila's survival was intricately linked to nature. And his survival was intricately linked to Lila. "Why make a bad situation worse? Who cares when we get to our destination? In fact, I just had an idea. Doesn't the Appalachian Trail run some of the way into the south? We can look at a map and see where we can hook up with it. We'll be in nature for a long time and see fewer bodies. I bet there are towns along the trail we can hit up for supplies."

For the first time, Ben saw some hope in Lila's eyes. She got up from her chair and came around to Ben, who stood up. She embraced him.

"Thank you," she murmured. "Thank you for understanding and thank you for your idea. I think that would be great."

With a plan in place, they set about their search. Leaving the sanctuary of Ben's house was difficult, anticipating the sights that awaited them. They had seen enough forensic crime shows to know that with each passing day, the bodies would look less and less life-like.

There were two bikes in Ben's garage. They figured the bikes would help them get the job done quicker. Their first stop was a AAA office down the road. They walked in as if it was still open for business. In a scene that was to repeat itself at every store they visited for the next couple of days, until the smell kept them from going in, the employees were all slumped over their desks, with a couple of customers lying on the floor. They gently stepped around the dead people and went about their business.

"I would say maps of any state we might go through, as well as any other information that might help us, booklets and things," suggested Ben. "Hopefully they have something on the Appalachian Trail."

"They do," replied Lila. "I just found it."

Their next stop was an Eastern Mountain Sports, where they figured they could find most of what they needed. They each picked out top-of-the-line backpacks and sleeping bags, as well as a tent that folded into practically nothing. They found a compass (not that either one of them knew how to read one), raincoats and hiking boots, as well as a good small propane stove and some bottles of propane. They picked out a large selection of freeze dried food. When they got to the knife department, they considered their choices carefully. They each settled on a Swiss Army Knife, a multi-function tool that included pliers, and a longer knife with a sheath that they could strap to their leg.

"We've got an awful lot of stuff," observed Lila.

"Yeah, I think we can say goodbye to the bikes for today. Let's lug it all outside, then we can go next door to the supermarket for a shopping cart."

Ben almost suggested that Lila wait there while he got the cart, but quickly realized that neither one of them wanted to be alone for even a minute at this point. To come back and find the other gone was just too terrifying for them to think about.

As they pulled out a cart Lila said, "I know this might be a stupid suggestion, but should we take some money while we're here? What if we do run across people? Would some of them still value money? Would we need it to trade for things?"

"I don't know, but what's the harm in having it. It doesn't take any space."

"I'll see if there are any registers open," said Lila. "Wow, do you notice how easy it's become to just take what we want?"

"We have to just keep thinking survival. It's the only way we can close our eyes to all this. Speaking of survival, I'm just going to pick up some cans of nuts or some chips," replied Ben. "I'll be right down Aisle um," he looked up at the signs, "Four."

"Do you mind talking as you go?" asked Lila.

"As long as you talk back," answered Ben. He turned into the chip aisle and stopped dead in his tracks.

Lila, noticing the silence, called out. "Ben, are you still there? Ben? BEN!!!" she screamed. She ran past the registers and reached Aisle Four. Ben was standing with his knees half buckled and was holding onto one of the shelves. In front of him was a woman still half standing, slumped over her shopping cart.

"Ben, are you okay?" Lila asked.

"My mother." It came out as a hoarse whisper. He then collapsed to the floor and sobbed with an intensity Lila had never heard from anyone before. This went on for fifteen minutes, Ben trying to catch his breath in gasps while alternately throwing up. Lila sat beside him and rubbed his back the whole time, not saying a word.

Finally he stopped and was silent for a few minutes before starting to talk. He spoke in a whisper that Lila could barely hear.

"Already, she doesn't look normal. She looks deformed. I expected to find her at the house. When I didn't, I accepted the idea that I'd never see her again. It's so much worse to run into her like this." Ben continued, and started to cry again. "And you know the worst part? The part I'm never going to get out of my head? She was just putting a bag of chips in the cart. I'm the only one in the house who eats chips, so her very last action in the whole world was for me."

"What would you like to do?" asked Lila gently.

"Could we just lay her down on the floor and cover her with something?"

Lila helped Ben pry his mother's fingers from the cart and rest her on the floor. It took a few minutes, but they found a plastic tarp in the back room and laid it over her.

"I love you mom," said Ben, his voice cracking, and he turned and walked out of the store, with Lila trailing behind.

They pushed the shopping cart home. Ben was lost in thought, so Lila let him have his time. When they got home, Ben went upstairs to the bed and lay in a semi-fetal position. Lila came up and got in bed next to him and held him tightly, as much for herself as for him. She worried that he might never come out of it.

The next morning, the emotions of the previous night had passed, but Lila knew that Ben had been deeply affected by the experience. He had slept soundly, but cried out several times in his sleep. When that happened, Lila had squeezed harder against him. When he woke, he seemed determined not to mention his mother.

I never realized just how much I loved my mother—how much I needed my mother—until that moment. She was always there to protect me from my father's compulsion to shape me in his image. She provided the sensitivity in my life. I realized that Lila reminded me of my mother. Maybe that's what attracted me to her. She had my mother's kind nature. And for that I was truly grateful. I also knew then that I had to get as far away from there as possible.

"I need to get out of here," announced Ben. "Do you think we could leave today?"

"I was going to suggest that," said Lila, with relief in her voice. "It's funny that yesterday we could just step over people and not give it a second thought. All of a sudden, I'm freaked out by it."

Ben pulled out a Massachusetts map. "You think we can ride our bikes with full packs? We'd make better time until we reach the Appalachian Trail."

"We can try, answered Lila. "What's the best route?"

"Let's see where we are. Okay, here's Newton. I think Great Barrington is the best place to pick the trail up. It looks like it's about 120 miles. It's a straight run along the Mass Pike." He looked up at her, gauging her reaction. "It's highway, but it'll get us to nature sooner."

"I can do it," said Lila. "How long do you think it will take?"

"Good question. How fast do bikes go? We'll be going slowly. Maybe ten miles an hour? If we put in two six hour days, that should probably get us there."

"Do we need guns?" asked Lila out of the blue.

"Yeah, I think we'd be stupid not to have any. But I have no idea if there's a gun store around here. I suppose we could take them off some dead cops."

Lila was shaking her head before he finished the sentence. "I can't do it. I don't know if it's because they're police or because I can't bear stealing something off a dead person. But I just can't do it. Not yet. I know that might change, but not now. How about we look in the phone book."

"I forgot they made phone books," said Ben. "I always just go online."

They found a gun store in the Yellow Pages that was only a few miles down the road, not far off the highway. They would stop on the way.

Their backpacks were packed within the hour. They had been able to fit everything in or on them, but they were awfully heavy, and Ben regretting having never had an interest in lifting weights to bulk up. He was pretty thin. That was one of his father's big complaints about him. They left the house, Ben knowing he'd never see it again. He refused to look back at it as they went to retrieve the bikes. He tried a few cars on the way, but they were all dead. Walking past the supermarket where they had left his mother was difficult too. All he could think about was getting away.

They picked up the bikes and mounted them.

Lila looked at Ben. "We're really doing this."

"We are."

With that, we started our new life. No fanfare. No goodbyes. A lot of fear. Some hope. But mostly a sense that we really had no idea what we were doing. We weren't survivalists. Suppose we had to shoot an animal for food? Assuming I could even hit one, which was doubtful, what would we do with it? We were unprepared for this. Wow, is that an understatement. It would have been almost comical if it weren't really happening to us. From the moment we left the "comfort" of my house, I realized one thing. If we were going to survive, we were going to have to toughen up ... quickly!

CHAPTER 3

The journey didn't get off to a good start. Ben hoped it wasn't an omen. The bike idea didn't work. Their packs were heavy and every time they made a turn the packs shifted, often causing one of them to wipe out. Finally, after Ben hit a curb and banged up his knee, they abandoned the bikes altogether. They thought about alternatives, including a wagon or an adult-size tricycle. They stopped at a bike shop, but it didn't have any of the tricycles. Finally, they just decided to walk.

"Once we hit the Appalachian Trail we won't be able to ride a bike or drag a wagon anyway," said Lila, "so we may as well get used to walking now."

"I still think the highway is our fastest route to the trail," said Ben. "The further west we go, the fewer cars we'll see, so hopefully it won't be too bad."

"As long as I know it's leading to the woods," replied Lila, "I'll cope with it."

We were trying our hardest to ignore certain things, such as the lack of electricity and the lack of mechanical noise. Every so often I would approach an abandoned car and reach over the driver to turn the key, just in case something started working again. Nothing did. The absence of traffic lights and headlights was still spooky to us. At night we would look toward Boston and see only darkness, interspersed with glowing pockets. The fires that destroyed much of the city had pretty much burned themselves out, but the smoke and the smell remained. The only breaks in the silence were the barking dogs. As long as we were near homes, the sound of the dogs was incessant. It was sad, but scary at the same time. Pets were going to die from hunger and thirst; zoo animals the same. There was nothing we could do about it. It would have been nice to have an animal with us as a companion, but the work involved was more than we could think about. We were both on overload. Just trying to pack cat or dog food would have been too much—our backpacks were heavy enough as it was. Lila brought up the fact that soon the dogs that were free would be running in packs, trying to find food. That made them dangerous. More than ever, the idea of carrying a rifle and a pistol was appealing.

We began to realize just how noisy our world had been: cars, music, TV, people talking, planes overhead, sirens ... the list was endless. While there was a part of us that appreciated the quiet (minus the dogs), we were children of the 21st century. Noise was a part of our existence. We didn't know if the electricity would ever come back on, but we had to prepare for it never being in our lives again.

It was all almost too much to think about. It was the same way with all the dead people. It wasn't that we were ignoring them, we just couldn't bear to think about them as human beings. That gave them personalities and lives and we couldn't deal with that. So we had to pretend we didn't care, knowing full well that deep down we cared very much.

They found the gun store and were once again faced with something they knew nothing about. So they decided to go with what felt good. They each ended up with a Sig Sauer 9mm pistol, based on a sign next to it that touted its quality. For rifles, Ben chose a Remington R15 Bushmaster rifle, because it was light, and, he had to admit, it was cool looking. After trying other small rifles, Lila ended up with the same. They considered shotguns, but everything seemed too heavy, and weight was a big issue. The Bushmasters had magazines that held four rounds, and the Sigs held ten. Finding the ammunition to go with the weapons was an adventure, but eventually they succeeded. They picked up a gun cleaning kit, then found some pamphlets on gun safety and shooting basics, and followed the directions on how to load the weapons. Ben felt embarrassed that he didn't have the faintest idea—other than from watching it on TV—how to handle the guns, and in fact, found himself much more nervous than he would have thought. Finally, they found holsters for the pistols and straps for the rifles.

As Ben put on his holster, he looked at Lila and smiled. She looked back at him and started laughing. There was something ridiculous about what they were doing, and they both sensed it. Two days before, they were just two really average teenagers. Now they looked like Bonnie and Clyde. The laughing was a gigantic release for them.

Two doors down was a large drugstore, so they went in and picked up a first aid kit and some other items. Lila went into the pharmacy to search for antibiotics. She looked for a recognizable name and eventually came away with some packages of a five-day antibiotic that she had remembered from when she had taken them a few months earlier. Ben, meanwhile, searched the shelves for anything that might be of use in their travels. He came across a display of condoms and, after a moment's hesitation, scooped up a handful and put them in one of the pockets of his pack. He was embarrassed, but was aware of how he was feeling about Lila. Who knew what might happen in the future?

They noticed now that when they went into an enclosed space, there was a faint sickening smell. It was time to keep as far away from the dead as possible, and was time to get on the road for real.

It was already mid-afternoon, so they knew they wouldn't get a lot of distance in, but if they could at least go far enough to be somewhat away from people, it would be a beginning. They started along the highway.

That first day they rested a lot. The packs were heavy and the hiking boots new. They knew that with time they would get used to carrying so much weight, but at this point, Florida seemed a long way away.

"I remember flying to Disney World one year," commented Ben during one of their breaks. "We got on the plane at seven in the morning, and were in one of the parks by noon."

"We'll be there by noon," responded Lila. "I'm just not sure what year."

"I wonder what we could have done differently with these packs," said Ben. "Should we try to find a wagon?"

"We've never been the last people on Earth before," replied Lila. "We're bound to make mistakes. We're bound to forget things—some really obvious things probably. We just have to hope that as time goes on, we get smarter. But no, I don't think a wagon would help. It would be awkward and would have its own problems. We're doing okay."

Although she was keeping it as light as possible, Ben could sense something was troubling her.

"What's wrong?" he asked.

"Everything," Lila answered, after a moment of contemplation.

"Why are we doing this? I mean, what's the use? Even if we make it to Florida alive, which is a big 'if', what do we do when we get there? Do we spend the rest of our lives foraging for food, living a life of … of what? Everything we've ever known is gone. Everything that made our life what it is no longer exists. Everything that was important …" She went silent, big tears rolling down her cheeks.

Lila's comments made me think. Really think for possibly the first time in my life. Where some of these thoughts came from, I don't know. Maybe it was simply fear, the fear that if Lila gave up now, it would be all over. Or maybe it was something else…

Ben took his time in answering. He was being forced to confront the answers to questions he didn't want to ask.

"Okay," he said. "This sucks, to put it mildly. But it could be worse. We could be dead." He held up his hand as Lila tried to interrupt. "Yeah, I know, maybe it would be better to be dead. But would it? I've never been very religious. In fact, not at all. But I do believe that we're on this planet for a reason. If we were here for a reason before all this happened, do we lose that reason now? Or, does the reason become even more important? Let's face it. We were killing this world. Maybe not you and me in particular, but humanity in general. There was so much hate, so much uncaring. Could it be that we're still here because we can somehow make a difference? It's not going to be easy. At any moment, one of us could refuse to go on. It will be up to the other to be the strong one. We don't know what's ahead of us, but I can only hope it will be something that will make us grow somehow. That we'll be happy. We might find some other people. Maybe we are the beginning of a new civilization. Maybe something good will come out of all of this. We don't know. But if we choose to die, we'll never know, and there's something wrong with that. Suicide has never solved anything. It's running away. Shouldn't we always try to live up to our fullest potential?"

Ben caught his breath. "Lila, I've never been so scared in all my life. The odds are stacked so far against us, it's ridiculous. We haven't talked about all the ways we could die on this trip, and you're right, there is no guarantee we'll even get to Florida. But doesn't that make you kind of mad? I mean, someone caused all this. Or maybe it was nature ... a sun spot. I don't know, and we probably will never know, but doesn't it make you want to stand up and say 'fuck you, I'm going to survive anyway!'? If something happens to you, then yeah, I'd pack it in and use one of these guns on myself. But as long as we're together, we have a chance to see what the universe, or whatever, has in store for us. Who knows? We could make a world around us that's better than what we had. All I know is that I can't do this without you ... I don't want to do this without you."

Lila looked up through her tears and managed a half-smile. "You know, you can be pretty deep." But then the cloud returned and she jumped up, picked up a stone, and threw it with all her might. She reached down and picked up a second, then a third. Ben just watched, knowing this was something she had to get out of her system. The tears were flowing heavily now, and with a look of sheer anger, Lila stuck her middle finger in the air, and screamed, "Fuck you! Fuck you! Fuck you! You can't stop us! You can't stop us ..." She collapsed to the ground, her head in her hands, shaking and sobbing. Ben started to approach her, but she waved him off.

Finally, she stood up shakily, looked at Ben with an expression he hadn't seen before, but one that told him that something within her had just changed, and quietly said, "Let's go."

At that point, fear turned into determination, for both of us. Lila blowing off steam at our invisible enemy confirmed that we didn't want to die. We wanted very much to live. For what, we didn't know, but the fact that we wanted to live was a victory in itself. For now we were emotionally okay, and that's all we could hope for. Our newfound sense of purpose came at the right time, too. Coming across the Whitmans the next day showed us just how debilitating fear could be.

Judging by the road signs, they figured they only covered about ten miles that afternoon. But that was okay. They were on their way. They got off the highway and found a secluded spot in a small grove of trees. They had stuck water bottles in their backpacks and poured a couple of them into a small telescoping pot they had picked up at the sports store. They heated the water on their tiny stove and cooked a couple of their freeze-dried meals. They had forgotten flashlights, and in fact, weren't even sure flashlights worked—were they considered electric?—but that was okay. Frankly, they were afraid to show a light at night. They didn't know who was out there.

They set up their tent, unrolled their sleeping bags and crawled in. They knew sleep would be hard to come by, but they had to try. As he lay next to Lila, Ben knew the shock was beginning to wear off. His body was stirring with feelings for her. Almost on cue, Lila leaned over and gave Ben a soft kiss on the cheek. She nestled up next to him and closed her eyes. Ben kissed her head and slipped his hand in hers. Surprisingly, they both fell into a deep sleep.

They woke up feeling rested for the first time since the ordeal began. Ben opened the flap of the tent, the dew dripping to the ground. They both had to go to the bathroom, but realized that they hadn't thought much about the logistics. Lila had remembered some toilet paper, but neither of them had thought of a shovel to dig a hole in the ground. They had no choice but to wing it. Lila found a sharp rock to use to dig a shallow hole. They knew that it really wasn't necessary to dig a hole—no one would be coming along this way, and considering all the dead people out there, a little poop wouldn't matter—but it was a sign of civilized behavior. Ben headed off in the opposite direction. He realized that it was the first time since the supermarket that they had been out of each other's sight.

They made a light freeze-dried breakfast—their appetites hadn't yet returned—and they used the water to wash their faces and brush their teeth. They rolled up their sleeping bags and folded up the tent and were on their way bright and early.

The trudging was tedious. Ben knew it would get more interesting when they reached the trail, but for now it was everything Lila had dreaded, miles and miles of concrete and cars filled with bodies. The smell—even in the outdoors—was ripe. At one point they came across a service area with a gas station and a convenience store. Lila found some vapor inhalers, used for stuffy noses. The menthol smell helped cover up the odor of decomposition. While they were there they grabbed some bags of chips and nuts, and some more waters and sodas. They also used a bathroom they found that contained no bodies. Even though they couldn't flush, using a real bathroom—even a service area bathroom—was a treat of sorts. They brought water in from the convenience store and spent some time washing up. They also noticed that already, they could use the bathroom at the same time without embarrassment.

Around mid-afternoon, they had dropped into a mindless gait when they were sharply brought back to reality by a cry from off the highway.

"Hey, it's a couple of kids. Wait! Stop!"

A middle-aged man and woman came over the rise, waving their arms at them.

I had thought that finding another person alive would be an exciting moment for us, but I found myself oddly annoyed. One look at Lila told me that she was finding it less than joyful, as well. Maybe it was being called "kids"—even after just a few days we had ceased seeing ourselves as kids—or maybe there was some jealousy of suddenly having to share Lila with someone else. Maybe if it had been anyone but this couple, it would have been different.

"Yoo hoo! Hold on there!"

Lila turned to Ben, made a face, and said, "Yoo hoo?"

They were stereotypes from a bad movie. He looked like he was on vacation, with a blue Hawaiian shirt and khaki shorts. He was wearing a bad hairpiece and had a pot belly. She was a bleached blonde with a poorly-fitting set of dentures, dressed in a flowered summer outfit.

"I can't believe we've found someone alive. Thank God!" said the man. He thrust out his hand. "I'm George Whitman. This is my wife Bunny." Ben knew that if he looked at Lila, he'd burst out laughing. They shook hands. "I'm Ben. This is Lila."

It's interesting that a situation we initially found funny could turn so pitiful so quickly. We realized that this couple may have survived the initial disaster, but they were destined to follow the rest of humanity—quickly. That much was obvious. I also wondered what we must have looked like to them; rifles slung over our backpacks, holsters on one leg, and long knives strapped to the other. I was hoping we looked a little scary. But the "kids" comment had put an end to that.

The Whitmans looked scared and confused. They hadn't yet been able to think rationally. Ben wasn't sure they ever would.

"We live in Worcester," began George. "We were in the middle of a home invasion and were in our panic room."

"When George insisted we should build one, I told him he was crazy," interrupted Bunny. "But he was right."

"So," continued George, "these people with ski masks broke into our house. We made it to the panic room just in time. We weren't in there more than a few minutes when all hell broke loose. Our lights went out and suddenly we couldn't breathe. It felt like the end of the ..." He looked around him, embarrassed. "Well, you know ... Anyway, none of our surveillance monitors worked and the phone died, so we couldn't call the police. We must've stayed in there about twelve hours ..."

"Not that we would know," piped in Bunny, "since our Rolexes stopped working."

"Finally we took a chance and came out," finished George. "Wouldn't you know they were all dead. Have you heard what happened?"

"There's no way to get information," said Lila, "so we really have no idea."

"No one else you've met had any idea?"

"You're the first we've met," answered Ben.

"A lot of Worcester burned down," said George. "We're headed for Boston. You should probably come with us."

"Thanks," said Lila, "but we just came from that direction. There's nothing back there. Just a lot of dead bodies."

Bunny started crying.

"You don't have to be so blunt, young woman," replied George in anger. "I'm trying to let Bunny know that it's not as bad as it seems."

"But it is," said Ben. Any patience he had disappeared when George yelled at Lila. "Look around you. How can this not be as bad as it seems? And I suggest you prepare for it. Shielding her isn't going to help the situation. You need to make a plan. Winter will be here in a couple of months. Are you sure you want to be here with no electricity? Do you have any food or water? Weapons?"

"But there has to be someone in charge," sniffled Bunny.

"There's nobody," answered Ben. "You have to be in charge of yourself."

"Well we're heading to Boston and I think you kids should come with us. You can't just wander around without an adult. How are you going to survive?"

Lila had had enough. There was nothing constructive she could say. She started back on the road west without a word, leaving the Whitmans behind. She knew Ben would follow momentarily.

Ben tried to reason with them one last time. "Please listen to me. You need to plan. You need to find supplies. And you need to stay away from the city. Disease will start to spread from all the dead people." He looked at them with sadness, knowing he was making no impression whatsoever. "We've got to go. I wish you both the best of luck." With that, he turned and followed Lila.

"No, you've got to come with us," yelled George. "You can't be out here alone."

Ben's last image of them was of Bunny sitting in the road crying and George throwing his hands up over his head in frustration. He caught up to Lila, who was crying as she walked, and put his arm around her.

How many more people were there like George and Bunny? People who didn't have the common sense to do what they needed to. I seriously doubt that the Whitmans lasted more than a month. I wondered if there was more we could have done, but there really wasn't. We were hardening ourselves to the reality of the situation, and while we would have gladly helped anyone who needed it, the Whitmans clearly didn't want it. That brought up the question: Of those who did survive the initial event, how many died within days or weeks, simply because they were unable or unwilling to live?

CHAPTER 4

They walked further into the evening than originally planned. Putting as much distance as possible between them and the Whitmans seemed like a good idea. The whole encounter had disturbed them.

"Well, on one hand," began Ben, as they journeyed down the highway, "it shows that other people did survive. But if they're all like George and Bunny, this world is in a lot more trouble than we thought."

"Do you really think they wanted us to go with them because they thought we'd be safer with them, or was it because they knew they would be safer with us?" asked Lila.

"Probably a little of both," answered Ben. "Mostly though, I think the whole thing is slowly driving them a little crazy. It's too much. They don't know how to handle it, so they don't do anything at all."

"We don't really know how to handle it either, but at least we're doing something," said Lila. "Maybe it's just the process of 'doing' that's the answer. As long as we keep trying, we're bound to make some right decisions."

"My mom used to say that people who kept their minds active, like playing Scrabble or doing crosswords" said Ben, "tended to be less confused as they got older. Maybe this is like that. As long as we keep doing something, we're better prepared to survive."

The further west in Massachusetts they went, the less congested the highway was. That came as a relief to them, as the smell dissipated slightly. As much as possible they ignored the dead people in the cars. When they did sneak a glance, they were sickened by what they saw. Many of the cars had their windows closed—the occupants had been using their AC—and the heat from the sun had bloated the bodies badly.

They came upon another service area. It took them close to an hour from the time they saw the sign telling them the service area was just ahead to the time they finally arrived. By car, it would have taken them a couple of minutes. Another reminder of how drastically their world had changed. They decided to check out the convenience store. Passing a car in the parking lot that had its door open and the driver lying on the ground, Ben picked up the driver's keys and tried the ignition. Nothing. Just what he expected.

"I still wonder what happened," he said as they entered the convenience store. They put handkerchiefs over their faces to help mask the smell. "What could have caused all this?" He picked up a five-day old Boston Globe. Lila was perusing the magazines and books.

"I don't know," replied Lila. "Is there anything in the paper that would give us an idea that they were expecting something to happen?"

Ben flipped through it. "Nothing that I can see." He was quiet for a moment.

"Anything wrong?" asked Lila.

"Not really. I just got to the sports page. The Red Sox lost an important game the night before all this happened. I was watching it and was really disgusted with how they played. Can you believe they're all dead now? It's the little things that keep popping up, like baseball or my favorite TV shows. They're all gone."

"I was just about to start driver's ed," said Lila. "I guess that's out. But," her eyes lit up. "I love baseball and was in a softball league. We should pick up a couple of gloves and balls. Maybe we can play catch sometime ..." She felt oddly guilty at suggesting it, and dropped the subject. She scanned the magazines again. "I love to read, but nothing is real anymore. I hope someday I can pick up a good novel again and enjoy it without thinking of the past."

"Hey," exclaimed Ben, who had wandered to the other side of the store. "Flashlights. The disposable kind. I wonder if they work. Nothing else seems to." He grabbed one off the shelf and switched it on. A bright beam of light shone across the room. "Wow, it does. Okay, so why does this work when just about nothing else does?"

"Don't know, but let's count our blessings. Flashlights will come in handy."

Ben grabbed four of them. They found some more chips and nuts, along with some cans of food, water, and soda, and a few more inhalers for the smell, then went to find a bathroom. To their dismay, the bathrooms were full of bodies. They knew it was time to stop thinking about using real bathrooms anymore.

They headed back to the highway and continued west. Dusk had arrived by the time they found a good camping spot. They chose a place up a hill by the side of the highway. It was in a small copse of overhanging trees, surrounded by boulders, and the seclusion made them feel safe. They set up their tent to the sounds of thunder.

"That's kind of a nice sound," said Lila. "Familiar."

"Some pretty dark clouds coming this way," observed Ben. "Let's hope the tent doesn't leak." He looked up at the branches overhead. "Although the trees should provide some cover."

They heated beef stew from cans they took from the convenience store, ate quickly, then crawled into the tent, exhausted from the day. They didn't use the flashlights, as they were still cautious about who, or what, was out there, and didn't want to advertise their presence. They settled into their sleeping bags, deep in their own thoughts.

The rain came in sheets. The thunder and lightning was violent, accompanied by a strong wind. Ben hoped the tent would hold. They had their backpacks in with them to keep everything dry, but it made for a crowded space.

The thunder and lightning eventually subsided, but the rain continued to pound on the tent, making it sag in places, but so far there were no leaks. Ben was lying on his side, facing Lila in the pitch black.

"Give me your hand," said Lila quietly.

"You going to read my palm in the dark?" asked Ben.

He could sense her smiling. She took his hand, put it under her shirt and placed it on her left breast. A shot of excitement coursed through Ben's body.

"You came to my defense when Richie made fun of my small breasts." She spoke in a breathless whisper. "I wanted you to feel them for yourself."

Ben's hand explored the area. He moved over to the other breast. Finally he had enough air to speak. His heart was pounding. He felt as if he was going to pass out.

"Th ... they're perfect. They're like peaches. They're beautiful."

"Thank you," she whispered. "In a real short time I've developed some pretty intense feelings for you. I feel like we're a part of each other, emotionally, spiritually, and physically. Maybe that's what they mean by 'soulmates'. I just wanted you to touch me. I want to touch you. We're all we have. We might be all we ever have." She was quiet for a moment before continuing. "But, as much as I want to feel your touch, I don't want to have sex yet. Is that okay? I know it's probably not fair to you, and I'm not trying to tease you. I'm just not quite ready. We may be two of the last people on earth, but I'm still sixteen. All the things I've ever looked forward to are gone. The future I imagined doesn't exist anymore. Maybe I still want or need something to look forward to. Does that make sense?"

"Uh huh," answered Ben, feeling a little dizzy.

"But don't worry," said Lila, squeezing his hand. "When I am ready, you'll be the first to know. Just please be patient as I work through it."

Ben finally found his voice. "You're amazing. That's all I can say. I have the same feelings for you. I think that's pretty obvious, but I also respect you deeply—your strength as we make this journey, your common sense, and your courage. I want to make love to you, but I'm willing to wait until you're ready."

He realized that his hand was still resting on her breast. He retracted it. She reached over and took his hand back, replacing it where it had been. He leaned over and kissed her on the lips. He hoped he wasn't too awkward. She responded tenderly. She slipped her hand under his shirt and hugged him. Then they fell asleep in each other's arms.

What can I say about that moment? The old clichéd line in books when two people are in love is: 'the world ceased to exist around them'. In our case, the world really had ceased to exist. But I wasn't so sure anymore that I wanted to find civilization. Could we build our own world? A world without the noise, without the petty problems? Or was I just basking in the feel of Lila's body? No, a change was happening within me. Of that I was sure. Here we had been on our journey for only a few days, and I was beginning to appreciate the peace that had come over the world. We hadn't yet talked about it, but I think Lila was feeling it too. Maybe that's why we were so disturbed by George and Bunny; they reminded us too much of the life we had left behind. Unfortunately, we were brought back to reality the very next day.

They woke up to bright sun, still in each other's arms. They had barely moved all night. Despite the devastation around them and all they had witnessed since that day in the freezer, they had smiles on their faces. They were determined to take any small joy they could find.

"Have you ever wondered about us ending up in the freezer together?" asked Ben when they had been on the road a few hours.

"All the time," answered Lila. "I think of Richie and what motivated him to have me help you at the last minute. Was it some divine intervention that he had no control over, or was he being his usual slimy self and he just accidently did a good thing? Sometimes I break out in a sweat when I think of how close I came to being one of 'them.'"

They had been trudging up a long incline for the last hour, and finally reached the top. They sat to catch their breath and drink some water. Below them, the trees of central Massachusetts were beginning to show their color. The expanse of highway cut through the hills like a long gray scar. Cars littered the road.

"It looks like time just stood still, doesn't it?" asked Lila. "In the movies they would all be wrecked, but here it looks like people just parked their cars in the middle of the road."

Ben couldn't speak. At that moment he was overcome by the silence. Other than a slight breeze scattering some leaves, there was nothing. It seemed that even the birds had stopped singing in reverence for the dead. There was a sudden lump in his throat and he felt tears trickling down his cheeks. He thought of his parents and his brother. The loss consumed him every day.

Lila reached for his hand, sensing his thoughts. "I don't know if there's a heaven or something else, but I know they are looking down on you. They know how much you love them. It goes beyond this world, I know it does."

"I don't know what I would do if you weren't with me," answered Ben quietly. "I've never been very brave. I'm trying. I'm really trying. But if it weren't for you, I don't think I would make it. I feel like such a coward even saying that to you."

"You are anything but a coward," said Lila. "Maybe you do need me, but I need you just as much, and you've been there for me. We're not going to get brave overnight, but each day we're going to get a little stronger."

They sat there for an hour, hand in hand, getting used to the new silent world before them. Finally they started back on their way, still unsure of what to make of it all.

A little while later they rounded a long bend and Ben's attention was suddenly taken with something in front of them. "Lila, stop. What's that?"

About a quarter of a mile ahead, the road was strewn with what looked like rocks. It was so out of place, it had an ominous feel about it.

"I don't know." They started walking again, but a bit slower. They finally got close enough to see more clearly. "Omigod! It's body parts," cried Lila.

Without thinking, they both covered their faces with their handkerchiefs and got out their nasal inhalers. There was really no way to avoid the mess—parts were everywhere. The source of the bodies became apparent when they saw a school bus stopped in the road. Its door had been pushed open and out of every open window hung entrails. It was most likely a school sports team headed for a game. Arms, legs, heads, and every body part imaginable lay in heaps all over the road and embankment. As if almost on cue, Ben and Lila heaved up their last dinner and breakfast. The smell was overwhelming and the sight was the worst either had ever seen.

"Dogs?" asked Lila.

"Or coyotes," answered Ben.

A moment later, from out of the woods bordering the highway, came a dozen coyotes, warily eyeing Ben and Lila.

People out west figure they have the market cornered on coyotes, but anyone in Massachusetts who has had a cat snatched off their porch can tell you that we have a surplus of Eastern Coyotes. They could often be seen at night walking down the town roads. I had always heard that coyotes didn't usually attack humans. But there was something scary about these. Like they hadn't heard that bit of news.

Ben slowly opened his holster and took out his Sig. It still felt unfamiliar in his hand. They hadn't even had time to practice with their guns. He cocked the gun by retracting the slide. Lila followed suit. For the first time, they felt they were in real danger.

"We should try to scare them off," whispered Ben. He held his pistol in the air and fired. He was surprised that the recoil was less violent than he was expecting. The animals scattered, but only for a moment. They quickly reformed their group, this time closer to the road.

Lila reached around for her rifle, putting the Sig back in her holster. "I think instead of shooting in the air, we should shoot at them." She aimed and shot at a coyote. She missed, hitting the concrete in front of the animals, scattering them.

"Let's keep moving as we shoot," shouted Ben. He wasn't watching where he was going and tripped over a pile of remains. He landed within inches of a dismembered, and fairly mutilated head.

The coyotes attacked. Lila shot her last three rounds, surprisingly hitting two of them. Ben quickly got up with his rifle in hand and shot all four of his rounds, hitting one. They set down their rifles and pulled out their pistols and started firing.

They weren't very good, but with all the rounds they somehow managed to hit half the coyotes. The other half retreated to the edge of the road to regroup. Ben set down his backpack and opened it, pulling out rifle and pistol bullets for each of them. He handed Lila hers and they reloaded. He put his backpack on and they started down the highway. He didn't think they'd attack again, but they did.

With fewer animals to shoot at, their hit count went way down. They managed to hit two between them with their rifles. One reached Lila and jumped on her. The others shifted direction toward the downed prey. Lila was momentarily managing to hold off her first attacker with her rifle between her hands, which he had in his teeth. With the animals bunched so closely, Ben took out his pistol and fired into the group, hitting two more. One took off, with the remaining animal focusing its attention solely on Lila. Ben ran out of bullets. He picked up his rifle and swung it like an ax, hitting the coyote at the base of its neck, killing it instantly. It fell into a heap on top of Lila.

Lila was screaming. Ben pushed the animal off, pulled her up and held her. But it wasn't enough. She was in sheer panic mode. She pushed away and looked around, wild-eyed. She wasn't focusing on anything in particular, but was walking in circles. Ben tried to talk to her.

"You're okay. You're okay. They're gone."

She tried to pull away, but Ben held on tightly. Finally, Lila collapsed in his arms, shaking so badly that Ben didn't know what to do. He began to wonder if the coyote had injured her.

"Did he hurt you? Are you bleeding? Look at me. Look at me!"

Lila looked at him through tear-soaked eyes.

"Are you okay?"

She nodded weakly.

"Okay, we need to get out of here. Can you walk?"

Again she nodded.

Ben collected their things. He put her Sig in its holster and strapped her rifle to her backpack. He put his backpack on and held onto hers with his left hand. It was extremely heavy, but he had to carry it or drag it. He helped Lila up with his right hand and supported her as they walked. She was barely conscious, but was somehow able to move her legs, allowing Ben to keep her moving down the road. He didn't know if it was emotional or physical trauma. They walked that way for more than an hour. When they were long past the carnage and, Ben assumed, past the danger, he moved Lila to the side of the road.

"I've got to set you down," he said gently. His back was killing him and his arms felt like lead weights.

Lila was nonresponsive. How she had walked that distance, Ben couldn't fathom. He turned and stretched, and found himself looking at a small lake on the opposite side of the highway.

"C'mon, just a little further. There's a lake over there. That'll be a good place to camp."

Ben helped her up and half carried her across the four lanes of highway to the edge of the lake. He let her sit against a rock while he scouted out a good place to camp. About 300 yards around a bend in the shoreline, far from the highway, Ben found a secluded spot. They needed a break, so he made the decision not to move from the spot the next day—maybe longer if Lila didn't come out of her private hell.

He went back for Lila and helped her along the water's edge to their new home for the next couple of nights. While she sat staring at the water—or nothing in particular—Ben set up the tent. After what they saw today, he knew neither of them would be hungry, so he helped Lila into the tent. He took off her boots, helped her off with her pants and slipped her into the sleeping bag. He thought about changing her shirt—the one she had on might have the smell of the coyote on it—and decided that she needed to wake up in something clean. He found the last clean one in her backpack, propped her up and pulled off her shirt. Replacing it was a bit more awkward, but he maneuvered her arms into the new shirt. She slept through the whole process. Ben knew that if she could wake up in something fresh and clean, it would make a big difference.

We had made it through our first life or death situation of the journey. I just hoped Lila would be able to see it that way. I was really worried. Maybe a night's sleep would help her come out of it. How many more of these were ahead of us? We had only been on the road four or five days—I had already lost track—and we had a long way to go. That's why we needed the next day to rest and regain our strength.

CHAPTER 5

The morning that greeted them was warm and sunny. Lila had woken up once during the night screaming and thrashing about. Ben calmed her down and held her til she once again fell asleep. He crawled out of the tent. Lila was still asleep. He took out the propane stove, the collapsible pot, some water, and made tea. He sat looking out at the calm lake.

"Any tea for me?"

Ben jumped at Lila's voice. He turned to see her head sticking out of the tent. She looked exhausted, but at least had the makings of a smile.

"Good morning," Ben replied, relieved to see her up.

"This is beautiful. How did we get here?"

"What do you remember?"

Lila frowned and looked down as she tried to recall. "I don't know. Not much. Fragments really. Like a bad dream, but I know it was real. Coyotes everywhere. A big one on top of me. I think he was drooling." She shuddered and looked down at her shirt, ready to rip it off. She looked up with a crooked smile. "This isn't the same shirt."

"I didn't want you waking up in the other shirt. Don't worry, I was a gentleman."

"No," she answered. "You're my hero. I don't know how you did this. I don't know how long it took you. You had to carry my pack too, didn't you? You did all that? Not now, but someday, I want you to tell me the story of the coyotes and how we got here." She knelt down behind him and gave him a hug, then looked around. "Can we stay here for the day?"

"We can stay for a couple of days, if you like. It's okay for us to rest. I think we deserve it."

Ben made her a cup of tea, and they just sat and admired the view. He was amazed at how upbeat she was. He knew that she really couldn't remember much of the experience, but he was also seeing an inner strength that was allowing her to move on.

"I like the peace," said Lila, observing some ducks idly swimming about. "My old life is starting to seem pretty meaningless now."

"I know. I miss my family a lot, but really, that's about it."

"I don't even miss my family that much," said Lila. "I think I was a loser in their eyes. How long would it have been before I started to believe it myself?"

"Do you miss your sister?"

"I was only six when she died, and she didn't seem to be around much. So no, I guess I don't. My parents might have been different before she died, but I really don't remember. All I know is that—and I know this is weird—I'm living more now than at any time in my life."

She stood up. "I haven't showered in a long time. Let's go for a swim. Race you!"

Lila whipped off her clothes and went running into the water.

Ben was awestruck at the sight of her naked body. He immediately felt the familiar stirring.

She splashed into the water. "A little cold, but not bad. You coming in?"

"Um," he began. "It's a little embarrassing. I might have to sit here for a bit."

Lila laughed. "Ben, we're soulmates, remember? We're two of the last people on earth, as far as we know. Nothing your body is doing right now is anything to be embarrassed about. The more we see, the more we know each other."

Once again, Ben was amazed at Lila's maturity far beyond her years. "Okay, then!" He tugged off his clothes, conscious of what Lila could see, and followed her into the water. It felt good after so many days on the road. He looked around. "I wonder if there are snapping turtles in here."

"If there are," answered Lila with a smile, "you have more to lose than I do."

They played for an hour, putting aside everything that had happened to them since that day in the freezer. Lila eventually got out and dug a bar of soap from her pack and came back to the water, Ben watching her longingly the whole time. They then spent another half hour washing themselves from head to toe. Ben felt like he was washing off the smell of death. It was a glorious feeling. Then they washed their clothes and set them out to dry. Afterward, they lay on the beach naked, just soaking in the warmth of the sun.

That night, they made themselves a feast of canned chili, crackers, and canned peaches, with packaged cupcakes for dessert. The day had allowed Ben to relegate the scene from the day before to a far corner of his brain, so he was able to eat again. Lila, luckily, still only had hazy images of the incident.

"That was filling, but we're going to have to start thinking about fresh food at some point," suggested Lila. "We forgot to pick up any books on wild game."

"We'll get a couple of fishing rods too," added Ben. "Hey, it's apple season. When we reach Western Mass, we can look for apple orchards."

"And anytime we pass a house, we can look for a garden and get some fresh vegetables," said Lila. "It's late in the season, but maybe there is something still left. Maybe there will be some farms. We'll just keep raiding gardens until all that's left are rotten vegetables."

As much as they loved their time by the lake, they decided not to stay an extra day. They both felt the need to get on the road, and went to bed that night feeling clean and refreshed.

As we lay next to each other, we knew we were deeply in love. It was scary though, because we also knew that we were it. If one of us died, the other would wilt and die too. There would be no reason to keep going. That can make life a very fragile existence. More fragile than it already is.

They were on the road early the next morning. The hours trudging along the highway on their journey were long, but with each passing day they found their endurance and strength increasing and they could walk a little faster. The frustration of making seemingly little progress eventually gave way to acceptance. Sometimes they would talk for hours on end about the past and the future—the future becoming the favored topic. Other times they would walk silently for long stretches at a time, often hand in hand without even remembering who reached out first.

As they walked, they took some time to study the manuals for their weapons and the how-to books on gun safety. They were determined to be more prepared in the future than they were with the coyotes. They spent a lot of time dry-firing their guns, and occasionally took some actual target practice, being careful not to use up too much of their ammunition. They also practiced taking apart and cleaning their weapons.

That day they encountered the city again, going through the Chicopee area above Springfield. They were wary of animals and of live people, but saw few of the former and none of the latter. At one point they ran across a pair of dogs that seemed ready to attack. A couple of shots in the air scared them off, however. Lila was bothered by them, images of her battle still in the dark recesses of her mind.

"Did you notice their eyes?" she asked. "They were weird. Kind of a hollow look. Scary."

"I did," answered Ben. "Something's happened to them. But just the bigger animals. The birds and smaller animals—like squirrels and things—seem okay."

The smell was once again horrific. The bodies were everywhere and were often torn apart. They hurried, not taking breaks, determined to find a relief from the carnage. It seemed to take forever, but the landscape eventually became rural again. They walked as long as they could beyond the city and camped that night by another lake, after finding a garden that provided them with tomatoes, green beans, and carrots. Ben looked at the map and realized that they could reach Great Barrington in two days at their present rate.

They were walking along the next morning when Ben was suddenly aware that he no longer heard dogs barking, the sound that had accompanied them at the beginning of the trip. He mentioned it to Lila.

"That's so sad," she said. "The ones stuck in houses or tied outside have probably died of hunger and thirst. If it's like this all over the world, just think how many that is. And that's just dogs. Billions of cats, birds, bunnies, hamsters ... all dead. Funny, I seem to be sadder about the animals than the people, except the children."

"I think we're looking at things differently these days. Could it be that we're sort of liking the world without people?"

"I kind of feel guilty thinking that way," said Lila.

"We didn't cause it. We're dealing with the fallout, so I guess we have the right to think however we do without guilt."

"Funny that it's the biggest event of our life and we don't even know what to call it," said Lila.

She was right. The world around us was dead and we didn't even know how to describe the disaster. What caused it? Was someone behind it? What do you call something of this magnitude? CNN would have had an important looking banner running across the screen proclaiming some original name their creative heads had come up with. FOX would have followed with a bigger and more important looking banner. Then the local news stations would try to prove to their viewers that they could keep up with the big boys and would design their own cool graphics. The race would be on to find the most shocking story from the disaster, or the one that would produce the most tears. The ratings quest would finally obscure the event. No, no names would suffice for this obscenity.

At the end of the day, they were excited to finally get off the Mass Pike and start heading southwest toward Great Barrington. The change of direction was a welcome feeling.

They had been walking most of the following day when they came across the sign announcing the Great Barrington town limits.

"We're here," sighed Ben. "Let's find a place to sleep tonight, then we can locate the trail tomorrow and start heading south."

They walked for a while longer, when Ben suddenly stopped and looked around. The smell of wood smoke filled the air.

"Do you smell that?"

"I do. I see it too." Lila pointed up the road to a church with smoke rising from its chimney. "Do we investigate or pass it by and make ourselves scarce?"

Lila never got an answer to her question. They heard a shout.

"Hey! Welcome!" A man in jeans and flannel shirt with a priest collar emerged from a side street and jogged toward them with a big smile on his face. "So good to see some living, breathing people."

He was a pleasant looking man. He seemed to be in his thirties, tall and well-built, with a sincere smile on his face. Ben and Lila couldn't help liking him immediately.

"I'm Father Phil. You can just call me Phil. I'm the priest of the church up the way. Where do you hail from?"

"Newton," answered Ben. "I'm Ben and this is Lila."

"Brother and sister?"

"No, friends," answered Ben.

"Soulmates," added Lila, squeezing Ben's hand with affection.

"Ahh," said Phil with a smile. "Well, you must come up to the church. I have lots of food and some clean beds. You can stay as long as you want. You're only the second people I've seen since it all happened. Sadly, the first group weren't doing too well—a couple of women and a man—and they took off. They were panicking pretty badly and nothing I could say helped. I haven't seen them again."

Ben and Lila both flashed to their encounter with George and Bunny.

"You seem to be doing well though," said Phil, eyeing their backpacks and weapons.

"I suppose as well as anyone could be doing at a time like this," answered Lila.

They followed Phil up the tree-lined street to the church. He took them through the back entrance, which led into a large room.

The back room was lined with supplies of all kinds—blankets, cans of food, bottles of water, medical supplies, personal grooming products, and a host of other items.

Phil looked embarrassed. "I've raided every store I can think of. I figured the Lord would understand. I wanted to be able to provide for any survivors."

"Come," he continued. "Let me show you where you can put your things."

He led them into a second, smaller room. There were a half dozen mattresses, each neatly made with clean sheets, blankets, and pillows. Phil had made the room as inviting as possible.

"I was expecting more people." His face sagged a bit. "Each day that goes by I begin to think that I never will get very many people. It's sad."

"You might be right," said Ben. "Like you, we ran across a couple of panicked people, but that was it for the whole trip ... until now."

Phil poured some water for them in a bathroom sink to wash up.

"The toilets, as I'm sure you've already found out in your travels, don't work. I dug a trench out back. Nothing fancy, but it will do the job. Toilet paper's by the door."

"Thank you so much for your hospitality," said Lila. "We really appreciate it."

"The Lord has let me find a way to help," he answered.

When they were finished stowing their gear—all except their Sigs, which they didn't want to part with for even a minute—they joined Phil in a kitchen off the big room. He was preparing a canned ham with some fried canned potatoes and fresh vegetables on a propane stove.

They sat down at a table and Phil asked them to join him in prayer before the meal. Out of courtesy, Ben and Lila bowed their heads.

"Thank you Lord, for the bounty we have before us. Thank you for bringing these weary travelers to the doorstep of your house. We are thankful for your love and guidance during these times of crisis. Please continue to watch over them. In the name of the father, the son, and the holy spirit, Amen."

Phil's prayer only succeeded in bringing up questions for me—and maybe that wasn't a bad thing. I had never been religious, but I did believe in God in some form. I felt very strongly that Lila and I had been brought together for a reason, but was it some God figure that did it, or was it something else altogether? I knew in my heart that it wasn't just some random happening, some chaos theory thing. But the God Phil was praying to seemed to have a personality. I imagined the old belief of some white-bearded guy sitting on a throne. So I was conflicted; I could see some kind of universal force behind everything—I couldn't understand it, but I could believe in it because it had no personality—but I had a real hard time with Phil's God. Why would he let this happen? Why would he let most of his children on this planet die? Why would he save us? Why would he save George and Bunny, only to let them slowly go mad with fear? If Lila and I hadn't been brought together, it would have been very easy for me to not believe at all. I guess the jury was still out on all of that.

Ben and Lila told Phil their story. Well, not all of it, Ben thought. After all, he is a priest. Ben also sidestepped around the coyote incident, to protect Lila. Phil then told his story. He had been a star college football player hoping for a chance in the NFL, when a trip to Rwanda with his local church group changed him forever.

"I saw all of the violence and destroyed lives and realized that I was destined for something more than football. I had to help the world in some way. When I graduated college I went straight into the seminary and studied to become a priest. That was a long process, and at the end of it I volunteered to do missionary work in third-world nations—Haiti, Guatemala, even back in Rwanda. Finally I came back to the states to receive my first assignment. Here it is. I've been here two years."

"So your background helped you in this crisis, knowing what to do," stated Lila.

"I'm not sure anything could have prepared me for this," he answered, "but I'm doing the best I can."

"What if nobody else shows up here?" asked Ben. "What then?"

Phil shifted uncomfortably and Ben immediately regretted asking the question. "Honestly, I don't know. I was put on this earth to do the Lord's work. He will find a mission for me."

Ben changed the subject. "Do you have any ideas on what happened?"

"Some," Phil replied. "I was a political science major in college, so I can't help keeping up on current events—not that any exist anymore." He stared into space for a moment. "Anyway," he was back, "about a year ago, there was a flap going on concerning the military about EMPs. That stands for electro-magnetic pulse. It comes from a nuclear device that can be detonated and affect anything electrical—anything with circuits. That's why all the cars have died. They all have computers. I bet though, that if you can find a classic car from, probably before the seventies, it would still run. They don't have the computers. Of course, finding gas would be a problem since all the gas pumps run on electricity. An EMP would affect so many things that you wouldn't think of—even the flow of water through taps and toilets, because it's all controlled electronically somewhere up the line."

He continued. "The threat of EMPs has been around for a long time, and there have been lots of articles and books—both nonfiction and fiction—written about them. But what I was reading last year was something different. The rumor was that some lab in the U.S. had come up with a new bomb that would emit an EMP more powerful than any before it. One that could potentially affect much of the earth. That, of course, had the conspiracy theorists yakking, and people who had heard about it were up in arms. Then any mention of it disappeared completely. I bet if I went online right now—if I could, of course—there would be no report of it at all."

"So," he concluded, "If I had to guess, I would say that somehow it was used on the world."

"Are you saying we—the United States—might have done this ourselves? Not terrorists?" asked Ben.

"Who knows," said Phil. "Another country could have stolen it, but why they would use it is beyond me. Terrorists could have stolen it. But remember, we had a lot of terrorists in our own country. They weren't all from the Middle East and Europe. It could have been a total accident. I just don't know."

"But from what you describe," interrupted Lila, "an EMP wouldn't kill people. Only electrical circuits. So what caused the deaths, and why only people, not animals?"

"Good question," answered the priest. "I'm of the opinion that this EMP was powerful enough to affect human circuitry—our own electrical system. After all, our brains are made up of electrical impulses. In a sense, it fried people's brains. If I had to guess, my bet would be on that."

"The other thing," he added. "I'm not so sure the animals—the larger mammals anyway—weren't affected by all this. I've seen some strange animal behavior of late—animals that normally wouldn't be aggressive, suddenly attacking out of the blue. Because their make-up is a bit different from ours, I would guess that their brains were affected, just not to the extent of the human brain."

Ben immediately flashed back to the attack by the coyotes, who were normally shy.

They talked for a while longer, then weariness overcame them. They promised Phil they would stay at least one more day. That would also allow them to find some books on hunting and fishing—light ones, preferably—as well as some fishing equipment. They retired to their mattresses, which they pushed together. They talked for a few minutes about Phil.

"I really like him," said Ben. "I wonder if we should invite him to come with us."

"I was thinking that, too, although I like having you all to myself." She squeezed Ben's hand. "It would be safer with a third person though. Not that I think he'll leave."

"You don't think so?"

"I might be wrong, but he's done a lot of work getting his church ready for survivors," said Lila. "I just don't see him leaving it."

"In that case, he'll probably ask us to stay here," commented Ben.

"How do you feel about that?"

"It's not what I was imagining for us. I was really picturing a warm beach and a tropical hut."

"Whew," said Lila. "Me too. I couldn't stay here. It would mean that our journey is over, and I'm really anxious to see what else is out there."

"I'm glad."

The long day of hiking had taken its toll and they were both asleep in minutes.

There it was. This was no longer a journey of survival. It was a journey of discovery. The old world was gone. What did the new world have to offer? I thought of Lewis and Clark and all of the trappers who made their way west in the early days of this country, having no idea what they would find, but being almost possessed in their quest anyway. We found ourselves using the word "scared" less and less, and the words "peace" and "beautiful" more and more. We had actually become excited for the future. I only hoped that we weren't romanticizing the whole thing to the point of letting down our guard.

CHAPTER 6

They woke up to the aroma of eggs frying. It was a wonderful smell that brought back fond memories. They wandered into the kitchen where Phil greeted them with a big "good morning." He had opened a can of corned beef hash and was frying it alongside the eggs.

"One of my parishioners kept chickens, so I've been feeding them. I'll have a never-ending supply of eggs," he explained. "I also catch fish, so dinner is usually taken care of. I try not to tap into the supplies here for my own use."

"When you get a chance, would you mind showing me how to filet a fish?" asked Ben.

"Be happy to. In fact, I'll take you to a good little fishing spot this afternoon."

"We never asked you," said Lila, "how you managed to live when everyone else died."

"God's will, I guess. I'm an amateur spelunker. There's a pretty cool cave about a half an hour from here. I was deeper than I had ever been and I guess it was enough. I didn't even know anything had happened, so it was devastating to come out and discover that my world had disappeared. First my car didn't work, and then when I found my first few bodies, I knew something of catastrophic proportions had occurred."

After breakfast, they walked into town to help Phil gather more supplies. It had been spared the destruction by fire that had affected so many other cities and towns. The fire would have been a blessing however. They had to wear hospital masks liberally coated in Vicks VapoRub to keep out the smell. But nothing could shield their eyes from the sight of the bodies. Flies were everywhere. The bodies they ran across were coated in them. Other insects had found them as well, as had larger animals. They could hear packs of dogs barking and growling. Ben and Lila thought things were bad before. Now it was to the point where they wondered if they'd ever be able to eat again without picturing the scene that was now before them. The thought of the Appalachian Trail, with fewer bodies to run across, was more appealing than ever.

They found a sports store that had freeze-dried meals—not that they had eaten many of their original ones—and Phil helped them pick out good fishing rods, reels, and lures, as well as some essentials such as a filleting knife. Phil also knew of a small gun store where they could pick up some more ammunition.

As they approached the gun store, two men burst out the front door, running right into Phil. They all went tumbling in a pile. The men were filthy and smelly, and their clothes—remnants of business suits—were tattered, Ben thought he was watching a scene from a zombie movie. They were clearly out of their minds with fear. They jumped to their feet and one of them stuck his newly acquired pistol in Phil's face.

"You can't stop us," he screamed. "Whatever we find is ours."

"It's okay ... it's okay," said Phil in a calming voice. "We're not here to stop you. You can have whatever you want. We were just walking by."

Meanwhile, Ben and Lila were very slowly pulling their Sigs from their holsters.

"No!" shouted the man. "The world has gone to hell. Don't trust anyone. Kill people in your way."

"No," said Phil. "Listen to me. I have a place that has lots of supplies. You can help yourself."

"You're lying!" screamed the man. "I'm going to blow your head off!" He was waving his gun all around.

The other man just stood there, not really a part of the scene.

Their guns were free of the holsters. Ben lifted the gun, pulled the hammer back, and fired it into the air, then he and Lila pointed them at the man.

"Drop your weapon or we'll shoot you," said Ben.

Both men were so scared, they let their weapons fall to the ground.

"I was telling the truth," said Phil. "Come with us. You can get cleaned up and have a nice meal. No one is going to hurt you."

Both men took off down the street without another word.

"Wait. Stop," shouted Phil.

Ben looked at Lila. They were both shaking as they reholstered their weapons.

"We didn't mean to scare them off," Ben said to Phil. "We just wanted them to drop their guns."

"I know," answered Phil sadly. "And I appreciate it. They were just like that first group I ran into, except in worse shape. They were so far out of their heads with fear, I'm afraid nothing would have convinced them to stay."

Once they had calmed down, Ben went into the gun shop to

find the ammunition they needed. He decided to take a few extra boxes, now that they had experienced some of the dangers that awaited them.

They picked up a few more things, but their hearts weren't in it, so they made their way back to the church.

Later in the afternoon, in an effort to cushion the earlier encounter, Phil took them fishing at a local pond.

"I'm not going to give you a course on how to fish. After you learn the basics of using the reel, you'll learn as you go. Our ancestors used a stick with a hook and a worm. You can use the lures, but in my opinion there is nothing like a good worm, which is why I had you pick up some hooks and bobbers. Just stick a worm on the hook, attach a bobber, and let it sit there in the water. It's very relaxing, too, and with the stress of your journey, a few relaxing moments might be nice."

They spent a couple of hours fishing, catching two largemouth bass. But the best part for Ben and Lila, was spending the time with Phil. He told them stories of his adventures in the Third World, and of his wild college days. They each felt they had found a true friend. There was none of the phoniness they had encountered with people in their previous life.

They talked about Richie and his decision to put Lila in the freezer with Ben and how they both felt it was not an accident. That brought up the subject of faith. Phil asked them what religion they were brought up in. Ben and Lila shrugged at the same time.

"My parents weren't religious," said Ben. "I remember we tried a few churches when I was young, but nothing consistently, so we just stopped going." He looked at Lila, as if to say, "your turn."

"My parents never talked about God … ever," said Lila. "I'm sure my sister's death had something to do with that, but I really don't know. I think I'm spiritual, but I couldn't tell you exactly what that means. I do know—and I hope I'm not insulting you, because you're not like that—but with all the things with priests and little boys in recent years and the cover-ups, I don't think very highly of churches in general."

"That was certainly a dark period," agreed Phil. "I haven't always been happy with the Church myself, and I haven't always agreed with the laws they've laid down."

"Then why have you stayed?" asked Ben.

"Because I have faith in God and in the Lord, Jesus Christ, to lead me in the right direction."

"Is faith the same as knowing?" asked Lila.

"We won't ever know until we're in heaven, so faith is all we have."

"What now?" Lila continued to probe. "There is no more church. You might be all that remains of the church. How does that affect you?"

"The church was God's vehicle on this planet, but it's not God. My faith remains intact."

"Because faith is all we have?" repeated Ben.

"Because faith is all we have," answered the priest.

As eager as they were to get on the road, Ben and Lila decided to stay an extra day with Phil. They were hoping to convince him to come with them. They also began to notice that, despite his cheerful demeanor and dedication to his religion, Phil had his own demons, and seemed at times to be hurting inside. They could tell that he craved their company.

That night, he showed them how to filet a fish, then cooked it with fresh vegetables on the side. Unfortunately, after seeing all the fly-covered bodies earlier in the day, they all just picked at their food.

At the end of the meal Ben said, "Phil, please think about this tonight. Lila and I would love it if you would come with us." Lila nodded her head in agreement.

"I appreciate the offer and will give it some serious thought," answered Phil, "but I'm not sure I'm ready to give this up yet."

After cleaning up, Phil went to his room and Ben and Lila got ready for bed. A short time later they were snuggled up together on the mattress. It was dark and quiet.

"Ben?" Lila said in a small voice.

"Yes?"

"I'm ready."

"Ready?"

"Remember I said I would know when the time was right? Well, I guess it's happened sooner than I thought. It's not the only thing I have to look forward to anymore. I have a life with you ahead of me."

"Are you sure you want to?" asked Ben, now scared to death.

"Very," answered Lila. "I feel safe with you right here. I don't know when we're going to feel safe again. Besides," she smiled, "Now you can use one of those condoms I saw you sneak into your pack back at the drugstore."

"You saw that, huh?"

"I did. Are you nervous?

"Yeah. You know I've never done this before," said Ben.

"I know." She gently touched his face. "We can figure it out together."

They embraced and slowly began their voyage of discovery. There was a lot of fumbling, some laughter, but mostly a tenderness brought on by the intensity of their love for each other.

At one point Ben suddenly lifted his head and said, "Are we supposed to be doing this in a church?"

Lila giggled and pulled him back down.

Much later, when we remembered that night, we talked about being ready versus not. In the world we had come from, we were way too young. We hadn't experienced enough in our own lives to consider a step like that. It would have been a mistake we would regret. But the world had changed, and we had to change with it or die. We had grown up exponentially in a very short time, and we didn't have a clue as to what the future had in store for us. We could be dead tomorrow. "Live for the moment" wasn't some overused bumper sticker phrase anymore, it was reality. We both knew we had to experience every good moment that came our way, because it was often going to be followed by an awful one.

The morning was angry. Thunder rumbled down upon them and they could hear the rain pounding on the roof.

"Whew, good thing we're not on the road," said Ben, as they lay in bed. They hadn't gotten much sleep, but when they did, it was restful and fulfilling.

"Mmmm," said Lila sleepily. "A good morning to stay in bed."

A brilliant flash of lightning, followed immediately by an intense crash of thunder, made them leap to their feet.

"Well, that woke me up!" exclaimed Lila.

"That one hit close by," said Ben. "Really close."

Phil ran into the room a moment later yelling, "The church has been hit. We're on fire. We need to save as many supplies as possible." He left as quickly as he had come in.

"We have to get our backpacks to safety first," said Lila. "Otherwise, we have nothing."

"I agree," said Ben, as he was putting on his pants.

They dressed quickly and rushed over to their belongings and gathered them up. They stuffed what they could in the packs and carried the rest. They made it out the back door and tried to find a somewhat dry area to stow them.

Ben looked up at the roof of the church. It had indeed suffered a direct hit. It was an old wooden building and already it was engulfed in flames.

"We're not going to be able to save much," yelled Lila. She was trying to be heard above the roar of the rain.

They could see Phil running in and out of the building, desperately trying to rescue some of the supplies he had so lovingly accumulated. They ran to help him, entering the church, not knowing what to save first, so they just grabbed what they could. They only made four trips before the flames reached the back of the church. Phil was going to go in for another run when Ben grabbed onto his arm.

"Stop! You're going to get killed if you go back in."

Phil stopped. It looked to Ben as if he was crying, but it could have been the rain.

*****

They sat in the rain for an hour, totally helpless, watching the church burn to the ground. Phil stared into space, saying nothing. Ben looked over at him often. He wasn't mistaken. Those were tears. Lila moved over to Phil and sat with him for the hour, her arm around him. There was nothing anyone could say. Finally, Lila helped Phil up and motioned for Ben to follow. She had noticed a detached barn that Phil used as a garage, and felt it was time to move somewhere dry. Ben followed with their packs.

The downpour was relentless. Ben couldn't remember seeing it rain so hard for so long. However, the power of the rain was no match for the intensity of the fire. Within a couple of hours, there was nothing left of the church but a few blackened beams.

While Lila comforted Phil, Ben ventured back into the rain to gather some of the supplies they had rescued. The cans were fine, but the boxes they were stacked in had disintegrated, so Ben had to carry the cans a handful at a time. They had saved some of the cases of water, as well, and Ben brought them into the barn. That was it. There was nothing else.

Later, Phil asked for some time alone and went into a dark corner of the barn. Ben and Lila sat near the door to give him as much space as possible, but even so, they could hear him talking to his God. He was questioning God's wisdom, cursing God's callousness, and asking for God's forgiveness, all interspersed with sobs. Lila cried just listening to him. Finally there was quiet. When evening came, Lila made her way into the back with a blanket she had found and covered the now sleeping priest. She came back and laid down with Ben. They both immediately fell asleep.

Ben woke up the next morning to the sound of Lila's screams.

"Ben ... Ben ... Omigod, Ben." She was almost choking on her words.

Ben ran to Lila, who was standing outside the barn, tears streaming down her face, staring into the woods.

Hanging by the neck from a thick branch, his body gently swaying in the breeze, was Phil.

CHAPTER 7

In the end, his faith just wasn't enough to sustain him. I think he was already struggling before any of this happened. He was at his best helping the poor in Rwanda and other countries, and I think he regretted ever leaving that. In some ways, this colossal event was a renewal of sorts for him. As devastating as it was, it gave him the opportunity to go back to the days when he was his happiest. With the church burning, all hope was lost. He no longer had a role in this life. I realized that he never would have come with us to Florida. He would have also never seen the people he wanted to help with his church—they just didn't exist in the towns. With or without the fire, Phil was doomed. He was no better off than George and Bunny. The fire just hastened his demise.

With tears in their eyes, Ben and Lila cut Phil down from the tree limb. Wordlessly, Ben retrieved a shovel from the barn and dug Phil a grave. They had passed thousands of people without giving thought to a grave—even their own parents. Somehow, though, they knew they had to provide one for Phil. When Ben had dug the hole deep enough, he and Lila gently set Phil in, and Ben covered him with dirt.

When they were done, Ben sat against a tree stroking Lila's hair as she rested her head on his thigh.

Lila finally spoke. "I was so happy last night. Making love to you; finding a true friend in Phil; the excitement of the journey ahead ... despite the devastation, I was seeing only beauty. Now I see only ugliness. What are we going to do? I'm so lost right now."

"I don't know," answered Ben. He was so deflated, he couldn't even think.

"I need you to know," pleaded Lila. "I need you to tell me what we're going to do now. You're my hero, remember?" She buried her head in Ben's lap and cried so hard she gasped for breath.

"I'm sorry. I'm trying. I'm not a hero. I couldn't stop Phil. If only I could've had a chance to talk to him, to tell him how much we cared about him."

"Why do people kill themselves?" asked Lila, between sobs. "Don't they know what they do to others?"

"I still can't believe Phil did that," said Ben. "Any other time, he would have experienced the fire and said something like, 'It's God's will.'

"Yeah, well fuck God!" exclaimed Lila. "I'm so tired of hearing about God."

Suddenly Ben came to life. He realized that Lila was on the verge of losing all hope. God or no God, they both knew they were together for a reason. He somehow had to remind Lila of that.

"Do you remember when we first started on this trip?" asked Ben. "We knew instinctively that we had to fall into survival mode or we'd be lost. We knew it wasn't going to be easy and we suspected there would be a lot of ugliness in front of us. We could have ended up like George and Bunny, or like the two we ran into at the gun shop, but we didn't. We didn't because our will to live was too strong. There will be beauty again. I'm looking down at beauty right now."

"I don't think I have your strength," said Lila. "I think of the night you saved me from the coyotes. You were strong. I wasn't."

"I was waiting to tell you this when you were ready to hear the whole story of that night," said Ben, "but I have to tell you now. Yeah, I carried you away from that scene, but I couldn't have done it alone. You were almost unconscious, and yet, you found the strength to keep moving. And in the battle itself, you calmly shot and shot and shot. You didn't panic. When the coyote jumped on you, you fought him off until I could help. Lila, you're just as much my hero. We're going to miss Phil, but we have to go on."

Lila lifted her head and looked at Ben. "You're right ... again. We have too much ahead of us. We have to keep going." Tears returned to her eyes. "This is so hard though."

"It is. I know. But I think we just need to pack our things and go. Like we did when we left home. There's nothing left for us here, so we have to keep going."

Lila sat up, sniffed, and wiped her eyes with her sleeve, then looked down at Ben's lap. It was soaked from her tears. "Did you wet your pants?"

Ben smiled and stood up, helping Lila to her feet. "We have our love for each other," he said. "We've got to let that carry us through these things, as hard as they are."

Lila put her arms around his neck and kissed him deeply. "It will."

They got their backpacks ready for travel. When they were at the sports store the day before, they had picked up a couple of good canteens each. They poured some of the bottles of water into the canteens, stuffed as many extra bottles into the packs as they could, then started on their way. The entrance to the trail was about four miles outside of town. They reached it in a little more than an hour.

There it was in front of us. The trail south. Nothing had looked so inviting. I felt as if we were stepping onto the yellow-brick road on our journey to Oz. Originally we thought we could make it here in two days by bike. How long was it? Nine days? Ten? It could've been more. All I know is that it was a long time coming. It felt like we had already lived a lifetime. We had found love. We had found a lot of death. We were hoping this would be the start of a new chapter in our new life. A good chapter, we hoped.

After the first mile, it was heaven. Near the entrance were more bodies than Ben and Lila had counted on, but once they started on their way, the bodies thinned out and eventually disappeared altogether. When they did run across remains, they looked the other way. Even with a few bodies, the difference between the trail and the highway was beyond words. Ben looked over at Lila. She was smiling and looking up at the sun, the rays reflecting off her raven hair.

Was she more beautiful than when we first met, or was it just my perception? Didn't matter. She was beautiful to me. Kind of funny, really. Less than two weeks earlier I didn't know when I was ever going to have my first date. Then the world fell apart and suddenly I was in love.

"What are you laughing at?" asked Lila.

"That I didn't have my first date until I was the last available man on earth," answered Ben.

Lila laughed. "What if I had said to you in the freezer that I wouldn't date you even 'if' you were the last man on earth?"

"That would stink."

"Yeah, for me too."

She changed the subject. "Were you scared when you pointed your gun at that crazy guy?"

"Big time," replied Ben. "I've thought about it a few times since then. What would I do if I ever had to fire it at someone? I don't know if I could. I take that back. I could if it meant saving your life."

Lila put her hand in his. "And I think that's what being in survival mode is all about. We don't live in the same society we did before. Everything and everyone we run across presents a potential danger. There is no 9-1-1. There's no police. It's just us. When you say that you could shoot someone if my life was in danger, I hope you also meant if your life was in danger too. We're a pair. We need each other. Let's hope we never have to worry about it."

The day passed quietly. The shock of losing Phil had hit them hard, and they lapsed into long periods of silence and reflection. By noon, a deep loneliness had set in.

Up to this point, it had been a process of getting use to our new world; dealing with the fear, the upheaval, and the sickening carnage all around us. Everything was new, and warranted our constant and wary attention. We had been alone since that day in the freezer, but not like this. The solitude of the trail forced us to confront the reality that we were IT. Just us. We would walk around a bend knowing that there would be no hikers to run into, no families out for a day's walk, no one at all. We began to look at the forest around us differently. At times, the trees, which had grown larger and starker in our minds, scared us. I felt more insignificant than I had ever felt in my life. There were aspects of this odyssey that we appreciated, including the silence. We were survivors. We embraced the strength to live with the hand we were dealt, and in many ways we could recognize—and even look forward to—the excitement of the adventure. But we couldn't deny the fact that there were times when we desperately missed the sounds of civilization.

That night they stayed in one of the shelters that appeared from time to time along the trail. Three sides of the shelter were made of stone, the fourth side open, and with a wooden roof over the whole structure. They felt more comfortable now using their flashlights. They decided part of that was because they were tucked away in the woods, but the other part was that they were more confident in their ability to take care of themselves.

They were ravenous. They hadn't eaten much of anything that day out of grief, and had only picked at their meal the night before with memories of the fly-encrusted bodies stuck in their brain. Lila said it was her turn to make dinner and opened a couple of freeze-dried meals.

"I was craving a burger, but this looks good," said Ben.

"Yeah, that's one of the many things we'll probably never eat again," said Lila sadly. "Let's not think about it."

Ben zipped the two sleeping bags together to make one.

They had settled themselves comfortably when Lila said, "I hear thunder."

"Again?" Ben heard it too. A flash of lightning appeared in the sky. "What's with all the storms?"

"I don't know, but I'm glad we're in here. I think we should use these shelters whenever possible."

They moved themselves further back into the shelter as the rain started. Just like the night before, and the night on the road, the rain came down in buckets. The thunder and lightning were violent and they heard some close strikes. Luckily, none started a fire.

The rain subsided a couple of hours later. Ben and Lila hadn't been able to sleep, but had used that time constructively—intimately getting to know each other better.

Suddenly they heard a dog barking, then a second. Soon a cacophony of barking filled the air.

"Dog pack," said Ben quietly, strapping on his holster and reaching for his rifle. Lila did the same and they sat near the entrance with their weapons ready.

The barking got closer, but with it came screams. They looked at each other. "There's someone out there," shouted Lila. Now they heard more than one voice screaming.

"Let's go," said Ben. Lila needed no prompting and the two made their way out into the now gentle rain. They ran back down the trail in the direction they'd come. Suddenly their lights picked up a gruesome scene. A small group of girls was surrounded by a pack of about six snarling dogs. A woman was lying on the ground bleeding from numerous wounds, and the three girls—Ben figured about nine or ten years old—were huddled around the inert form.

A German Shepherd was lunging toward the figure on the ground when Lila coolly took aim with her rifle and shot the dog. It died on the spot. The other dogs hesitated. Ben shot and missed, and the dogs dispersed.

They ran over to the group. Ben asked the girls if they were hurt, but got no response. Lila, meanwhile, checked on the wounded adult.

"She's alive, but she's in bad shape," said Lila. "We need to get her to the shelter."

They slung their rifles over their shoulders and picked up the woman. Ben took her upper body and Lila grabbed her feet.

"Follow us," called Ben to the girls. At first they didn't move, but some growling from the woods shook the inertia from them and they quickly followed behind.

Carrying the dead weight was hard, especially since the woman was fairly overweight, and they had to set her down once. But they had just done the same thing that morning with Phil, so the weight came as no surprise. They made it to the shelter and laid the woman on top of their sleeping bag. Lila pulled some first-aid supplies from her backpack and used her flashlight to assess the situation. Meanwhile, Ben herded the girls into a corner and reached into his pack for some bottles of water, which he handed to them. They drank like they had been dying of thirst, but still said nothing.

He heard movement in the woods and went over to the shelter opening with his rifle and flashlight. He held the flashlight against the barrel of the gun, like he had seen in cop shows, so that the rifle was pointed in the same direction as the light. He heard a growl about twenty feet away and swung the rifle barrel in its direction. He caught sight of some fur and fired. He heard a yelp and the animal scurried away. Over the course of the next fifteen minutes, he fired twice more—missing both times, but scaring the dogs away.

"How's the woman?" he asked at one point.

"I don't know what to do here," replied Lila in a panic. "She's bleeding in so many places. She's had whole hunks of skin ripped off. I'm trying my best."

"That's all you can do. I'll come help you. I think we've scared them away."

A couple of minutes later, Ben moved over to where Lila was trying to put bandages on some of the flowing wounds. It was an awful sight. An ear was missing, as were some fingers, and there were numerous bites all over her body. But Lila was right. They weren't just bites. Whole areas of flesh had been torn away.

Already we had changed. Just a few days earlier, we would have been heaving all over the place at the sight of her. But compared to what we had been witnessing, this wasn't even enough to make us gag. That was one way we were measuring our progression—if that's what you could call it—the things that still bothered us and those that didn't.

The woman suddenly started shaking.

"I think she's having a heart attack," shouted Lila.

"I don't know CPR," said Ben.

"I do," replied Lila. She knelt over the woman and pushed hard and fast on her chest. The woman stopped moving and Ben checked her neck for a pulse while Lila worked on her.

"No pulse," said Ben

Lila kept at it. Five minutes later, Ben touched her arm.

"Lila, there's still no pulse. She's gone." Lila stopped and looked at Ben. There was no emotion in her face. This wasn't like Phil, or her parents. She didn't know this woman. She refused to let herself get emotional over her. They had seen too much death for that.

"You have blood all over your hands," said Ben. "I'm going to heat up some water for you to wash with." Lila nodded wearily.

The three girls were still quietly huddled in a corner, so Ben and Lila moved the woman's body out of the shelter, then took the time to clean up. When they had washed the blood off as best they could and disposed of the dirty water, they turned their attention to the girls.

"Are you hungry?" asked Lila. Two of them nodded their heads. Lila pulled out some meals from her pack and heated up more water. "What are your names?"

There was only silence.

"You're safe now," Lila said gently. "Was that your mother? I'm sorry she died."

"Our teacher," one of them whispered.

Lila wanted to keep them talking so they would be less scared. "Where are you from?"

"Williamstown," the same girl replied, in a little more than a whisper this time.

Lila knew now who to focus her attention on. "What's your name?"

"Caitlyn."

"Nice to meet you Caitlyn. I'm Lila and this is Ben. We're from Newton."

She finally got the names of the other two girls—Megan and Brooke—and some semblance of their story, mostly from Caitlyn. Like Lila and Ben, they were saved by a freezer. The apocalypse happened on a Sunday, but they were with their teacher at school, preparing for a bake sale. They had gone into the walk-in freezer in the school's kitchen. There were two other girls in the group at first. One went crazy and ran away the next day—they spent hours looking, but never found her. The second girl was dragged away by dogs when they were first attacked, a few miles back. That was where the teacher received most of her wounds.

They were still in shock, but were also famished, and wolfed down the meal Lila served. Ben separated the sleeping bags and threw away the bloody one that had been on top. Dawn was still a couple of hours away and it was cold. They opened up the remaining sleeping bag and covered the three girls.

"You're safe here," Lila told them again, "so try to get some sleep." She moved over to the shelter entrance and put her arm around Ben, who was guarding against dogs.

"I don't think they've slept in days," she whispered. "What a horrible thing to see one of their friends dragged away by dogs."

"So what do we do with them?" asked Ben. "I know. Stupid question. Obviously we have to take them with us. But it's going to be a lot harder with them. We don't have the food and water we need for that many people. And we're going to have to find a town to get them some warmer clothes, sleeping bags, and other things."

"This wasn't how I envisioned our trip south," said Lila. "But I guess we really don't have any choice, do we?"

We didn't have any choice at all. They had to come with us. It really sucked. It made the journey far more dangerous for us, and it was going to slow us down a lot. And the fact is, I couldn't stand kids. On the other hand, it was pretty selfish of us to want to avoid people altogether. If in fact there was some purpose in our living when so many others died, what possible difference could we make by traveling alone? On the other hand, maybe we didn't want to make a difference. Maybe we just wanted to create our own little world.

CHAPTER 8

We learned two things that night. First, with roving packs of dogs—and who knows what other animals—we had been pretty naïve to think that we could just fall asleep together. Did it mean we were going to have to take turns standing guard while the other slept? The second thing was that it was already starting to get cold at night. We needed to stay ahead of the winter, and we were still only in Massachusetts. We had been hoping to pick up the pace. Now with the girls, that wouldn't happen.

Morning came and Caitlyn was still the only girl doing any talking. The other two would mumble comments from time to time, or add a word or a phrase to a story Caitlyn was telling, but for the most part, they just stared into space. Each girl had a small, dirty backpack—the kind used for schoolbooks—something Ben and Lila hadn't noticed the night before.

"They can carry some of their own food and water in their packs," said Ben.

"If we can find some," replied Lila.

Ben was looking at a map. "The trail crosses a road soon, before we hit some bigger hills. Maybe there will be a convenience store or something."

There was. Ben and Lila had the girls sit outside while they went in to raid what they could.

They were able to stock up on water bottles, some canned food, granola bars, and lots of cans of nuts. They brought out sodas, chips, and packaged cupcakes to the girls. It wasn't nutritious, but it was filling, and that's all they could count on for now. They hadn't yet found a looted store, and while comforting that they wouldn't starve, it added to their fear that they were almost completely alone in the world.

There were no dead customers in this store, but the clerk behind the counter was covered in bugs, and his body had seemed to collapse into itself.

They helped the girls fill their packs.

"I know these are heavy now," Lila explained to them, "but you're going to have to carry them."

Ben was impressed with Lila's gentle, but firm touch with the girls. They did whatever she said without question. He felt sorry for them. As much as his own life had been turned upside down, it must've been so much harder for kids their age.

When they were back on the trail, Lila asked Caitlyn how they chose to come this way.

"My teacher decided. Everyone was dead and my teacher said she had a brother in Connecticut. She said we wouldn't see so many dead people if we took the trail. So that's what we did. I think they're going to be dead in Connecticut too, aren't they?"

"I think so. I'm sorry."

Caitlyn went silent at that point.

The next three days passed uneventfully. Ben had to give the girls credit, they didn't whine or ask to take many breaks. It was actually a bit spooky, he thought. Megan and Brooke rarely said anything, and continued to stare as they walked. Caitlyn would open up for short periods at a time, then join the other girls in their silence. They still hadn't replaced their sleeping bag, so they gave the one they had to the girls to share. They were able to make it to a shelter each night, and on the third night they decided to set up the tent in the shelter for some extra warmth, and privacy from the girls. While they didn't take turns keeping watch, they did notice that they were each sleeping much lighter than before.

On the fourth day, black clouds once again appeared on the horizon. They weren't in the vicinity of any shelters, so they hurriedly set up their tent. Ben and Lila put the girls in, as well as their own backpacks to keep dry. Meanwhile, they sat under a tree, huddled together under a couple of rain ponchos. As with the other storms, it was violent. The lightning was dangerous, and the rain soaking. The thunder was so loud they couldn't even talk to each other.

When the storm had subsided somewhat, Ben said, "You know, when it gets colder, these might be blizzards."

"It's still the end of September ... I think," replied Lila. "So I imagine we still have a couple of months. We should be able to get to the warmer weather by then. What do you think is causing these?"

"I was thinking about that as we were sitting here. Remember Phil's theory about the EMP?" Lila nodded. "Let's just say he was right. If it was as powerful as he described, that means a massive nuclear weapon was exploded in the atmosphere. Couldn't that change the weather patterns?"

"I suppose," said Lila. "But if so, is this the extent of it, or just the beginning?"

And that was a good question. We had witnessed the breakdown of electronics, the end of humanity, the change in animal behavior, and now what? Was it responsible for this too? Was it hastening an already changing climate? What more were we going to have to deal with? I never once envied those who had died, but I did wonder if our life was eventually going to get easier, or whether this was what we could expect until we, ourselves, joined the others.

On the fifth day with the girls, they reached the Hudson River. Ben and Lila hugged and held onto each other as they looked out across the river at Bear Mountain on the other side. It wasn't that they had reached a particular destination, but that it was a milestone, of sorts. Crossing that river meant that they were finally out of New England.

According to Ben's map, once they crossed the river, the trail wound past Hessian Lake. They thought that would be a good place to camp for the night. As they reached the other side of the bridge, they came across a handmade sign—painted on plywood—that read, "Survivor camp ahead—at Hessian Lake."

"Omigod," said Lila. "Real live people?"

They had fallen behind the girls.

"I don't know about you," said Ben quietly, "but I have no interest in joining another group of survivors. But maybe someone there will take the girls."

"My thoughts exactly," replied Lila.

If this were a movie, a strong bond would have formed between us and the girls. Leaving them with someone else would have resulted in tears and painful goodbyes. The truth is, we felt no closer to them at that moment than we did the night we saved them from the dogs. Megan and Brooke had spent the last five days in space. They couldn't have said more than a few dozen words between them. Caitlyn had been more communicative, but there was no closeness, and we never expected any. They had gone through a horrific experience. It might be months before they started communicating—maybe never. If there were some other kids their age in the camp, and/or a nurturing adult, there might be some hope for them.

There were a couple more signs, and then they heard the group before they actually saw them. They rounded a bend and there, spread out along the edge of the lake, were what looked to be close to a hundred tents of all sizes.

"Wow," said Ben. "There must be two or three hundred people here."

They walked down the main path between the tents. Many people stopped what they were doing to take a look at them. It was obvious they were newcomers.

Here it was, our first real contact with what was left of society. I honestly don't know what we were expecting, but what we found filled us with an overwhelming sadness. Individually, their faces reflected the utter sorrow they had encountered since that awful day. But it was the collective group that had the strongest effect on us. As one, they had no idea what was to come next. Was there even a next? It was obvious that they saw no future, and without a future, how could you live in the present? How many of them wished that they had died with their friends and family? And yet, among them, we saw isolated faces of determination. If there was to be any hope at all, it would come from those few souls who refused to give up.

They approached an area of increased activity around a crudely made plywood building.

"Hey there." A tall, distinguished-looking man came out of the hut and stuck his hand out. "Welcome to the survivor camp. We haven't given it a real name yet. That's under debate. I'm Paul Flynn, one of the board members."

"I'm sorry?" asked Ben.

"We're trying to make this a safe haven for people, so we established a five-member board to help govern the camp. It's getting bigger every day, so we need to have rules." He looked at their weapons. "Um, the first rule is that residents have to turn in their weapons for safe-keeping." He laughed. "We sure can't have people going around accidently shooting each other." He turned serious. "Or themselves. Suicide is a real problem."

"That's okay," said Lila. "We're actually just passing through." She had sat the three girls under a tree, out of earshot. "We came across these girls and were wondering if there was anyone here who could take them. We think they would be better off here, than with us."

"Sure, we can do that. We have a group of children without parents that we care for here. I'm sure we can add them. Sally," he called to a girl not much older than Ben. "Could you go get Mrs. Davenport?"

When Sally walked off, he said, "Come. Sit. Have some dinner. He ladled some beef stew out of a large pot into bowls and handed them to Ben, Lila, and the girls. Caitlyn, Megan, and Brooke went back under the tree to eat.

"So where are you from?" asked Paul.

Ben and Lila told him their story, and that of the girls.

"Most of the people here are from the city. A lot of them

survived because they were in subway cars that happened to be in the right place. In many cases, the people in one car survived, when everyone else on the train died. Right spot, right time. Who can explain it? We're camped out here until the towns become better suited to habitation, then we'll move before winter. We still haven't decided to go across the river to Peekskill, or upriver to West Point."

"Aren't you worried about the winter?" asked Lila.

"It's a concern, but there's plenty of wood out there and most houses have fireplaces—some have woodstoves. We figure if our ancestors could do it, so can we."

"Hey Flynn. You gonna make them give up their guns?"

Ben and Lila turned to see three guys in their early twenties, dressed in Army fatigues and boots. The one who had spoken had the look of a body-builder; the second was tall and skinny, with a long scar on his cheek; and the third was an obvious druggie—scrawny, with unhealthy, almost yellowish skin. They definitely weren't military.

Ben noticed that Paul was suddenly uncomfortable.

"No, Tank," Paul replied. "They're just passing through. They're not staying."

"Too bad," said the one with the scar. "I'd like to have her around," pointing to Lila. "I bet you and me could have some fun."

"Ah, she's not your type, Slash," said Tank. "I bet she likes 'em with muscles." He rolled back his sleeve and made a huge muscle with his heavily tattooed bicep. He pointed to Ben and said to Slash, "You can have that girl."

The three of them laughed. Ben felt himself flush. Lila grabbed his hand, as if to say, "Just don't do anything."

The problem was, I wasn't going to do anything. Tank and his friends scared the crap out of me. They were saying things to Lila that no boyfriend should put up with. But what was I going to do? It was three mean guys against one wimpy teenager. I had done some growing on this trip, but not that much. I thought of the gun on my hip. I couldn't very well shoot them. They hadn't really done anything yet. That wasn't the kind of person I was. Besides, I'd most likely miss.

"C'mon, Tank," said Paul. "Just move on, okay?"

They laughed, and as they started away, Tank looked at Lila, pointed to her, made an obscene gesture, and winked.

"Oh, they're trouble," said Paul, after the three had walked away. "The board would love to expel them from the camp, but frankly, they scare us. Nobody wants to be the one to tell them." He changed the subject. "Aren't you two a little young to be making a journey by yourselves? I think you'd be better off staying with us. It doesn't look like much yet, but we're planning big things. We want people to feel comfortable here. And when we move to West Point or Peekskill, we hope to establish a real town—get schools started, churches, get people into businesses again—it won't be exactly like our old life, but it might come close."

Ben glanced at Lila and could see the look. She wanted to leave as quickly as possible.

"Well thank you for the offer," said Ben, "but we have our own plans."

"Will you at least spend the night. It'll be dark in a few hours."

"I think if we can get the girls taken care of, we'll probably just head out," answered Lila. "But thank you."

Paul seemed disappointed, but accepted their decision.

"Here comes Mrs. Davenport now."

She was a woman in her thirties. Ben thought she had probably once been a soccer mom, but the past few weeks had taken their toll. She looked fairly bedraggled. Her once permed hair was now hanging limply, and her designer clothes now dirty and torn. However, it was obvious that she was trying her best to cope.

After a few minutes' discussion, she said she would be happy to take care of the girls. Ben and Lila approached the three girls and tried to explain that they would be happier there, but got no response in return, not even from Caitlyn, so no hugs were called for. They said their goodbyes to Paul and wished him well, and were on their way.

"I couldn't wait to leave," said Lila.

"Yeah, when he started talking about making it close to what it used to be, he lost me," replied Ben.

About a half an hour out of the camp, Ben stopped and listened. "Do you hear that?"

"Gunfire?"

"Automatic weapons. That's not somebody hunting," said Ben.

"Do you think we should go back?" asked Lila. "Maybe it's coming from the camp."

"We could, but ..."

"I know. I agree," said Lila. "We can't fight other people's battles. I just hope whatever is happening isn't too awful."

They heard a few more bursts of gunfire, then silence.

They picked up their pace to put as much distance between them and the camp as possible.

When it started to get dark, they set up their tent next to a shelter. They wanted the intimacy the tent provided, but the shelter nearby in case the weather took another turn for the worse.

They were exhausted, and since they had eaten Paul's stew,

they didn't need to make any dinner. They covered themselves with the sleeping bag they salvaged from the girls, and slept in their clothes for extra warmth. They knew that soon they were going to have to find a town to get a couple more sleeping bags.

They were asleep within minutes.

*****

Ben was awakened violently at dawn by hands yanking him out of the tent by his ankles. Lila screamed as she too was pulled from the tent.

"Hey honey," said Tank, looking at down at a terrified Lila. "I've been dreaming about you."

We couldn't have imagined a worse nightmare.

CHAPTER 9

Tank grabbed Lila and carried her over to the shelter, violating her body with his hands as he went.

"No! Please no!! Just let us go," cried Lila.

"The way you came on to me at the camp?" asked Tank. "Hell no. I could tell you really wanted it from a man, not some kid playing G.I. Joe." He turned to Ben. "You think parading around with those fucking guns makes you a man? I'll show you what makes a man. Slash and Coke are gonna get some of the action too. But if you're really good, we'll let you watch us have fun with your girlfriend for a few hours before we kill you."

"You shoulda stayed at the camp," piped in Slash. "Maybe with all those guns, they woulda elected you to the Board."

"Yeah," said Tank, still holding the struggling Lila. "All five Board positions suddenly opened up last night."

"Like they could tell us to shove off," said Slash. "Who did they think they were?"

The one they called Coke got behind Ben and put a choke hold on him with the crook of his arm. With his other hand, he held a gun to Ben's head. Slash and Tank laid Lila across a picnic table in the shelter, and Slash held her down by her shoulders. Lila was kicking and screaming and calling out Ben's name. Tank ripped her shirt off and undid her jeans and pulled them off along with her panties. He held down her legs with one hand, as he undid his own pants with the other, revealing a large bulge in his underwear. Coke, meanwhile, was watching the entire scene with anticipation on his face, a little drool at the corners of his mouth. The gun was still at Ben's head. Lila stopped screaming.

I think it was her eyes that changed me forever. Lying there, splayed across the table completely naked, being held down at the shoulders by Slash and at the legs by Tank, she turned to me with a tear running down the side of her head, and with an expression of resignation in her eyes that said "I'm done. How much worse could my life get?" Then I snapped. Oh God, did I snap.

Ben stomped down hard on Coke's instep. Coke cried out in surprise. At the same time, Ben grabbed hold of the gun, while reaching for Coke's pinkie finger. He yanked back on the finger until he heard a loud crack. Coke screamed in pain.

Coke's attention on the proceedings was the only thing that had saved Ben. It gave him that extra second to do the two simplest things he could remember from karate class. He then twisted the gun away from the still screaming Coke, held it point blank in Coke's face, and pulled the trigger. The noise inside the shelter was deafening. Coke's head exploded and blood and pieces of his brain sprayed the walls.

Ben turned his attention to Slash, who had let go of Lila and was reaching for a gun. Lila, meanwhile, rolled off the table onto the floor of the shelter. He aimed at Slash's midsection and pulled the trigger. His aim was off, and the bullet caught Slash in the throat, almost severing his head from his body. Ben spun and looked at Tank, who was trying to pull up his pants to get to his holster. Again he shot at the midsection and this time hit what he was aiming for. Tank went down with a grunt.

Ben ran to the tent to get the sleeping bag. He returned with it and placed it over Lila, who was curled up in a corner. He heard a noise and saw Tank crawling for the shelter opening. The rage within Ben was all-consuming. He walked over to Tank and viciously kicked him in the face. Tank flopped over on his back, his nose flattened and several teeth stuck by blood to his face. Ben couldn't even speak. He pointed the gun at Tank's crotch. Tank's eyes widened in fear. Ben pulled the trigger and Tank opened his mouth to scream, but nothing came out.

Not finished yet, Ben destroyed both kneecaps with shots. He pointed his gun at Tank's elbow and was about to shoot when he heard Lila scream his name. "Ben, please stop!" She was sobbing. "Oh, please stop! Please…" Her voice trailed off. She sat there with her face in her hands, shaking uncontrollably.

Ben looked at Tank, who had lost consciousness, then looked down at the gun in his hand, and dropped it to the floor. He was covered in blood, mostly from Coke's head. Smoke hung heavily in the shelter, his ears were ringing, and the smell of gunpowder was so pungent it burned his nose.

He stepped over to Lila and sat down beside her. And then he began to cry. They held each other for an eternity. Finally, Lila rose and picked up her pants and the remnants of her shirt and put them on. She came over to Ben and pulled him up. They walked over to the tent and retrieved their boots, backpacks, and their weapons, all without a word. They left the tent where it was, the sleeping bag in the shelter, and walked back to the trail. As they were about to embark, a group of men with rifles came up the trail at a run.

"Hey, stop," yelled one of the men. They approached Ben and Lila, who had turned and looked at the group sightlessly. The ringing in their ears was still intense from the explosions of the guns in the enclosed space. They could hear the men, but everything was muffled.

Looking at Ben's blood-covered body, one of the men said, "Shit, what happened to you?"

Getting no response, he said, "You're the two who were in camp talking to Paul yesterday, right? We're looking for Tank, Slash, and Coke. Have you seen them? They killed Paul and the other members of the Board last night."

Ben pointed in the direction of the shelter, and he and Lila turned and continued on their way.

As they walked, they heard, "Holy mother of God!" behind them.

I honestly don't remember much of that day or the next. We walked and just kept walking. I don't know if we said two words to each other. I didn't know who had been scarred worse from the experience. We got off the trail at some point ... at some town ... and wandered the streets until we found a sporting goods store. We picked out a tent and a couple of new sleeping bags. There were probably other things we should have looked for, but we were in no shape to think clearly. We got back on the trail and headed south.

Toward dusk the day after the shooting, they came upon a lake. It was an idyllic spot nestled in the green hills. They both knew they had found their healing place. They chose a location far from the trail, on a sandy bank. Without a word, they set down their packs and took off their boots and holsters and emptied their pockets. Lila dug in her pack for a bar of soap, and they walked into the water fully clothed. They spent the better part of an hour taking off each piece of clothing and washing it thoroughly. Then they washed themselves, then each other, then themselves again. Finally, when they felt that they had washed off the memories of the day before, Ben threw the soap onto the grass, and they turned to each other and hugged and kissed and cried. They walked out of the water and dried themselves, then sat wrapped in their towels watching the sun go down.

They finally talked that night, and it was if the floodgates had opened. They didn't fall asleep until almost dawn. They talked about the experience, but also about their childhood, their future, and most of all, their love for each other.

"I know that I was nearly raped," said Lila at one point, "and if that had happened even a few weeks ago, I would have spent years in therapy. But I'm okay. I don't know why, but I'm okay. Maybe it will hit me later. I don't know, but I think it has more to do with being in survival mode. It's not the world it used to be, and I'm not the person I used to be."

"Your strength has kept me alive," said Ben simply.

"And your actions the other morning have kept both of us alive."

"In some ways it was the easiest thing I've ever done, but the hardest thing I'm ever going to have to live with," said Ben. "I don't care that it was three scumbags who more than deserved to die. It was the fact that I pointed a gun at someone and pulled the trigger. I'll probably have nightmares of that for the rest of my life."

"I don't think so," said Lila. "I've watched you gain massive strength since that day in the freezer. If you were the person then that you are now, Richie never would have called you a dumb schmuck. He wouldn't have even been able to look you in the eye. There's a confidence in your eyes ... in your whole being. There will come a time when you'll remember back to this and just know that you did what was necessary."

They finally slept, waking up in the early afternoon. Setting up their camp with the expectation that they'd be there more than a couple of days, they cleaned out their backpacks and hung clothes on tree branches to air them out. They dug a fire pit in the sand and gathered wood. No longer did they feel the need to hide their presence. While they had no desire to see anyone, they refused to be scared. They were going to live life on their own terms.

They were running low on water, so Lila decided to take a chance and start boiling lake water to drink. They didn't know how polluted it was—it looked clean enough—and they took time to walk some of the shoreline to make sure there weren't any bodies contaminating the water. They ran across a canoe and paddled it back to their camp.

Ben decided to try his hand at fishing. They were sick of freeze-dried and canned food. He took Phil's advice and dug for worms, attached one to a hook, and cast it out into the lake and let it sit. He caught something almost immediately. He had no idea what it was, but it looked big enough to eat. A half an hour later he caught a second. Altogether, he came away with four fish. Lila had found a flat log that they could use to filet the fish, and they decided to cook them over the open fire using skewers they fashioned out of long slivers of wood.

The fish was a welcome relief to their palates. They ate just the fish—no canned food to go with it—and at the end felt like they had accomplished something significant. They had provided for themselves. They knew that a real sportsman would laugh at their accomplishment, but for two former suburban teens, it was life-changing. The next step would be hunting game.

They spent a week healing. They slept a lot, fished a lot—Ben experimented with lures and became quite successful—and took the canoe out to the middle of the lake and just let it sit there as they soaked in the sun. They talked, made love, and swam in the chilly water. They could have stayed indefinitely, but after a week of unusually warm weather, they could again feel the signs of winter approaching. They also needed to stock up on all sorts of supplies.

They had three violent storms during the week, but were almost getting used to them. However, they couldn't shake the feeling that the storms were only the beginning of something more dangerous.

They had to travel several miles off the trail to find the next town. They located a drugstore and stocked up more thoroughly on first aid supplies. They had each gained a lot of muscle weight and found they could carry much heavier packs. Lila picked up a supply of tampons and other female items, and Ben took that opportunity to strip the store of all of its condoms. He had run out the last day by the lake—definitely a sign that it was time to go. Lila also decided to find a couple of paperback novels.

"Maybe it's time to see if I can read a novel without it being too nostalgic," she explained. "What I'm really afraid of is that it won't have any meaning to me anymore. Can I read a novel and actually enjoy it?" As she said that, she changed her mind and decided that she wasn't ready to read one. However, at a bookstore nearby, they did find three valuable books: a practical guide to first aid, a book on deer hunting, and another on small game hunting.

Then they found a sporting goods store and stocked up on some of the items they should have picked up the day they got the new tent and sleeping bags. At that point, they felt they had reached their weight limit in their packs, and decided to head back to the trail.

The following evening they were starting to search for a place to camp—they were no longer looking for wooden shelters—when they smelled campfire smoke off the trail. They investigated and discovered a group of eight people: two men, three women, and three children. Normally they might have walked on, but there was something pleasant-looking about the group, so they thought they'd stop by.

"Approaching the fire," called out Ben. He heard a couple of guns cock, but they showed themselves anyway.

"We're friendly," said Lila, and stepped into the clearing.

Seeing that they didn't have their weapons in their hands, the men put down their own.

"We don't mean to barge in," said Ben. "We smelled the smoke and thought we'd stop. We might end up seeing each other on the trail, so we thought it would be good to introduce ourselves. I'm Ben and this is Lila."

The adults looked at each other. "If I'm not mistaken," said one of the men, "you exterminated some vermin about ten days ago. Am I right?"

Ben looked at Lila. "Um…"

"Three mean ones?" added the man.

"I guess you could say so," said Ben hesitantly, not knowing where this was going.

"Then come and sit," said the other man. "You're welcome here anytime."

The group turned out to be from the survivor camp. Two of them looked to be married, but the rest--including the children--had just come together along the way. Most of them remembered seeing the two teens when they came in and talked to Paul. They told the story of the night the two left the camp.

"We'd been having problems with those three ever since they showed up," explained Dan, the first one to speak when they had walked in. "But, everyone was afraid of them. The board just wanted to form a decent community. There are always some problem people, but these three were pretty extreme. Finally, the night you left, the board decided to do something about it. They told them they were being evicted. They left quietly—or so we thought—and came back later that evening with weapons and hunted each Board member down one by one."

Ben and Lila were sad. They had liked Paul.

"The Board wasn't particularly strong," said Dan, "but they were trying. It's hard to form something out of nothing. They made some mistakes, but eventually they might have gotten something going with the community."

"Is the camp still there?" asked Lila.

"It is. They formed a new board after the group came back to report what you'd done to those three."

"We heard it was pretty gruesome," cut in Gordon, the other man.

Ben just nodded. He didn't know what to say.

"Anyway," continued Dan. "It was time we moved on. We decided to head south, as did a number of the people, once they knew they wouldn't encounter Tank and his gang. You did a service for a lot of folks. Thank you."

"Actually," said Gordon, "You're pretty famous. The story is spreading down the trail of the two mysterious teenagers who faced down the scum of the earth, and left many grateful survivors in their wake."

And that was how we became folk heroes.

PART 2:
THE LEGEND OF BEN AND LILA

CHAPTER 10

Time had worked to weed out the weakest of the humans. The George and Bunnys of the world—and even the Phils—had died out, leaving only those whose will to live was strong enough to sustain them. It didn't mean that there weren't any crazy people out there, it just meant that they were "strong" crazy people. And of course, you had the "Tank" types, who felt they could take advantage of those who were weakened by the disaster. The fact is, we were all weakened by it, but Lila and I had found the strength in each other to somehow grow in the process. But could we still grow if we found ourselves without each other? Early in our journey, I thought we would wilt and die without the other. Was that still the case?

They stayed the night with Dan and company, and were off early the next morning. They walked for days, occasionally encountering others on their own journeys. They ran across a small camp from time to time, usually within the proximity of an urban area. They ranged in size from a half dozen to a couple of dozen people. Nobody seemed particularly happy, but all appeared determined to make it through the ordeal. Whereas in the days following the disaster, people were curious as to how others survived, nobody cared anymore. They were alive, and that was all that mattered.

Almost all of them had heard of Ben and Lila. They were greeted with a mixture of respect, awe, and even a little fear. The story of their incident with Tank and his buddies had taken on a life of its own—exaggerated each time it was passed on to another. Since nobody really knew what had happened—the few people who had been at the scene after the fact could only surmise—it lent itself to interpretation. Wild interpretation.

At first they tried to set the record straight, without going into personal details, but after a while they decided not to bother. The first reason being that nothing they said seemed to have any effect on the version of the story people wanted to believe. The second was that they might end up being safer if people feared them a bit. A reputation could be a good thing in the world in which they were now living.

They began to realize for real just how few people had survived. Assuming that most either headed for the country—the forests or the mountains—or to the sea, and abandoned the cities due to the sheer numbers of dead and the risk of disease, they were seeing around them what was left of the country's population. Ben's unscientific guess was that for every million who died, maybe a hundred survived. Maybe.

They tried to camp near water, so they could fish, which was becoming a staple of their diet. At night they read their books on small game hunting. They weren't ready to tackle deer just yet, figuring it was way more meat than they needed while traveling.

They also read another book on edible wild plants. If they were going to live in this new world, they needed to garner as much knowledge of the wilderness as they could.

Once in a while they would venture into a town to find a bookstore and add to their library, throwing away cans of food from their packs and replacing them with survival books. During one of their forays off the trail, Ben located a gun shop and once more stocked up heavily on ammunition. As he turned to leave, a selection of crossbows caught his attention. While most were too large to conveniently carry, he discovered a smaller version—only about 18 inches long and weighing about two pounds—called a pistol crossbow. Immediately falling in love with it, he picked up a quiver and a supply of arrows—or bolts, as he learned they were called.

He showed his new possession to Lila, who could sense his excitement.

"One of the disadvantages of the rifle," he explained, "is the noise. If I can get good at this, it'll really expand our options for hunting."

Eventually, they crossed the Susquehanna River and knew they were making progress. The violent storms still came on a frequent basis to slow them down, and once, they could have even sworn that they felt the ground move under them.

They often took target practice, and Ben practiced with his crossbow until he was feeling pretty confident. They never argued, and in fact, found their love growing deeper each day. They began to know what the other would do or say before that person would even know it themselves.

Sometimes they would venture far off the trail just to experience the peace of the forests or the vistas provided by the cliffs. It was during one of these expeditions that they finally decided to try hunting. They were emerging from the forest into a large meadow when they spotted a small flock of sheep not more than 50 feet away. They hadn't made the conscious decision to start hunting that day, but encountering the sheep sealed it for them.

"How did sheep get here, in the middle of nowhere?" asked Ben in a whisper.

"I'm actually surprised we haven't seen more farm animals," answered Lila. "Any that made it past the fences would have looked for good sources of food and water."

"Should I go for it?" asked Ben.

"We've got to get it over with sometime. You know we've been putting it off. How is it that we can walk past thousands of dead humans, but the thought of killing an animal disturbs us?"

"Okay, well here goes," said Ben, lying down on the grass. The sheep either hadn't noticed them, or didn't care. Ben figured that being farm animals, they were used to the scent of humans. He got into a comfortable prone position, bracing his elbows on the grass, and aimed at the closest of the sheep. He took a deep breath and slowly let the air out. He pulled the trigger, the sound of the rifle a rude interruption to the peace and quiet of the meadow. The sheep scattered and birds exploded from the trees. A lone sheep lay in the grass motionless.

He looked at Lila and saw tears in her eyes. They slowly got up and approached the dead animal.

The tears were now rolling down Lila's cheeks. "He's so beautiful," she said quietly. "I feel horrible."

"I do too," said Ben. "But if we're going to survive, we're going to have to get beyond this."

"I know," replied Lila. She put her hand on the sheep's head and started talking to the animal. "Thank you for giving up your life for us. We are truly grateful for your sacrifice." She was silent for a minute, then said, "Okay, I guess I'm ready. I know it'll get easier. I just didn't expect the first one to be so hard."

"Why don't we do what we need to right here?" suggested Ben. "We can take the meat we want, then leave the rest for the bears, or dogs, or coyotes."

Lila agreed, and they got to work.

It was a disaster from the very beginning. Using a book that gave explicit instructions for slaughtering the sheep, Ben slit the sheep's throat to allow the blood to drain from the body, then tied a cord to its back legs to hang it from a branch. It was a lot heavier than they anticipated, but after a lot of effort, and two broken branches, they managed to hang it from the tree. Everything seemed messier and more difficult than they had hoped for, and Ben made numerous wrong cuts. They also realized that they lacked a saw to take off the sheep's legs and head. However, they kept at it until Ben sliced into the sheep's intestines by mistake and fecal matter gushed over everything. They knew the meat would now be contaminated.

Ben flopped down on the ground, frustrated and exhausted.

"We ended this sheep's life for nothing," he said.

"It wasn't for nothing," replied Lila. "Look at what we've learned from this. The biggest thing is knowing that we can do it. Okay, so maybe the first one didn't work, but the next one will, and with each time we do it, it'll get easier. At least we know that because of everything we've seen over the last few weeks, this didn't gross us out as much as we thought it would. Next time let's try something smaller and work our way up. It'll also be easier when we find a place to settle down. We can find the right tools and do it the right way."

The next day they shot a rabbit and the day after Ben got a squirrel with his crossbow. Cleaning the smaller animals was a lot easier, and when they ate their first meal of rabbit, the pride of accomplishment they felt was beyond anything either of them had experienced before. Hunting the animals also became easier. They no longer allowed feelings of guilt, only appreciation for what was coming into their lives.

Yet, while they found themselves adapting to the wild, they still craved certain amenities from their old life. Soap, toothpaste, and razors were essentials. Lila had to shave her legs, and Ben was determined not to grow a mountain man beard. That wouldn't happen though, as Lila often teased him, because his whiskers still didn't grow that fast, and when they did, they came through in clumps. Certain areas of his face just didn't grow hair.

They began to cover fewer miles in a day, simply because of their side trips off the trail. But that was okay. They no longer felt an urgency to get "somewhere". Where they were at any given moment was where they needed to be. They were happy. They could honestly say that they were the happiest they had ever been.

And then the rains and the winds came. The weather had worried us for a while, so when the mega-storm finally hit, it was almost anti-climactic. The resulting set of circumstances, however, was something we hadn't anticipated.

It crept up with very little warning. They had just set up their tent and were making a fire pit when they felt raindrops. The night sky had hidden the approaching clouds. With the raindrops came the wind. They quickly moved their backpacks into the tent—this one had a little more room than their first tent—and closed the flap.

"I guess it's a can of nuts for dinner," said Lila, rummaging in her pack.

As usual, the lightning and thunder were intense, and it went on all night. By morning, Ben was starting to worry. None of the storms had lasted anywhere this long, and it showed no signs of letting up. They decided to get comfortable. What could have been a romantic time in a tent in the rain, however, was spoiled by the viciousness of the storm.

The storm lasted three days, with no let-up. Late on the second day, the wind suddenly picked up to a ferocious roar.

"What is that?" yelled Lila.

"Sounds like an engine. A plane or a train," Ben shouted back.

They looked at each other, terrified. The minute Ben said the word 'train', they both knew what it was. They had heard enough news reports of tornados where witnesses said it sounded like a freight train.

"Hold on!" yelled Ben.

He barely got it out of his mouth when the tornado struck. The whole tent was uprooted and thrown a hundred feet down a hill into a batch of scrub brush. The small, hard branches ripped the tent to shreds. They continued to tumble down the steep slope, finally coming to rest in six inches of water in a small grove of trees. The tornado disappeared as quickly as it had arrived, but the fury of the rainstorm continued.

Ben saw blood in the water, and heard Lila scream, "Omigod, Ben. You're hurt."

He looked down and saw one of his crossbow bolts stuck deeply in his thigh. He hadn't even felt it go in. Now he did. The pain was excruciating. Lila tried to locate the first aid kit in all the mess. It was nowhere to be found.

"The first aid kit is gone," she shouted. It was hard to be heard above the roar of the storm. She rummaged through Ben's pack and found a reasonably clean t-shirt. "I can try to use this as a bandage," she said.

The pain was so unbearable, Ben felt like he was going to pass out. "You've gotta get the bolt out."

Lila quickly assessed the situation. Luckily, Ben had chosen tips that were smooth as they came to a point, rather than the flared kind, so she was able to pull the bolt out the way it went in. She told Ben what she was planning.

"Go for it," he said through clenched teeth. She pulled and he screamed. It came out accompanied by some soft tissue and a lot of blood. Lila put his t-shirt on the wound and pressed down hard. Ben passed out. Lila kept her weight on the wound, in some ways happy that Ben had lost consciousness so he wouldn't feel it. It eventually clotted and Lila found a second t-shirt to replace the first one.

Meanwhile, the rain continued to come down in buckets, but Lila was able to pull what was left of the tent over them for a little protection. Ben regained consciousness and they found a somewhat comfortable position, where they stayed until the rain finally stopped the next day.

Everything was a mess. The woods further down the hill had become a swamp from the rain. While Ben sat against a tree, Lila searched for their belongings. Luckily, all of their weapons survived the deluge, as did their packs and canteens. The contents of the packs, however, weren't so lucky. She recovered bits and pieces, including a few cans of food, and some she found as far as a quarter of a mile into the woods. But many of their possessions had been lost.

"A lot of the missing stuff we can eventually replace," said Lila, after taking an inventory. "What concerns me the most is the loss of the antibiotics. We took them exactly for a situation like this. We thought ahead. And now we don't have them. I could kick myself for not closing and tying my pack."

"We didn't know," replied Ben. "Maybe it won't get infected."

It did. The next day, the wound had turned red, with pus oozing out.

"We've got to get you some antibiotics," said Lila in alarm when she pulled up the bandage. "Can you walk at all?"

"I can try." Lila helped him up and he used his rifle as a crutch. Immediately, he felt dizzy, and when he set his foot down, he almost collapsed from the pain. "No way," he said.

"Maybe I can make a stretcher or one of those Indian things ... a travois."

"We don't have anything to tie it all together," said Ben. "Plus, you'd have to get me up the hill first." He held her hands and looked into her eyes. "Lila, we have a choice. We can wait this out and see if it heals on its own, or you will have to go find some by yourself."

"Do you remember where we are?" asked Lila.

"The map is gone, but I think we're near a place called New Kingstown. I have no idea how big it is, but I think Mechanicsburg and Harrisburg aren't too far from it."

"Okay," said Lila. "I think I should go."

"This will be the first time we've been separated," said Ben.

"That's okay," replied Lila, smiling. "I was getting kind of sick of you anyway."

"Take your weapons, just in case," said Ben.

"I will," answered Lila. "But that's all I'm taking. I can move faster that way. I've left you a canteen and a couple of cans of beef stew, in case you get hungry. I guess you'd have to eat it cold, but I won't be long, so I don't think you'll have to worry about it. Do you need anything before I leave?"

"Nope. Just hurry back to me. I love you."

"I love you too." They kissed. "I should be back in a few hours at most."

Famous last words.

CHAPTER 11
(Lila)

Lila climbed the hill and found her way back to the trail. She took out her knife and made some large notches in a tree to remind herself where to find Ben. "Just my luck," she said to herself. "I'd come back with the medicine and spend the next month looking for him."

She headed down the trail at a run. She had gotten so used to traveling with the heavy backpack, she had forgotten the freedom of being unencumbered. However, the thought of Ben, sitting all alone deep in the woods in debilitating pain, was all too sobering. An hour later, at what looked like the most appropriate spot, she got off the trail and made her way toward town. A number of buildings had burned, including the first drugstore she came to, but the next block down was intact, and she saw another large drugstore.

"Nice thing about this country," she said aloud. "No shortage of drugstores."

For the first time on their trip, the store she entered was a mess and had been heavily looted. Her heart sank. She headed for the pharmacy and started sifting through piles of medicines. The good ones had all been taken. She was left with prescription mouthwashes and hemorrhoid suppositories. She kicked a pile in anger, and bottles and tubes went flying. As she turned to leave, she noticed the bags of filled prescriptions. They were unopened. She let out a little scream of joy and started to rip open the bags. In no time she found the antibiotics she was looking for.

She ran through the store, out the door, and smack into someone standing there. She hit the ground hard, her rifle bouncing back into the store opening.

"Well what have we here?"

He was tall and blonde, carrying an M-16, and wearing Army fatigues. Lila looked around. There were three others, all sitting in an old convertible looking at her lying on the pavement.

"You a junkie?" asked the blonde man, in a slight southern accent. "Looking for a fix in the drugstore?"

Keep cool, Lila thought to herself.

"Sorry I ran into you," she replied to the man, as she stood up. "My boyfriend is hurt and I was getting him some antibiotics."

"You expect me to believe that?"

She dug into her pocket and held out the drug. "See? He really is hurt. I need to get back to him quickly. Nice to meet you, but I've gotta go."

"Hold on there," he said. He had sergeant stripes on his uniform, and seemed to be in charge. "You can't be out here all by yourself. You should come with us. We have a camp set up with a lot of people. You'll be safe there."

"I appreciate the offer," said Lila, who was growing increasingly uncomfortable, "but I'm okay, thanks."

"Hey, look. We'll pick up your boyfriend along the way. We're not going to hurt you. We're the good guys. We have a doctor at the camp."

I was torn. They made me nervous, but there might have been something sincere about their motives. I wasn't sure. I wanted to be back with Ben—just the two of us—but was that the best thing for Ben? Would he be better off being seen by a doctor?

"Okay," she said hesitantly. "Can we go now, though?"
"Sure can. We even have a car. Climb in."
It was strange for Lila to be in a car again. It looked like it was from the 1950s. Phil had been right about the pre-computer cars. They took off in the direction she had come from. Too late, she thought of her rifle in the doorway of the drugstore.
"This is Mike, Brian, and Ray," said the blonde man. "My name is Walt. We belong to a camp about ten miles down the road. It's organized and safe. The head honcho is Major Wells. You'll like him. So where's your boyfriend?"
"He's a few miles up the Appalachian Trail. In fact, there's the entrance over there. That's where I came out. Stop. Stop!"
The car kept driving. The four men looked at each other.
"Oh, sorry," said Walt. "We're not allowed to go on the trail. I'm afraid we won't be able to pick him up. I thought he was in a house or something."
"Then let me out. Please! I'll take him the medicine myself."
"Well, I'm afraid we can't do that either," replied Walt. "We're under strict orders to bring everyone back to the camp that we find. I'd be really punished if it got out that I let you go. I'm sorry."
Lila started crying and screaming, "Let me go! Please! He's hurt. He's going to die if I don't get to him." She tried to jump out of the moving car, but one of the others grabbed her.

"We're doing this for your own good. You have to trust us," he said, holding her in place.

I watched with horror as the entrance to the trail got further and further away, picturing Ben's face as he started to wonder if I'd ever come back, and what could have happened to me. I saw him three days from now, looking at his leg as it turned gangrene, the realization hitting him that he was going to die alone in the woods. My heart was breaking. My whole world was ending.

And yet—and maybe this was the survival mode that Ben and I had so strongly embraced—I had to start planning my escape. This wasn't going to be how my life ended. But I couldn't read these guys. Were they taking me somewhere for a rerun of the Tank incident, or was there really a camp? On one hand, they seemed like they thought they were really saving me from something. But on the other, there was a sort of cult-like feeling about them—people doing bad things with good intentions.

And through it all was the thought: "I'm sorry Ben. I'm sorry I let you down."

There was a camp. It appeared to Lila to be a long abandoned armory. It was in an open field about a half a mile in diameter; a few smaller buildings grouped around a much larger one. The important feature, at least to Lila, was the tall fence with barbed wire at the top. They had picked their spot well. There was one entrance, with two guards manning the gate. Lila could see a few other vintage cars and trucks parked outside the compound. Inside the fences were close to a hundred people. They had set up makeshift shelters throughout the compound. She tried to guess the number of guards without luck. But there didn't seem to be too many.

The car pulled up to the gate. "We have a new guest," said Walt.

"Welcome," the guard said to Lila. "Major Wells will be happy to meet you."

"If I could meet him soon, I would appreciate it," said Lila, trying her best not to create any animosity.

"In due time," answered the guard. "We have to process you in first."

Her traveling companions climbed out of the car and moved her along toward one of the buildings. She had the thought that if she could get away even for a moment, she would start shooting at her captors, regardless of the result. As if reading her mind, the one called Ray slipped her Sig from its holster as they walked.

"We'll keep this for you," he said. "Don't worry. We won't lose it."

Lila looked around. Many of the "residents" had come over to check out the new person. Suddenly, she saw Dan, Gordon, and the rest of their group. One of the women put her hand over her mouth in surprise. Dan whispered to the man next to him, who whispered to the people around him. Soon they were all murmuring. She heard the names "Lila" and "Ben" more than a few times. That made her walk with more of a swagger. She and Ben had somehow made a positive impression on folks who had heard their names. Lila felt that it would be good to keep up the image. Somewhere down the line, it might turn out to be one of the smarter things she'd done. These people looked trapped. Whatever power the guards wielded, it was enough to keep everyone in submission. They would need a leader. Lila already had the reputation. If she could build on it, maybe she could get them to follow her in an uprising.

Meanwhile, her heart ached. She thought of Ben every minute. If only she had looked before running out of the drugstore. If only she had pulled out her gun the minute she met the men. If only…

However, she needed to stay focused. Ben would expect her to stay focused. If she could escape tomorrow and steal a car, she could still make it to Ben in time. A big if. As they walked, she slipped her right hand into her pocket and halfway pulled out a tiny Swiss Army Knife, the kind used on a keychain. She slipped it into the small watch pocket in her jeans.

They entered the building. It consisted of one large, drab room, with some long tables set up in the shape of a square, and one table at the door with a file cabinet, obviously the check-in point. A very officious-looking man, dressed the same way as all the other guards, asked for her name.

She thought of using a fictitious name, but then realized that her real name would eventually come up with the "residents," which would make its way back to the guards. That could have a negative backlash on her.

"Lila Martin."

"Home?"

"None in particular."

The guard frowned. "Where are you from?"

"Massachusetts."

The guards looked at each other.

"How'd you get here?"

"I walked with my boyfriend. He's hurt on the Appalachian Trail. Could someone go with me to pick him up? He needs a doctor."

"Sorry, we don't go on the trail."

"Why not?"

"Too dangerous. The possibility of ambush is too great. Other groups have died. It's just not worth the risk. I'm sorry about your boyfriend."

They had heard the stories! They just hadn't put Lila's name to them ... yet.

"Please take that knife off your leg and empty your pockets."

"Why?"

"To keep order here, there mustn't be any weapons."

"But you have weapons." Lila suddenly didn't care what they thought of her. This unemotional little toad was getting to her. "I don't even want to be here. I'd like to leave."

"I'm sorry. I can't allow that. It's for your own good."

She lost it.

"My own good? Listen, you insignificant little pissant. It's a good thing you're taking this knife, because if you didn't, I would shove it up through your nostril and out the back of your head."

The man turned pale and the other three laughed. "Oh, we have a feisty one here," said Ray. "The major is going to like her."

She emptied her pockets, making sure not to touch her watch pocket. Ray patted her down, but was not particularly thorough and missed the knife.

"You will be in shelter number 32," said the toad stiffly. "The others can tell you about the meal schedule and bathing privileges. Through that door. Pick up a pillow, a blanket, and a bag of personal items on your way out."

She grabbed the items he mentioned and walked out the door into the compound.

"Ben, if you can hear me," she whispered, "please stay alive. I'm so sorry."

What was this place? Why were we here? Did they have a purpose in mind? I looked out at the residents, who were all watching me. They were scared. No doubt about it. Something terrified them. At first glance, the men looked weak. The women had retreated into themselves. It was going to take a Herculean effort to get this group to do something. Emotionally, they had already been beaten down.

The first one to approach her was Dan.

"Lila, I'm sorry you're here. Where's Ben?"

She looked at him with tears in her eyes. She was trying hard to hold it together.

"He's sitting under a tree far off the trail, waiting for me to return with antibiotics," she answered, her voice catching as she talked. "His leg is infected. I know he's wondering what happened to me."

"What did happen?" asked Dan. He had subtly moved her away from the rest of the crowd, so now it was only Dan and Gordon with her.

Lila explained how she arrived there, then asked them what had happened to them.

"We came off the trail too," explained Gordon. "Actually, not too far from here. The trail passes less than a mile that way," he said, pointing past the fence. "We were met by some guys in a truck, who told us they could get us a hot meal and a hot shower. Well, that was enough for us. We were thinking of the kids. They needed a break. So, we got in with them and the rest is history. We've been here almost a week."

"What exactly is this place?" asked Lila.

"Hard to say, exactly," replied Dan. "The best we can figure is that this Major Wells …"

"Who, we're not sure is a Major at all," cut in Gordon.

"We think it's all about power," continued Dan. "The oldest story in the book. He sees that the country is in shambles. Somebody's got to lead. The problem is, if you're going to lead, you need followers. So, where to get your citizens? In his case, he hijacks them. He sends teams out to pick up stragglers, brings them back here, and expects them to become loyal subjects over time. He probably figures that somewhere down the line, once he has their loyalty, he can move out of the camp, back into towns."

Lila was confused. She was also hurting badly. She wanted to get out of there to help Ben, but couldn't do a thing about it. Inside, she was weeping. Outside, she had to show strength. It was killing her. "Two things I don't understand: Where did he get his little army; and how does he expect the people here to follow him?"

Gordon looked away.

"Second question first," explained Dan. "He deprives us of everything. He feeds us enough to keep us alive, but we have to earn things. We have to volunteer to help out in some way. He doesn't ask. I think he figures that if we come to him offering our help, it's more effective than him asking us. It puts us in a more subservient position. So we can earn more food, the occasional cold bath—in bath water that has been used by people before you, of course—an extra blanket on a cold night, things like that."

"Tell her," said Gordon.

"I will. Give me a minute," replied Dan. "The children get as much food as they want. Wells figures that if he's good to the children, they'll grow up admiring him."

He continued, "As for your first question, I think he had a couple of followers starting out. He may have actually been the leader of a small cult—but I can't be sure. I think he made deals with various men along the way; if they worked for him in establishing a new regime, they'd get special treatment and would be assured a high post when it all gets established. I've overheard some of the guards talking, so that's where I get this."

"Tell her," persisted Gordon.

"In a sec. Wells is the leader here, and he's not too awful, in his own way. I have a feeling his original intention, though misguided, was genuine. The thing is though, he has a second-in-command who wields the real power. I think it's just a matter of time before he takes over. His name is Captain Sharp. He's real mean. You don't cross him. There were some guys who did, and he made a public showing of their punishment. He made sure not to kill them, but it wasn't pretty. Major Wells stays away from that stuff."

"Tell her!"

"Tell me what?" asked Lila.

"I told you that they make us ask to help," said Dan. "They also keep the men down through beatings and intimidation. Keep us weak and fearful. The women, however are kept subservient a different way."

Here it comes, thought Lila.

"Wells and Sharp choose whatever woman they want for the night ... every night. Sometimes they let some of the guards have their pick too. Gordon's wife has been given to the guards twice already. What she's had to submit to is beyond criminal. It's heinous."

Gordon was crying.

Dan continued. "Rewarding his guards with a woman every once in a while keeps them hungry and loyal. So really, it's the two oldest things: power and sex."

"The thing is," added Gordon, wiping away his tears. "Wells

likes his women young. He's going to take an immediate liking to you."

Not if I had any say in the matter.

CHAPTER 12
(Lila)

As Lila was talking to Dan and Gordon, she noticed the furtive glances by many of the other residents. Dan caught it too.

"They all know who you are, although many are confused because it's just you, and not both of you. I think some of them are hoping that you can somehow save them from this place. Others have made comments that they are disappointed that, besides being alone, you are smaller and younger than they thought you'd be," he explained. "On the other hand, one of the citizens—that's what Wells calls us—was near the door and heard your comment to Bill about shoving the knife up his nose. That made its rounds almost instantly, reviving people's hope in you."

"One person can't do it alone," said Lila. "They have to be willing to do their part."

"And that's the problem," replied Gordon. "They are already so beaten down and frightened, I just don't know how much help you'd get. You can count on Dan and me of course, and we know of a few others, but after that ..."

"Here's the other thing," added Dan. "Be very careful who you talk to. Some of the citizens have become informers in the hopes of getting extra privileges." He put his arm around her shoulders. "We'll walk you to your shelter. I'm sorry about Ben. He's strong though. You never know. He could pull out of that on his own."

"Even if he did, he'd never know where to look for me."

"I've watched you two," responded Dan. "You have a really strong connection. If he's alive, you'll find each other."

"I want to get out of here as quickly as I can and get to him."

Ben and I were a team. It seemed so strange to be without him. We always made decisions together. But, we were always on the same wavelength, which told me that whatever plan I came up with would be one that Ben would agree with. So I just had to pretend that he was here with me. He WAS here. His enthusiasm, his bravery, and his spirit were so much a part of me, he could have been standing right next to me. I wished he was.

Changing the subject because it was just too painful, Lila said to Gordon, "How's your wife holding up?"

Gordon looked as if he was going to cry again. "She's ashamed. She doesn't talk much anymore. I don't know what we're going to do."

"If she's willing," said Lila, "I'd like to talk to her. I think I might be able to help."

"Thank you," replied Gordon. "I'll tell her."

They reached Lila's shelter, such as it was. A tiny A-frame, just big enough for one person to sleep. It had been shoddily put together. It was damp, probably from the last storm, and Lila could see the sky through large gaps in the wood. It would be useless in the rain.

She looked at Dan. "You said a while ago that Wells wasn't

awful. Why? Because he's not as violent as Sharp? Don't kid yourself. He's just as bad—maybe worse because he hides his ugliness behind Sharp. Anyone who would do this to people," she swept her hand to indicate all of the people and the shelters, "is evil. It's a crime that with all the good people in the world who died that day, people like Wells and Sharp and Tank would survive. Well, we took care of Tank. Now it's time for Wells and Sharp to pay."

I remembered the fury with which Ben exacted his revenge on Tank, Slash, and Coke. I had pleaded with him to stop because his rage scared me. I didn't like what he had become that day. Now I understood. I had the same rage, only I realized that I was more calculating than Ben. He let his out in a firestorm that annihilated everyone in his path. Mine was building slowly. When I took my revenge, I was going to enjoy it. Every minute of it. I was going to make them pay for what they had done to Ben, to my life with Ben, and to people like Gordon's wife, who deserved none of it. If it meant I had to work alone, so be it. If it meant I had to die in the process, I wanted the name Lila to become a rallying cry for all who refused to put up with evil in this new world.

And how would I try to do all this? With a one-inch blade on my Swiss Army Knife!

Dan nudged Lila. "Here they come."

From the large main building came a small group of men. The one in front was in his late forties or early fifties, average build, and a shaved head. Next to him was a much younger man, overweight, with a scowl. They were surrounded by four armed men.

"Wells is the bald one and Sharp is the fat one," said Dan.

They were walking as if they were the president and vice

president, expecting people to cheer for them. No one cheered, but it didn't seem to faze them. There were, in fact, a few of the weaker citizens who were trying to shake their hand, so as to ingratiate themselves and maybe get rewarded. Wells and Sharp ignored them.

As they approached Lila, she was torn as to how she would handle it. Does she play it cool or take it right to them? She finally figured she'd wing it.

"Welcome to our camp," said Wells, holding out his hand. She shook it. "We've been hearing about you; the famous Lila."

"I've gotta say you don't look like much," put in Sharp.

"Captain Sharp," said Wells, "I am sure you're familiar with the saying, 'don't judge a book by its cover.' Let's not misjudge Lila. Now you're not going to cause any trouble, are you?"

"All I want," she replied, "is to get back to my boyfriend. He's hurt and he needs my help. Can't you just let me go?"

"I'm sorry," said Wells. "We can't do that. You see, a country must protect its citizens, and this is the safest place."

"Who put you in charge?"

Sharp slapped her so hard across the face, she hit the ground and rolled about ten feet.

"Don't you ever talk to our leader like that again," he bellowed at her. "The next time you do that, there will be serious consequences."

Lila got up slowly. She had tears in her eyes and her jaw ached, but she was determined not to show any emotion.

"I'm sorry for Captain Sharp," said Wells. "He can be a little overprotective. I'll invite you over to my quarters one of these evenings for some nice conversation. I hope you'll come."

Like I have any choice, thought Lila. But to Wells, she said, "I'd be happy to. I look forward to your invitation."

"Good. Good. Well, I must be off."

Off your rocker, Lila wanted to say.

The group turned almost as one and headed back to the main building.

"Are you okay?" asked Gordon. "You're bright red where he slapped you."

"I'll be fine, thank you," she answered.

The funny thing is, I was fine, except for the devastation I felt over losing Ben. I had a mission to free the people here and to make Wells and Sharp suffer as horribly as possible. And I would do it.

It suddenly hit me that I was starting to believe my reputation.

Lila had work to do. She could almost laugh at the thought that a few weeks earlier, she was still in high school, waiting tables in a little chain restaurant, and now she was planning murder and a jailbreak, with a hundred people counting on her to succeed.

"I need to know," she said to Dan, "how many guards there are in total, and how many at any one time are on duty."

"That I can tell you," he answered. "We thought about an escape attempt a few days ago, but scrapped the plans. There are sixteen guards in all. They take twelve hour shifts, so there are eight on duty at a time. Here's the thing: of those eight, four of them are often gone looking for new citizens—like how you were found. That means there are often only four guards on duty during the day."

"But," he continued. "They have M-16s and are always keeping an eye on us. They don't get close enough for any of us to overpower them, and they are usually outside the fence. We've thought about running en masse at the gate, but we'd get mowed down. I doubt if anyone would make it."

"No," said Lila. "We have to plan something they wouldn't expect." She looked around. "Where do they store the gas for the cars?"

"Over there," said Gordon, pointing to a building close to the fence. It was next to the building Lila was processed in. "You have to understand, Lila, that we're with you a hundred percent. However, if your plan—whatever it is—doesn't work, they will take it out on the citizens here."

"Like they're not already?" asked Lila, with a flash of anger. "Look, if there's one thing Ben and I have learned to do since IT happened, it's to survive. I fully expect us to make it through this, but with survival comes risks. That's how you get better at it, by taking risks. If people here aren't willing to take a risk, then they're not worth saving. They have to want it. Otherwise, I'll just work on getting myself out of here."

Gordon was embarrassed. "You're right. I'm sorry. How could things possibly get any worse for us here?"

"What are the other buildings used for?" she asked.

Dan answered. "One is for supplies. It also houses the kitchen. The other is a bunkhouse for the guards. The building they processed you in seems to be used for meetings, as well. As for the big building, we don't really know. We do know that Wells and Sharp each have their quarters there, but as to the rest of it, maybe they're planning on expanding as the citizen population grows."

The annoying sound of an air horn came across the compound.

"That's the signal for dinner," explained Gordon. "You might want to eat. You don't get much around here."

She got in line with the others and held out a tray. The

expressionless woman serving the food slapped a spoonful of rice on the tray, followed by a smaller spoonful of canned peas and a plastic spoon. It seemed that most of the people just stood around and ate right where they were, piling their trays on a table when they were done. Then they wandered back to their shelters.

It made me angry to watch this happening. I thought back to school and learning about the various "camps" throughout history: the Nazi death camps; Manzanar; the relocation camps in South Africa; and countless others. Did I pay any attention, other than to learn it enough to pass a test? Yeah, right. Did it have an effect on me whatsoever? Of course not. This was going on all over the world and I couldn't have cared less. Maybe I would've cared if I had taken the time to really study it. But I had other things that were important. Maybe I was paying my penance now.

But I was also angry at the "citizens" here. How bad does your life have to get before you fight back? These people were like sheep. No, at least sheep make some noise. These people seemed to have given up the minute they walked in the gate. You have to fight back. You have to.

During one of our many conversations, Ben had admitted that he spent most of his life a chicken. He was always bullied and was too scared to do anything about it. Look what happened when he fought back. Look what happened when we both said, "We will survive!" I had to somehow instill in these people a will to live. And it wasn't going to be easy.

Lila walked back to her shelter alone, lost in her thoughts. She was thinking about Ben, lying there all alone in the dark woods. She waited until she was in the privacy of her shelter before she allowed herself to cry.

She was tired, but forced herself to stay awake. She wanted to get an idea of where the guards posted themselves during the night.

She realized that at night, there would be a full complement of eight guards, with nobody driving out. They stationed themselves at intervals outside the fence. Going over or under the fence at night didn't seem the best idea. She finally fell asleep, only to be awakened by the air horn at seven the next morning.

The next five days were frustrating for Lila. It seemed that every idea she came up with for escape was countered by an obstacle that made it either impossible or too risky. She couldn't help thinking that Ben was dead or dying. She thought about what Dan said, that she and Ben had a strong communication. She would lie in bed at night trying to communicate with him. The only thing she felt was his distance.

Meanwhile, she would see Wells and/or Sharp walking around the camp during the day. Sharp was just plain mean. He was always beating a man for some minor infraction. For the most part, he left the women alone. They had other uses. Wells was different. She never saw him strike anyone, but he was equally as foul. In addition to parading around like a king, he found every opportunity to degrade the men, usually in front of the women. He emasculated them time and again, obviously in the hopes of breaking them. He would approach women he had spent time with and describe their night to their husbands. Sharp was a bully. Wells was just plain evil.

The only positive happening was her talk with Gordon's wife, Melissa. Melissa sought her out one evening as Lila was sitting outside her shelter watching the guards. She approached Lila from the darkness and sat down next to her, not saying anything. Lila said hi, but decided to let Melissa have her space. Although Melissa was a good twenty years older than Lila, her confidence had been battered to the point where Lila could tell she was barely hanging on. Finally, after several minutes, Melissa said softly, "Gordon suggested I talk to you, that maybe you can help me."

Lila touched Melissa gently on the arm. "I don't know if I can or not, but seeing you so beaten down infuriates me. I can't stop them from doing the things to you that they do, but maybe I can help you get through it."

The tears were streaming down Melissa's face. Lila knew that if she couldn't get through to her, Melissa wouldn't last much longer.

She continued, "Our life turned upside down in a moment, and of the few people who did survive, some of them couldn't take it and they let themselves die. I'm sure you ran across a few of them."

Melissa nodded.

"So survival is the key word. You survived when millions didn't. You were surviving up until these people showed up. You had plans, whatever they were, and these assholes took that away from you. Your plans aren't dead. You're not dead."

She proceeded to tell Melissa the story of her near rape. "Ben and I decided that our survival—mental as well as physical—was the key. Yeah, now I find myself in the same situation as you, but they will never kill me. They will never kill my spirit. If I get called to Wells's room and am expected to do what he has done to all the other women here, I'll decide what to do at that time. If it means I have to go through with it to make it to that day when I kill him with my own hands, then I will do it."

She paused. "Melissa, our world changed. That means a lot of other things changed, maybe even our attitudes toward sex. The chance for survival can make us strong. Forget your old ways. It's a new world. The old world is long gone. If they make you do it again, do it with the secret knowledge that you, ultimately, will be in control. Wells and Sharp are only in that position temporarily."

"But what about Gordon. It's killing him to see me get led away, knowing what they are about to do."

"It's killing him because he sees that it's killing you. Let him know how much you love him and that you are doing this to survive. I think he'll understand."

"How old are you?" asked Melissa. Her voice seemed a bit stronger.

"Sixteen," answered Lila. "Actually, I guess I'm seventeen now. I was only a month or so away from my birthday when it all happened."

Melissa attempted a smile. "You're seventeen going on forty. You're mature way beyond your years. Thank you. I needed to hear that. Lila, whatever you plan, be careful. This new world needs people like you. We can't afford to lose you."

They stood up and hugged, and Melissa slipped away into the night.

The next day at breakfast, one of the guards approached Lila. It was the toad. He had a nasty smile. "Major Wells has picked you for tonight. We'll escort you after dinner." He knocked the bottom of the tray, so that her rice spilled over her front. "Have fun tonight."

"I will," answered Lila. "I'll be picturing you lying in a ditch with a bullet hole in your head."

He stopped, as if to come back and strike her, then changed his mind and walked away.

I had wondered what I would do when Wells called me in for my turn. When I was talking to Melissa, I assumed I would just do as he said and bide my time. But I had been there almost a week now, with no plan formulated and no realistic hope of escape. Something drastic had to be done, and it was up to me to do it.

Only one of us was going to walk out of that bedroom alive that night.

CHAPTER 13

Ben woke up for the fifth, or maybe the sixth time. He kept passing out. He had horrible dreams: exploding heads, and people hanging from trees—Lila was one of them. Where was Lila? She had left hours ago. Ben knew that there were towns not too far from there. Could she not find any antibiotics? And where did all the flies come from? They were landing all over him. The pain was unbearable. Finally, he passed out again.

It was dark when he awoke. He wondered if Lila had gotten lost. From the trail, it all looked the same. He heard a stick snap. He pulled his rifle closer to his body. Nothing now. Maybe it was a squirrel or something. He was suddenly cold. He wrapped the tent remains around him. It didn't help. He was shaking. His leg hurt. It felt like it was on fire.

It was light again. Had he slept through the night? Everything was still wet from the storm. He was freezing. Where was Lila? A shiver of fear shot through him. He hoped she was okay, but he knew she wouldn't have left him unless something was wrong. Why did he let her go? He passed out again and when he woke it was midday. Where did all these flies come from? They were landing all over his leg. He tried to cover it, but he just didn't have the strength. Now he was hot. So hot. He was sweating. But he knew that when it turned dark, he would be cold again. You've gotta drink, he told himself. He unscrewed the top to the canteen and took a swig. He had forgotten how good water could taste.

He could no longer keep track of time. He would be awake for a painful hour or so, then lapse into unconsciousness. When he passed out, he had no idea for how long. He remembered taking sips of water. He remembered being scared of animals. If they came, he'd never be able to defend himself. How long had he been lying here? Hours? No, much longer. He realized it had been days, but he had no idea how many. He remembered looking down at his leg at one point and seeing his wound covered with maggots. He had panicked and tried to swat them off, but he didn't have any strength left. And once again, unconsciousness had prevailed.

Ben woke up starving. How long had it been since he'd had a meal? How many days had he been out here? And most of all, was Lila okay? He realized that he was thinking clearly for the first time since she left. He wasn't hot … or cold. He was feeling better. But how? He looked down at his thigh and almost gagged. Maggots were all over the wound. He let out a grunt of repulsion and went to sweep them off, but stopped. He was a child of the TV generation. He'd seen this before on some forensic show. Maggots weren't bad. They healed wounds. But how? He couldn't remember. Yes he could. They ate away the dead or infected skin. Something like that. He could see the edge of the wound. It was no longer bright red. They were helping him.

"Eat away, boys," he said in a half croak. He actually found himself watching them work. They tickled a bit. Even as disgusting as they were, he was so hungry, he knew it wouldn't affect his appetite. He reached down for a can of food. Beef stew. He pulled the top off the can and used his fingers to eat the stew. It tasted so good. When he finished eating, he fell asleep.

It was daylight again when he awoke, but he knew it was the next day. He looked down at his friends, but most had gone. In their place, they left a clean-looking wound. It was still there, but it was healing nicely. It was time to go and find Lila.

He left whatever maggots were still there on his leg. He'd let them eat. Eventually they'd fall off. Holding onto the tree, he slowly stood up. The wound still hurt, but nowhere near enough to keep him there. He decided to leave the backpacks and carry only what was necessary: his Sig in the holster; his rifle; his crossbow; his knives; and his canteen. Anything else would just slow him down. He draped the crossbow and quiver by their straps around his neck, so that the only thing he had to hold was his rifle, which would be his crutch. Then he began his journey up the hill.

It took an hour, as he was favoring his leg, but he finally made it to the trail. Immediately, he saw the blazes Lila made in the tree. She wasn't lost. That meant something had happened to her. Ben started down the trail. He was surprised his leg didn't hurt more. But it was still painful enough that he had a pronounced limp. At least he was alive and he was walking.

He had no idea how many days it had been since Lila left, but he was going to somehow pick up her trail. A few hours later he reached the open spot in the trail that led to the town. The first thing he saw was the burned out block, but then saw the drugstore sign on the next block. He reached the store and was about to go in when he saw Lila's rifle lying in the doorway.

He checked out the store and evaluated the scene and decided that she had been abducted. If it had been an animal attack, there would have been blood. Her gun still had a full magazine, so it hadn't been fired.

I knew then—or maybe I just hoped real hard—that she was still alive. It was almost as if she had left the rifle as a sign that she was okay. My heart was pounding. I had to find her.

While he was there, he grabbed some candy bars—he needed sugar—and a bottle of warm water, as well as a box of bandages and some antibiotic cream. He sat to rest his wound, and looked down to see a few of his friends still doing their job. Now the big question: Which way? He was going to have to guess. He had no idea what the situation was.

Luckily, a few minutes later, he no longer had to wonder. He heard yelling, and, struggling to his feet, grabbed Lila's rifle as well as his own. He pulled some of the bandages from the box and stuffed them in his pocket. The yelling was coming from the next street over. He limped around the corner to see a 1950s Chevy convertible with four soldiers standing next to it. At least they dressed that way. The way they were acting, the probability was that they weren't soldiers at all. They were surrounding a man, a woman, and a young teenaged boy. He crept up so he could hear the conversation.

"But we don't want to come with you," said the man.

"You're not safe out here," answered one of the soldiers. "We have a camp with a lot of people. You'll be protected there. You need to come with us."

"What if we refuse?"

"You can't refuse. The major needs you to help start this country again. You have no choice. C'mon, let's go." They started pulling the three into the car.

Ben was now only twenty feet away, hidden by a dead car. He stepped out from behind and cocked his rifle. The four soldiers spun in his direction.

"It seems to me," said Ben, inching closer, "that these people don't want to go with you. I think you should listen to them."

"Who the hell are you?" asked one of the men

Ben suddenly realized what a sight he was: mud from head to toe; one leg of his jeans ripped up to the crotch; an ugly wound; limping; and carrying a pistol, two rifles, and a crossbow.

"Eeww, shit," said one of the men. "He's got maggots on his leg."

Oh yeah, I forgot that part, thought Ben.

"Hey," said one with sergeant stripes. "I bet you're the boyfriend. Lila's boyfriend."

"I am."

"Then you should come with us. Your girlfriend is at the camp. She'll be real glad to see you."

"I'm sure she didn't go to your camp willingly," responded Ben.

"Well, not at first, but now she's real happy there."

"Yeah, I'll bet," Ben answered sarcastically. He aimed his rifle. "How about you set down your weapons, then let these people go."

"One of you against four of us," said the sergeant.

Ben fired and the redhead flew against the side of the car, then fell to the ground.

"Three of you."

"Shit!" exclaimed one of the soldiers. "He killed Ray."

The man and his family pulled themselves away from the soldiers and stepped back. The kid pulled a pistol out of his belt.

His hand was shaking.

"Don't worry about it," Ben said gently. "I've got it. Today doesn't have to be the day you kill your first scumbag." He addressed the soldiers. "Now who's going to tell me where your camp is?"

"Go to hell," spit the sergeant. Ben shot him in the chest. "I repeat my question."

"About ten miles down that road," said one of the two remaining soldiers.

"You idiot," said the other. "Don't tell him that." He raised his M-16 and Ben shot him. He fell to the ground.

"Please don't shoot me," pleaded the other. "I just joined them because I had nowhere else to go."

"Leave your weapon and take off that uniform. You don't deserve to have that on." Ben thought of his brother as he said that.

The man stripped to his underwear.

"Now go. Go in the opposite direction from the camp. If I see you again, I will kill you. Run!"

He hustled away, looking over his shoulder as if Ben was going to shoot him in the back.

"Thank you," said the man. "I'm Art. This is my wife Joan, and my son Pete."

"I'm Ben."

"And your girlfriend is Lila. We've heard stories about you."

"I'm sure they were exaggerated," replied Ben.

Art looked at the dead men, then back at Ben. "I don't think so."

"You look hurt," said Joan. "Is there anything we can do?"

"No thanks. I may look a mess, but I'm actually healing."

"Gross," exclaimed Pete. "You really do have maggots on your leg."

"I do," said Ben. "They saved my life."

"I can't believe you just shot those guys," continued Pete. "You didn't even look scared."

It occurred to Ben that he wasn't scared. People like that no longer frightened him. Maybe because his own death no longer frightened him. In his old life, these fake soldiers would be considered a nuisance. They'd be slapped with a fine for their various crimes of stupidity, or spend some time in jail. It was a new world. Ben had no patience and felt no kindness for men like that. The sooner they were dealt with, the better off everyone would be.

He looked at Pete. "You want to help me drag these guys off the road? If they have friends who come looking, I want them to wonder what happened to them."

Pete obviously didn't like the idea of touching the dead guys, but Ben could tell that he was trying to grow up. A few weeks ago, his life consisted of video games and TV. Probably nothing in his world was real. Now it was all real, and the transition had come way too fast.

Together, and with the parents' help, they pulled the bodies into some trees. They weren't visible from the road. Ben searched through their pockets for anything that he could use. He found a couple of packs of cigarettes and lighters. He kept the lighters, figuring they might come in handy.

"I'm going to take the car to rest my leg while I get closer to this camp they talked about," explained Ben. "You're welcome to take it after me."

"Thanks, but I think not," answered Art. "It could only bring us trouble if his friends see us in it. We live in Harrisburg, and now that the bodies in the city have gone a long way toward decomposition, we're going to see if we can move back into our house. We don't know what we're going to do, but at least we're together."

Ben could see tears in his eyes.

What would they do? They could move back into their home and try to make adjustments in their living habits, but for how long? They were trying to pick up from a life that didn't exist anymore. Wouldn't it be better to start fresh in some mountain cabin or ocean beach house? I felt sorry for them. For Lila and me, our life started the day of the disaster. For these people, it ended. How do you start fresh when you haven't let go of the old?

They said goodbye and thanked Ben again. He left them with the suggestion that they take the M-16s from the dead men to protect themselves. One solitary pistol stuck in a belt wasn't going to do it. He thought about taking one of the M-16s, but he was comfortable with what he had. Then he drove off. It felt strange to be driving again.

In some ways, it was a culture clash. Walking and experiencing the quiet of the world around us had become our new life. Driving like this was like fingernails on a chalkboard. As time went on, I had less and less desire for the conveniences of our old life. The only thing I wanted right now was to find Lila. She was alive! Now I just had to get her out of there. And of course, if everyone else was being held against their will, I'd have to free them all. The life of a folk hero wasn't easy.

When he had gone about eight miles, according to the odometer, he found a driveway off the road. He pulled right into an open garage, left the keys on the seat, and closed the garage door. The four men from the camp officially ceased to exist.

He finally applied the cream and a bandage to his wound. The last of the maggots had fallen off, and he wished them well and thanked them for their healing. He hoofed it the rest of the way. It was slow going, as his leg still hurt, but he didn't want to chance getting any closer in the car and be seen or heard.

He smelled wood smoke and knew he was getting close. He got off the road and traveled through the woods until he reached an enormous clearing with buildings, a fence, and dozens of people, all milling about. Darkness was beginning to set in and he could see people lining up for a meal. No sign of Lila yet. Wait! There she was, in line with those guys from the trail, Dan and Gordon.

I wanted to jump out of the woods and run up to the fence shouting, "Lila, it's me." I knew she was worried about me and probably felt guilty about leaving me, so I wanted her to know I was alright. However, I had to do this the right way. I had to see how many guards I was dealing with and come up with a plan to free her. For the moment, she was fine, so I had time.

Ben was suddenly exhausted. He found a soft spot on the ground, far from the sight of the guards and curled up and fell asleep.

The next morning he was up early watching the camp.

He observed as Lila was eating her breakfast—it looked like slop—and a guard came over to talk to her. He saw him dump her tray over her front. Ben imprinted the man's face in his brain. He wasn't going to live long.

He saw some guards open up a building and carry cans of gas

out to an old pickup. That might be valuable to know, he thought, looking at the building and thinking of his lighters. The building was wood. But it was also inside the fence, which might present a problem. Two men got in the pickup and took off. Ben could see Lila, with Dan and Gordon, watching the morning's events. Ben knew they were going off to look for their missing buddies.

He spent the rest of the day just observing. The pickup returned a couple of hours after breakfast and there was definitely some panic among the guards. Good, he thought. He hadn't come up with a plan yet, but decided it was time to deplete the opposing forces a bit. That night he would take out a few of the guards.

After dinner, he saw a guard escorting Lila to the large building. She didn't come out.

When it got dark, he decided to move. He left the two rifles in the woods, got out the crossbow, and exited the woods, quietly sneaking over to the compound. He had practiced a lot with the crossbow, and was fairly accomplished with it. A lot of their meals had come from its use.

He saw a guard near the gate. No one else seemed to be near. He took up position behind the pickup, and when the guard was close enough, Ben let a missile fly. It struck the guard in the temple and he crumpled to the ground.

Ben hurried over to him and pulled the lifeless body into the woods. Then he went back and tried to cover up the drag marks with a branch. He retrieved his bolt from the man's head and wiped it off in the grass, then went hunting again. He was able to get one more victim over the next few hours. At one point in the middle of the night, he thought he was going to be caught. There was activity in one of the buildings, and four guards ran out the door. However, they were headed toward the big building. What mischief are you up to, Lila, he asked himself.

Finally, his leg throbbing, he rested for the remainder of the night.

He woke up the next morning to the sound of an air horn blasting away. He heard the guards yelling, "Get up. Everyone up!" Once most of the people were up and standing around expectantly, the door of the big building opened.

Surrounded by guards, Lila came walking into the compound.

She was covered in blood!

CHAPTER 14
(Lila)

Rather than head back to her shelter after breakfast, Lila stayed near the kitchen. Something was going on. The guards seemed agitated and she wanted to see if she could learn why. She saw Dan and Gordon and made her way toward them.

"Do you know what's happening?" she asked.

"I just heard one of the guards say something about 'them' not coming back. Not sure who they're talking about yet," said Dan.

Two guards loaded some gas cans into the back of an old pickup and took off down the road. Nothing happened for a couple of hours and none of the guards were talking. Finally, Lila saw the pickup returning. She could hear a few bits of conversation from the guards in the pickup to the others.

"... Nowhere to be found ..."

"... Dropped off the face of the earth ..."

Between assorted citizens, they were eventually able to piece together the story. Walt, Ray, and the other two who had picked up Lila, had gone out the day before on one of their normal searches and had never returned. Wells didn't want the guards driving at night, so they had waited til morning to search for them, bringing along cans of gas in case the group had run out. The men in the pickup had searched all along the normal route and had found no sign of the others.

Lila, Dan, and Gordon took a walk around the perimeter.

"What do you think happened?" asked Dan.

"I think they took off," answered Gordon. "I think they got tired of Wells and Sharp and they just hit the road."

"I don't think so," said Dan. "I mean, they didn't have the easiest life around, but it sure beat the alternative. They had meals—which are a hell of a lot better than ours—occasional women, and power. They don't look like the kind who would survive very well on their own. No, I think something happened to them."

Lila was silent.

My first thought was, "Could it be?" All I knew was that if Ben was alive, his one and only thought would be to find me. He'd be likely to shoot first if he ran across a bunch like them. I knew that I was probably projecting my hopes, but I needed something to hold onto.

"You think it was Ben, don't you?" Dan was looking at her.

"I don't know. I don't want to get my hopes up. He was in really bad shape when I left him. If I think it's him and then it turns out not to be, it would devastate me. I'm better off not hoping."

"I understand."

Lila spent the rest of the day by herself in her shelter. She allowed herself a good cry over Ben, then her thoughts went to the evening ahead. The whole camp knew she had been chosen by Wells and they were all giving her space. Lila appreciated it, but at the same time felt very much alone. She had no idea what she would do once she was in the room with Wells. She knew what she wanted to do, but was she really capable of murder? Even if she was, did she really think she could overpower Wells? No, she knew that eventually she was going to have to submit to his will, just like every other woman there. When she reached that conclusion, she began to shake uncontrollably. She was losing her confidence. This place had sapped her of all her strength. The shaking continued for over an hour, and she felt herself becoming like the rest of them. Lila, the folk hero, was no more.

By the time the air horn sounded for dinner, she had regained some of her composure, and trudged over to the kitchen. Individually, Dan, Gordon, and Melissa came over to her and hugged her or squeezed her hand, but otherwise, everyone avoided her.

Lila had just finished her meal when the toad approached her and told her to follow him. Everyone followed her with their eyes as she made her way to the large building. Lila wondered if some were disappointed that she was apparently allowing herself to submit to this.

Then she thought to herself, why should I care what they think? And yet, she saw their faces. There was no hope in that compound. It wasn't fair. They survived the greatest catastrophe ever to happen to this planet, only to be controlled by a madman. She knew then that it had to end tonight. She couldn't go on living this way. Anything had to be better than this.

Lila had found the strength she'd been searching for all day.

I was tired of death, but I knew that I really had no choice this time. I needed to be free. We all needed to be free. I was hoping, but I didn't really know if Ben was alive. If he wasn't, this man was to blame. I didn't believe in heaven or hell, but I did believe in some sort of accounting. You can't do these horrible things and get away with it. I hated the expression "an eye for an eye," but was it far from the truth? We need to take responsibility for our actions. I don't know if Phil would have agreed with the accountability. He would have said something like, "it's in the hands of God" or something about "judgment day." Well, the major's judgment day had arrived.

They entered the building. Offices lined the walls of the first floor, most of them long since abandoned. The first office though, had a handmade sign that read "Major Wells." Across the hall was Sharp's office. At the end of the hall was the entrance to some sort of gym. It reminded Lila of an old school. It even had that smell. If she could catch a faint whiff of cafeteria food, then she really would think she was in school.

The toad took her up a flight of stairs. On the second floor, Wells and Sharp had set up living quarters on opposite sides of the hall. They had even decorated the hall to look comfortable. She figured they had raided a furniture store to outfit their rooms, and wondered what the guards felt about Wells and Sharp living a life of luxury while they lived in barracks. After all, it was probably the guards who had to get all that stuff and lug it up there. However, she refused to ask the toad the question. When the time came, she'd communicate with him her own way.

"Hold on," he said, as they were about to go in the major's room. "Hands up in the air while I frisk you."

She had transferred the knife to her boot. The toad frisked her thoroughly—a little too thoroughly, she thought—then told her to take off her boots.

"Why," Lila asked.

"Do you usually do it with your boots on?" he asked sarcastically. "Take off your boots. You could be hiding something in them."

She took off her boots slowly, hoping to figure out how to hide the knife from the guard. She couldn't think of anything.

"Your feet stink," said the toad.

"Yeah, that's what happens when you're not allowed a bath. Want to get a little closer? You can have one down your throat."

"Well, what do we have here?" The toad found the knife. "What did you think you were going to do with this?"

Lila had run out of smart responses. She just stood there silently.

The guard knocked on the major's door, then opened it. Wells was sitting in a chair next to his bed, writing something in an ornate notebook. He put the notebook and pen down on a bedside table and stood up.

"Come in, Lila. Make yourself comfortable." He looked at the guard with disdain. "You can go now."

"I found this in her boot." He handed him the knife.

Wells looked at Lila and raised his eyebrows.

"I felt like I might need some protection, just in case," she said, trying to make up a reasonable sounding excuse.

"You don't have to worry," answered Wells. "You don't have to fear me."

"Okay," mumbled Lila. It was important to seem as submissive as possible.

The guard left. Lila looked around.

"In case you're wondering," said Wells, as if reading her mind, "I don't keep any of my weapons in here. Please sit." He motioned her to a chair. "I'm really nobody to fear."

"But what if I didn't want to do this tonight?"

"I would think you would look at it as an honor," answered Wells. "You may not see it that way yet, but you will."

"Can I ask you a question?" said Lila.

"Of course. You know, you're the first woman to actually engage me in conversation. Most of them just sit there limply. You have intelligence. I like that. What's your question?"

"Why? Why all this? It must be obvious to you that the people out there aren't happy. And yet, you keep them locked up against their will."

"Let me read you a passage from my book."

"Your book?"

"Yes, I'm writing a history of the beginning of the new Republic. Who better to write it than the man responsible for forming it?" He reached over and picked up the notebook he was writing in when Lila showed up. He flipped back a few pages, then began reading:

> "I look out my window at the throngs below and it pains me to see their expressionless faces. They are like children, looking for someone to mold them, to tell them what is right and what is wrong. And like children, sometimes they get angry and throw their fits. They complain about the food; they complain about the living conditions; but do they really understand what awaits them outside these gates? No. They need to be trained first. They need to know hardship to be able to appreciate abundance when they earn it. And they will earn it. The Republic of America, with me as its founding father, will guide

them into the future. And they will be grateful for the firm hand and the clear vision. They will understand that they are the first citizens of this new land, and that the hardships they suffer will one day be looked upon by their children, and their grandchildren, and their great-grandchildren, and generations down the line, as a most worthy sacrifice."

He put down the notebook and looked at Lila. "Now do you understand?

Yeah, I understand that you're loony, Lila thought to herself.

"I guess so," she said, for lack of anything better to say.

Suddenly, his whole demeanor changed. He stood up with anger plastered across his face.

"Now get over here and take care of me!"

"Excuse me?" Lila was confused by the sudden transformation.

"I am the president! You will abide by my wishes. You will service your president!"

Lila stood up, realizing just how sick and twisted the man was. She crossed the room slowly, not knowing what to expect. She stood before him, and he slapped her, much the same way Sharp had slapped her on her first day there. She fell to the bed.

He climbed on top of her fully clothed, trying to put his hands under her shirt to take it off.

She had had enough.

What is it about some men and their need to dominate? Whether it's emotionally, physically, or sexually, it's a scary trait. It's a perverse trait. I looked at Wells, then I thought of Ben, a quiet, introspective, sensitive man, who had a power within him that was magnificent. That was, of course, if he was still alive.

Wells was so excited, he was almost drooling. He had his eyes closed in ecstasy, his hands under her shirt on her breasts. His display of power was a turn-on for him. Lila could only imagine the sick things he had in mind. While trying to fight him off, she reached over to the bedside table, fumbling for his pen. She had it! She reached back and without hesitation, drove the pen through his right eyeball, into his brain. He let out a scream of agony, then collapsed on top of her.

Blood gushed over her. She pushed his still twitching body off the bed and onto the floor. The life was seeping out of him. She was trying to catch her breath, and was gasping for air from the adrenaline of the moment. Slowly she calmed down. Finally, she sat up and looked over at Wells.

"Not all of your weapons were in another room," she said to the dying man, her voice cracking.

Now what was she going to do? She hadn't thought beyond killing him. She put her boots on and crept to the door. Suddenly it burst open and Sharp and the toad were standing there. The toad grabbed her around the neck and twisted her arm behind her, totally incapacitating her.

"You are so predictable," Sharp said to Lila. He looked over at the dying Wells. "He was an idiot." He walked over to where the major was lying. Wells had a dying glimmer of recognition in his one eye. But even that was almost gone. Sharp kicked him in the head and spat on him. "He thought he could tame you like he had done the others. I knew better. I had heard the stories. But even more than that, I had looked into your eyes. You were someone to fear. Wells was too stupid to know that."

Lila found her voice. "Why didn't you warn him then?"

"Because this is exactly what I wanted to happen. The guards too. They know that life will be better for them under me. I should be in charge, not him. I should be leading this country. I was just biding my time. You have no idea how you've helped. Not only did you get rid of Wells, opening the door for me to take over, but you've given me another way to keep the masses down."

Lila looked at him with wide eyes. She had a sense of what was coming.

"You can't be treated like the other women," said Sharp. "You'll never be conquered in the bedroom. You're too dangerous. But everyone here looks up to you. If they see you crumble, no one will ever try to rebel again. And the best way to do that is to punish you. I could kill you, but that would just make you a martyr and empower the others. No, I have something better in mind."

They led her into the hallway. While the toad held her, Sharp reached into his doorway and pulled out a long metal wire.

"A car antenna," he explained. "You have any idea how much this is going to hurt when we whip you with it? Oh, and I don't mean just today. Every day. Every single day, until your eyes become lifeless and I'm convinced there is nothing left in your soul. We're going to whip you and let everyone watch the hope drain out of you. We'll wait until morning though."

The toad pushed her into a small empty closet and shut the door. She could see his shadow under the door as he stood guard.

She sat down in a corner and wept, wondering how her life had come to this. Eventually, exhaustion set in, and she fell asleep.

She woke up to the faint sound of the air horn. The door opened and Sharp and a guard pulled her roughly from the closet and led her down the hall.

They were met at the bottom of the stairs by two more guards, and they waited there while the toad called a meeting of all the citizens, while still blowing the obnoxious air horn. Finally, when everyone was gathered, they led Lila out.

As they paraded her in front of the crowd, one of the guards came over and talked quietly to Sharp. Being so close, Lila caught most of it. The guard was explaining that two of the night guards were missing from their posts. They found some blood near where the gate guard stood.

It's Ben, thought Lila. I know it is!

The day suddenly didn't look so bleak.

CHAPTER 15

When he saw the blood, Ben wanted to charge in with guns blazing, but quickly, he realized that it was not Lila's blood at all. It was obvious, however, that Lila had done something significant and that they were going to make an example of her in front of the other prisoners. He had to think fast.

He needed to get closer to the action if he was going to make a difference, so he evaluated the situation. They were taking Lila to a small platform that had been set up near the kitchen, obviously the place from which they made speeches. The kitchen was on the left as you went through the gates. His spot in the woods was to the right of the gates. The vehicles were parked outside the fence behind the kitchen.

He could sneak down from the woods to the fence and have a clean shot, but he would also be in the open for anyone shooting at him. He looked at the cars. The gasoline cans were still in the back of the pickup. The guards were so thrown by the events of the day before, they never got around to emptying the truck. He now knew what he was going to do, but he had little time to do it. They were approaching the platform. He grabbed both of the rifles and headed through the woods away from the camp, then crossed the road at the narrowest point, hoping he wouldn't be seen. He was now on the same side as the truck. He hurried through the woods on that side, then furtively crossed the small open space to the truck. The nearby guard's attention was on the proceedings through the fence.

Once at the truck, he carefully lifted one of the cans out and opened it. He also opened a can in the truck and turned it on its side, so that the gas spilled all over the bed of the pickup. He then poured gas over the side of the truck and onto the ground under it. This would be the hard part, and timing was everything. They hadn't replaced the gate guard yet, so he could run past the gate to the other fence to give himself a clear shot. He planned to make a gas trail, then light it before he started shooting. However, it would all depend on him not being seen. He heard the one in charge begin to speak.

"Last night, this citizen of the Republic of America committed anarchy. She assassinated our president." A smattering of applause sounded from the braver ones in the crowd. "As the new president, I say we cannot condone this kind of rebellion, and it must be dealt with swiftly. She must be made an example of. This morning, and every day before breakfast, she will be whipped ten lashes by me, until we decide she has been punished enough. Anyone seen giving her any kind of aid or comfort will suffer the same fate. To maintain order in a society, punishment must be severe for those who break the laws. We look forward to the day when each of you will become free and valued citizens of the Republic."

The speech obviously over, Ben knew the time had come. Strapping the rifles over his back, he picked up the gas can and slopped the gas out in a steady stream as he headed to the other fence. So far, no one had noticed him. He reached the other side in time to hear the man in charge say, "Take her shirt off and tie her up." That was the first Ben noticed the t-shaped post built onto the back of the platform.

They knew they were going to have to use it, thought Ben. They were planning to punish people all along. Some republic, he thought. He lit the gas on the ground with one of the lighters lifted from the guards in town, just as they were moving her into position. Ben aimed his rifle through the fence at the officer in charge. He also saw the guard who had dumped Lila's tray yesterday. He was going to be the second to die.

The flame shot across the yard and made contact with the gas on the truck. A giant whoosh sounded as the truck caught fire. He heard a guard yell. He shot and missed the officer, but destroyed the face of the one who had abused Lila. He went down with a scream. Explosions erupted from the truck as, one by one, the other cans and the truck's gas tank succumbed to the heat. There was bedlam in the compound. Lila, thinking fast, had grabbed the pistol of the downed guard, and was pointing it at the one in charge. Ben couldn't hear what he was saying, but looked to be pleading for his life. Lila shot him in the chest.

Shooting into the compound was now difficult, with all of the innocent people running around, although many had dropped to the ground for safety. Instead, he focused his attention on the guard behind the fence by the kitchen. His first shot missed, but his second scored. The man dropped in his tracks.

It was over as quickly as it began. The remaining guards, seeing Sharp down, dropped their weapons and surrendered. Ben limped through the gate, still looking like something that had emerged from a swamp, and made his way toward Lila. She jumped off the platform and ran to him, almost knocking him over as they embraced.

"I knew you were here," she said in between kisses.

"I had to find you," replied Ben. "I was so scared I'd lost you."

"So was I," said Lila. She held him at arm's length and stared. "We've gotta go clothes shopping for you."

Ben laughed for the first time in an eternity. He looked out to see the whole compound quiet, everyone staring at them.

"Everyone," said Lila to the group, "this is Ben."

Then they all started talking at once. Dan and Gordon came over and gave Ben a hug. Suddenly, there were three shots in succession. They turned to see Melissa, Gordon's wife, holding a pistol on the group of guards. Three of them were writhing on the ground bleeding. The other five were frozen with fear. Melissa didn't have the stomach to finish the job, and dropped the gun at her feet. Gordon went over to comfort her. She was sobbing. Dan picked up the gun and instructed the remaining guards to drop their gun belts and lie on the ground.

He looked at Ben. "What should we do with these five, as well as the injured ones?"

Ben looked at him with exhaustion in his face. "It's up to you guys. We're done." He looked at Lila. "You ready to go?"

"More than ready," she replied. "Just one second."

She went over to the building she was processed in. Ben heard a door splinter inside. She came back a few minutes later, strapping on her Sig and her knife. "All of your weapons are inside that building," she said to the group. She came up to Ben. "Now I'm ready."

They said their goodbyes to Dan and Gordon. Lila gave Melissa a hug, and they walked out the gate. Ben went over to retrieve his crossbow and the canteens. Lila pointed out where Dan said the trail was. They had walked about a hundred yards in that direction when they heard five shots in succession.

"I can't believe they shot the remaining guards," said Ben.

"You can't believe what they went through," answered Lila.

They held hands and looked in each other's eyes as they walked. They were together again!

That night, they found a quiet spot off the trail and just laid there; no tent, no food, just each other. They looked up through the trees at the night sky, and they shared their stories of survival. Afterward, they fell asleep in the peace and quiet, and the comfort of each other's arms.

The next day they left the trail in search of some stores. They found a shopping mall and were able to totally restock, from backpacks on down to new boots. Normally, they would have steered clear of a mall, simply due to the large number of bodies, but most of the bodies had reached a state of dried skin and bones, and they were able to ignore them for the most part.

They had fun picking out clothes. They had been stuck in the same outfits for so long, they almost had to peel them off. They were still filthy, but hoped to find a lake or pond later that day to clean up.

They lucked out. Heading back toward the trail, they ran across a hotel. Lila had the bright idea of checking out the swimming pool. It was an indoor pool, and while the emptiness of the building seemed spooky, the need to get clean was overriding. The pool had a layer of film and a funky smell. Using a net, Ben skimmed the surface to open up a spot in which to swim. The water was cold, so they bathed quickly, but afterward felt somewhat clean again. They took that time to dress Ben's wound properly, as well.

Their whole excursion off the trail had only taken them four hours, so they had plenty of daylight left. By the end of the day, they were deep in the hills again in southern Pennsylvania. They found a small lake and set up camp far from the trail. It was cool, but clear that night, and they lay there, watching the stars.

"Remember when this first happened?" asked Lila, lying with her head on Ben's shoulder. "Remember how scared we were? We didn't know what to do."

"And yet, we didn't stop," said Ben. "We didn't give up."

"No, we didn't. But we still had some of our innocence, and I miss that." She was silent for a moment. "Ben, I'm tired of what we've become. I'm tired of the killing. I'm tired of our reputation. We're the violent do-gooders. People are either scared of us or expect us to perform miracles—or both. I don't want to be that anymore. I killed a man by jamming a pen through his eye socket. I shot another at point blank range. And neither of the killings bothered me. You've killed close to a dozen men, and you probably have no regrets. It's all very surreal, but really disturbing too."

"Isn't it interesting," started Ben, "how one incident can change your life? If it hadn't been for Tank and his crew, maybe we wouldn't be looking at the head count we are."

"The thing is," said Lila, "we've come a long way in our confidence and our ability to take care of ourselves. I wouldn't give that up for anything. If it weren't for our survival instincts, we'd either be dead from Tank and his gang or in that prison camp in a hopeless situation. We know how to hunt and fish. We know how to protect ourselves. We're probably two of the most competent people alive right now …"

"Which is why others look to us for help," cut in Ben.

"It is," agreed Lila. "And I don't mind helping people. I mind killing people, and I mind having others look at us as though we were super beings. I understand all we've gone through and all we've become. I understand the skills we've acquired and the ability to think clearly in stressful situations. I understand all of that, but ..." She was at a loss for what to say.

"But you want life to be simple again," finished Ben.

"I do."

Lila put into words what I was thinking. When I shot the three guards by the car, or the guards at the camp, I felt nothing. I had ended a life—a lot of them, actually—and felt nothing. Nothing at all. Shouldn't there have been some remorse, or some sensitivity? I knew that our whole world had turned upside down and that to survive we had to be stronger than most of the other people. And we were. And I couldn't say that we had lost any of our humanity, because we were willing to help anyone in need. But the killing part bothered me. Tank, and Slash, and Coke, I could understand. That was pure rage. And if I looked at the other killings, logic told me that we did the right thing ... the only thing that we could do to survive. Why then, did it bother us so much now? It wasn't remorse for what we'd done, but rather, guilt for the fact that we were able to do it so easily. That's not who we were.

I remembered learning in karate that the reason self-protection doesn't come easily for most people is because we are civilized human beings. It goes against our nature to be violent. But in that same lesson I was also taught that to survive, sometimes you had to bring yourself down to the level of your attacker.

I knew right then we'd be okay. The fact that we could even talk about it, and that it bothered us, was a sign that we hadn't lost that essential part of ourselves. I said that to Lila and I think she appreciated it. She needed to hear it. We both did. We now knew that if we had to kill to survive, we could as a last resort, and it wouldn't mean that we were any worse as human beings because of it. We may have lost our innocence, but we hadn't lost our soul.

They walked a few more days without seeing anyone. Twice, they felt small tremors. Ben remembered feeling one during one of the violent storms, as well, but these were a bit stronger. On the fourth day, they met Nick and Jason.

They were cooking a rabbit for dinner that Ben had shot with his crossbow, when they heard someone hail the camp.

"Two friendly people out here. Can we approach your fire?"

Their hands immediately went to their guns, but Ben told them to come on in. Nick and Jason walked in and introduced themselves. Like Ben and Lila, they had full backpacks and carried weapons. But there was nothing menacing about them, and the teens felt at ease right away—as much as when they had first met Phil.

They introduced themselves to their guests. Both seemed to be in their mid-thirties.

"Ah, yes," said Nick. "There are all kinds of stories going up and down the East coast about you two. Sounds like you're quite the heroes." He could see their discomfort and changed the subject. "But we're just happy to meet some fellow travelers."

"Where are you headed?" asked Ben.

"Eventually to the coast," answered Nick. "But we've been kind of exploring in all different directions on our way there. We've been passing along information whenever we can."

"What kind, and where are you from?" asked Lila.

"I come from St. Louis," said Nick, "and Jason comes from

California. We were two of the lucky ones ... twice. Three times for Jason."

Ben and Lila looked confused.

"Let us explain," continued Nick. He looked at Jason and touched his shoulder. "You go first."

Ben got the idea that they had told this story a few times before.

"California doesn't exist anymore," began Jason.

Immediately, Ben's thoughts went to his brother. Any hope that his brother might have survived were gone now. Lila sensed his thoughts and held his hand.

"A few days after the event, an earthquake struck. It was the 'big one' they've been warning about for decades. Ironically, the death toll was low because there were very few people left alive to experience it."

"Can I interrupt?" asked Lila. "We've been assuming everyone got zapped by this, but we've only met people on the East Coast. So you can confirm that it's nation-wide?"

"Most likely world-wide," said Nick, "but definitely nation-wide."

"Anyway," continued Jason, "I was lucky. I had found an old truck from the early '60s, and a supply of gas cans and loaded it up. I was west of LA and already on my way east when it hit. How I made it, I'm not really sure. It was a mess. Sometimes I had to go for miles to circumvent the fissures. I know that half of California behind me went into the sea. It stayed messed up through Arizona and New Mexico, then finally cleared up. I was on fumes when I hit St. Louis."

Nick took up the story. "We met up in St. Louis and Jason told me what had happened, and I knew immediately that we had to head east. You see, I'm a meteorologist—I worked for a local TV station—and a seismologist. I had suspected for a while what was coming and Jason only confirmed it."

"Why did you suspect it?" asked Ben.

"Well, I can go into that later, but I think a massive nuclear weapon was involved in all this."

Ben and Lila looked at each other.

"Someone else we met had that theory too," said Lila. "But go on."

"California has the San Andreas Fault, as well as many others, but the Midwest has the Madrid Fault. I figured the chances were good that because of the magnitude of the first earthquake, it would trigger a chain reaction that would continue on to the next weakest fault. A chain reaction like that isn't common, but it's not unheard of either. Or maybe it's not a chain reaction at all, but just a case of each fault being affected from the initial blast, and the strength of the fault determines how quickly the quake hits."

"Whatever the reason," he continued, "I knew we were in trouble in the Midwest, so we found a stash of gasoline and I accompanied Jason east. We felt the quake hit when we were in Tennessee. From the force of it there, I knew it was pretty massive in the Midwest. We eventually ran out of gas, so we started hoofing it. And here we are."

"So what you're saying is that most of the country is pretty much in shambles?" said Lila.

"No. What I'm saying is that it's going to hit here too. It's only a matter of time before the whole country is destroyed."

PART THREE: REVENGE

CHAPTER 16

Lila shook her head. Not in disbelief, but in amazement. They had something more to look forward to?

"When?" she asked.

"That I can't tell you," answered Nick. "It could be weeks, but more likely months. Hell, it could even be years, but I don't think so. I think the earth is falling apart—not completely, of course. It's not going to break into pieces and float away, or anything like that. But if I'm correct and it was a massive nuclear device that delivered all this, then I think it was large enough to have severely jolted the Earth."

As if on cue, the ground moved slightly. They looked at each other, and Nick gave a sad smile.

"Anyway," he continued. "I think it sent such a powerful shock wave against the Earth, it weakened it. Sort of like a beam in a house during an earthquake. If it's new and sturdy, it will hold up longer. If it's unstable to begin with, chances are it will collapse right away. The faults are like that."

"What about the wild weather?" asked Ben.

"We've had a bit of a reprieve for the last couple of weeks," answered Nick, "but don't get used to it. It'll be back. I think the blast had a significant effect on the weather patterns, too."

"What do you suggest about the earthquakes? Where's the best place to be?" asked Lila.

"The simple suggestions seismologists usually make wouldn't work in this case, because it's going to be too devastating. Obviously, the cities will be the most dangerous places to be. I can't tell you where the safest place is. We're headed for the coast. I'm hoping that will get us away from the worst of it."

"What about tsunamis?" asked Lila.

"We'll take our chances. No matter where you are, you're really just taking a chance."

"So how is warning people helping?" asked Ben.

"I don't know," answered Nick. "I guess all I can say is, wouldn't you rather know or would you rather it came as a surprise?"

"I see your point," said Ben. "Although, there are probably people out there who would rather not know."

"There are," agreed Nick. "But I guess that's their problem."

We were entering a strange new world. With every passing day, our old life in Newton was fading, becoming a wisp of a memory. In some ways, we just didn't have time to think of that life. And in others, we avoided thinking of it. When we did, sometimes the memories were sad, but more often they were repellant. It was an ugly world we had left behind, made ever so clear when we camped at night and soaked in the sounds of solitude. Our new world had glimpses of paradise, and we hungrily sought out more. But sadly, it also contained too many reminders of the world left behind.

We, the human race, had a chance here for a fresh beginning. But the universe had played a cruel cosmic joke on us all by sparing some of the worst of society. Were they put here to provide challenges? As if just existing wasn't challenge enough. I thought back to our discussion of killing. By doing away with the scum, were we cleansing the world or just adding to the negativity?

Nick's warning about the earthquakes had surprised us, but really hadn't scared us. Overlooking the fact that we—humans—were responsible for them this time, earthquakes were simply a force of nature. Lila and I, in some perverse way, looked forward to them. It was nature at its most powerful. We could respect that. We just wanted to live in harmony with the natural world. If only the human race would let us.

They invited Nick and Jason to set up their tent and share their campsite. It turned out that Jason was a veterinarian. Ben brought up the subject of the strange animal behavior. Jason felt that it would return to normal.

"My guess is that it's a temporary affliction. Besides," he added, "you'll have a whole new batch of young ones who weren't around to experience the event. They should be perfectly normal."

Nick and Jason were tired and headed for their tent. Ben and Lila sat up a while longer, enjoying the peace and watching the flames of the fire.

"I've been thinking about Florida," said Lila. "We've changed a lot in the weeks since we left home. It was a good idea at first, and it got us moving, but is that still where you want to end up? Because I'll be honest, I'm not sure I do."

"Me neither," replied Ben. "I've kind of had this fantasy that we are like the pioneers in the old west trying to find a homestead, looking out over thousands of miles of untouched land. But the reality is that we don't have all that land to choose from. Being on the trail like this is deceiving. We're traveling through hills and forests, but we're often only a few miles—or less—away from towns and shopping malls. Sometimes it depresses me knowing how close we are to all of that."

"And Florida would be that to the extreme," said Lila. "Whew! I'm glad you're feeling the same way. I have to say though, that the idea of the ocean is really appealing to me too."

"We're young," said Ben. "What's stopping us from finding a place to settle down, then moving on whenever we want? I think right now, we're both loving the forest, so let's look at a map tomorrow and talk to Nick—as a meteorologist, he might have some ideas—then go from there."

That settled, they moved to their tent, where they made quiet, passionate love amidst the sounds of the night birds and animals. While they were still awake, Ben whispered to Lila that it was too bad everyone couldn't have the love they had.

"I feel sorry for Nick and Jason," he said very softly. "Two guys without women to keep them company."

"You're joking, right?" whispered Lila. "Ben, I don't think they want any women with them. I think they're very happy just the way they are."

It took Ben a minute, but he finally caught on. "Oh. Well then, I guess I don't have to feel sorry for them."

The next morning over breakfast, they got into a discussion about the population that was left.

"The way I see it," said Nick. "There are three groups of people left in the world. The largest group is made up mostly of those we've all run into. They are struggling to get by. They might have some skills, but not a lot. They are doing their best, but I'm afraid a lot of them will die before they ever acclimate themselves to this new world. Many already have. Then there are those like us; we've adapted to the changes and are constantly learning new ways to survive. We are most definitely the smallest group."

He went on: "The other is one made up of those who need to have power, or need to follow someone with power. They feel that the only way to survive is by amassing a group under or around them. Sadly, that kind of group, even if started with the best of intentions, usually becomes a mirror of the worst part of our former society. I would have thought that to be the smallest group, but I think it was only wishful thinking. It's getting bigger. They start poaching from the first group, who slowly come over to their way of thinking because they have no choice. They know they won't survive otherwise. That's what your Major Wells was trying to do. He just didn't do it very well. He tried to imprison people, rather than absorbing them into his group. If the change is gradual, people won't notice. He tried to change them with force."

"What are you saying?" asked Lila.

"I'm saying be careful. People are desperate. They want to live, and if that means doing things they never would have thought of doing before all of this happened, then so be it. It's the mob mentality after a disaster. They don't allow themselves to think about it."

"We want to avoid people," said Ben, "and we want as much nature around us as possible. Forgetting about the potential for an earthquake, where do you suggest we go that will keep us far away from towns?"

"The Great Smoky Mountains," said Nick. "And the trail leads right to them. From this point on, you're going to see some beautiful country. The Blue Ridge is gorgeous, but you'll often be looking down at towns and farms. But you can really get lost in the Great Smoky Mountains. Great Smoky National Park or any of the national forests around it. A lot of that is pretty much untouched. If that's what you're looking for, there's your answer."

Leaving Nick and Jason was hard. They had developed a strong connection in less than twenty-four hours. But they were heading in different directions, with different journeys ahead of them.

"I hope we meet up again sometime," said Ben, after they had hugged.

"Call me on my cell," replied Nick.

They all broke into laughter.

Nick and Jason started on their way and Ben looked at Lila. "I guess we have a new destination."

"And we don't even have to leave the trail to get there," added Lila.

They began the next leg of their trip with light hearts, and the next three days were peaceful ones. The weather was good and there were no tremors. They saw no other people. Ben would often hunt with his crossbow, or fish if they ran across some water. The evening of the third day, they tried pheasant for the first time. It tasted delicious, but the next morning, Lila woke up feeling sick, and threw up.

"Okay," she said. "No more pheasant."

Later that day, they came across a sign pointing the way to a lake with a public beach. They took the trail, and, as they approached the beach, heard the sound of people. They quickly got off the trail and made their way through the trees to scope out the scene.

There were about two dozen people, including about eight

children of various ages. Some of the kids were playing in the sand—at this point, the water was too cold for them to swim. Most of the adults were sitting. Some were by the water with crude fishing poles made from branches. Two of the men were arguing.

"What do you think?" asked Ben.

"Look at the people," answered Lila. "Look how skinny they are. They're starving. These people seem to have no skills at all. Ben, remember when we were talking about killing people and helping people? These people need our help. Can we see what we can do for them? Who cares if we get to the Smokies a bit later than we thought. Besides, that pheasant really did a number on me. I've felt sick all day. This might be a good place to spend the night."

"I'm good with that," said Ben. "Let's go introduce ourselves."

They got back on the small trail, so as not to scare them by emerging from the woods. As they reached the beach, Ben called out, "Hello the camp."

Folks stopped and stared. Ben suddenly knew what Lila was saying. The people looked like pictures he'd seen of the holocaust. They were emaciated and obviously hadn't had a decent meal in weeks.

"Looks like you could use some help," said Lila.

"Oh, thank God someone came," cried a woman. "God heard our prayers."

One of the two men who had been arguing came over and shook their hands. "You're a sight for sore eyes. I'm Reverend Tom Wilson, and these are my people. Welcome to our camp."

Ben and Lila introduced themselves, and Lila said, "You all look like you're starving. When was the last time you ate?"

"We have met with some misfortune," said the reverend. "We ran out of food some time ago. We've been trying to fish, but haven't had much luck."

"I've been trying to get us to leave and find a town," said the other man. "My name is Jack Brennan. Reverend Wilson here didn't want to leave. Now it's too late. The nearest town is too far away. No one has the strength to make the journey."

"I will admit that I misjudged the situation," remarked the reverend. "But look who God sent us."

Oh boy, thought Ben. Aren't there any normal people left in the world?

"We'll do what we can to help," offered Lila. "Have you been boiling water for drinking?"

"We did think of that," said Jack. "I feel embarrassed though, that we have so few skills among us. We're city people. I'm an accountant. We have two salesmen, a bunch of store clerks. I guess we never got out much ... obviously not like you two."

"Believe it or not," said Ben, "we didn't get out much ourselves. We just knew we had to learn quickly or we'd die."

"Some of us don't learn so fast, I guess," replied Jack.

"I don't mean to sound blunt," said Ben, "but you've got to learn or you will all die. We've seen a lot of people survive the initial disaster, but not make it after. Do you have any guns?"

Jack looked down at the ground. "We have a couple of rifles, but we didn't pick up the right ammunition, so they're useless."

"I don't understand why you didn't try to make it to a town," said Lila.

"You want to answer that, reverend?" asked Jack.

"I must say that I don't like your accusing tone," answered Reverend Wilson, looking at Jack. He turned to Lila. "I had a divine message that we should avoid the cities."

"Nothing wrong with the message," said Ben. "Avoiding the

cities is a good idea, but that's after you get supplies. With no skills, how did you expect to live?"

"God sent you, didn't he?"

Lila was already frustrated with the reverend. "We will help you get some food in your bodies and give you some hints for staying alive, but it'll be up to you to take it from there. Then we're moving on. We weren't sent from God, trust me."

Later, they talked to Jack alone. He was troubled.

"I used to believe all the things Reverend Wilson told us," he said. "Now I'm not sure I believe anything. I mean, look where he led us, all because he said God guided him here."

Lila softened. "I believe in some sort of God, or a spiritual force. But I don't believe that you just sit back and wait for God to deliver. And you can't just blindly follow what someone else says. You have to take care of yourself. We've found that the opportunities present themselves if you're willing to do the work."

By the look on Jack's face, Ben knew the advice was too little, too late.

That night, they set up their tent in the woods near the trail, and far from the group.

"How're you feeling?" Ben asked Lila.

"It comes and goes," Lila answered. "I'm sure I'll feel better tomorrow."

They were almost asleep when they heard whispered voices from the trail leading to the beach. They grabbed their weapons, quietly opened the flap, and stepped out of the tent. Three figures were carefully moving down the trail.

"It'll be like shooting fish in a barrel, " whispered one of them. "We can get them all together and take what we need. They're so helpless, they'll let us do whatever we want."

Ben and Lila loudly cocked their weapons. The three stopped dead in their tracks.

"Hi there," said Lila. "My name is Lila. My friend here is Ben. You don't want to go any further."

"Oh shit," said one of them.

Ben and Lila approached the three, shining their flashlights on them. They weren't any older than Ben or Lila, just a lot scruffier. They had obviously had a hard go of it, but Ben surmised that they probably didn't look too much different now than from before the world changed, except for the weapons. Even though they each carried a full arsenal; a rifle each, a couple of pistols each, and assorted knives, Ben sensed that they weren't particularly dangerous. Probably more scared than anything else, he thought. They also carried backpacks.

"We know who you are. Everyone does. Look, we were just kidding. We just wanted a place to sleep tonight. You don't have to kill us."

"We're not going to kill you," said Ben. "However, I want you to take off your backpacks and your weapons, and lay them on the ground."

They quickly complied.

"Now I want you to turn around, go up the trail, and keep going. If we see you again, we will kill you."

"But you've left us defenseless," protested one of them.

"Just as defenseless as that group you were going to rob," said Lila. "I'm sure you'll find food and weapons somewhere. Just not here. Now move. And remember, we don't want to see you again."

Without another sound, they moved up the trail and out of sight.

They looked in the backpacks and found a good amount of

food, and, as Ben suspected, ammunition. No one in the camp had noticed the encounter.

"I guess sometimes that reputation of ours can be put to good use," remarked Ben. "Nobody got hurt and all we had to do was say our names."

"You realize that when we bring all this stuff into the camp, Reverend Wilson is going to say it's a gift from God, don't you?" said Lila.

"Hey, maybe it is," answered Ben, with a smile.

The next morning, Ben woke to the sound of Lila throwing up outside the tent.

"Are you okay?" he asked, when he stuck his head out.

"No," answered Lila. She looked at him with fear in her eyes. "Ben, I think I'm pregnant."

CHAPTER 17

I had been thrown for a loop before, but nothing came close to the feelings of total surprise, followed by sheer panic, I felt at that moment. How did it happen? I mean, I knew how it usually happened, but we had been very careful, and I had always used a condom. I will admit to a brief thought that maybe something happened in that camp that Lila hadn't told me. But I quickly realized two things: it hadn't been long enough in the past for her to already be feeling this way; and our communication was too good. If she had had to do something against her will, she would have told me. Nothing much embarrassed Lila anymore. No, it had to have happened early in our trip—maybe even our first time.

But I knew there was no sense in asking those questions. The fact was, we had to deal with it, just like we had to deal with everything else. And yet, this was bigger. It was going to affect us in ways that nothing else could. Nothing much scared us anymore. This terrified us!

Ben just stared, his mouth hanging open. What could he say? Congratulations? Neither had any illusions. This was the worst news possible.

"You're sure?" he asked feebly.

"I can't tell you definitely," she answered, "but I'm pretty sure."

"What do we do?"

"What else can we do? We don't have the options available to us that we had a couple of months ago. We've just got to see it through."

Although it was said calmly, Ben knew that she was feeling anything but.

How could we raise a child in this world? Assuming it even lived into childhood, what kind of life would it have? I thought about my own childhood, and all the fun I had. What fun would this kid have? Everything was based on survival. On the other hand, with us as parents, he or she would learn to be self-sufficient at an early age. I had to get the thoughts of my own childhood out of my head. It would do no good. This was a far, far different world. Then I thought of the ridiculousness of the situation. A couple of months earlier I was hoping to have a first date. Two months later I was thinking of my first child. What a strange path my life had taken.

There was nothing much they could do about it now, so they picked up the prizes from the night before and walked into the camp. Normally, campers by a lake would be up and buzzing about. Ben looked around him at the lethargy. These were people in their final days, accepting of their impending deaths. He shook his head in disgust and called to Reverend Wilson.

"Reverend, could you call your people out here?"

Seeing that Ben and Lila were loaded down with weapons and the backpacks, he quickly called his to flock. "Come quick, God has bestowed gifts upon us."

"What did I tell you," Lila said to Ben.

When they had all assembled, Ben launched into a speech.

"We came upon these things last night, and thought you might be able to use them. In the backpacks are various food items. These will help you for now, but they won't last long. You need to learn to fend for yourselves. Luckily, we have some weapons here. We can teach you how to shoot and clean your prey, but you have to want to learn."

I felt like I was speaking to children, children who had already decided that they didn't want to do any of the work. I didn't hold out much hope.

They spent the next week at the camp. Ben would take some of the men out hunting—the women had no interest—and Lila would teach those left at the camp survival techniques and how to find edible plants. At night, they would lie in their tent shaking their heads at the futility of it all. It would have been funny if it wasn't so life-threatening. The group was hopeless. Some of the men refused to shoot animals, while those who were willing couldn't get the hang of the rifles.

Lila had as much trouble with her students. No one seemed willing to learn. Some stared at her with blank looks, while others just parroted Reverend Wilson's stock phrases. The reverend was their biggest obstacle. He had evening services where he would go on and on about God's greatness. Ben noticed that Jack—the one person who was determined to succeed at hunting—no longer attended the services.

One night, at the end of the week, Ben confronted the reverend after one of his sermons.

"You're not doing these people any good," he said. "You spout all these words, but you're not teaching them anything useful."

"We all have our roles," answered the reverend. "You teach them skills they can use in the physical world, and I teach them about the glories of God."

"Look around you at the devastation," said Ben angrily. "Is this the glory of God? Maybe that's why you led them here, so they wouldn't see what the rest of the world looks like."

"I notice you are out here, as well."

"We are," said Ben. "But we choose to be. We've prepared ourselves for living out here. You've done nothing. We've tried to teach them, but they have no interest. Well, we're done. Lila and I will go out hunting tomorrow and find some food for you, then you're on your own. We've tried our best."

"And we thank you. God will reward you for all you've done."

Ben just shook his head and walked away.

That night, as they were lying in their tent, they reviewed the week.

"Do you feel we've done any good here?" asked Ben.

"No," replied Lila. "I had great hopes when I first saw them, but how can you help people who don't want to help themselves? Jack is the only one who seems willing to work at it."

"He asked me today if he could come hunting with us tomorrow. I think he's going to ask if he can go with us when we leave here for good."

"He's married. What about his wife?" asked Lila.

"He said earlier this week that his wife is so devoted to Reverend Wilson, they no longer have much of a relationship. I don't think they would miss each other. How would you feel about him coming with us?"

"Well, if there really is a reason for everything, maybe we

weren't here to save all these people. Maybe we were just here to save one of them," said Lila. "I'd be okay with it."

"I know we haven't talked much about it lately, but you've seemed better this week," observed Ben.

"It comes and goes," said Lila. "But it's not too bad right now. We'll have a lot of time to talk about it."

Holding each other, they fell asleep.

They were up bright and early the next morning and made themselves breakfast. Jack joined them. Although he was middle-aged—Ben thought in his mid-forties—he didn't seem embarrassed to be looking to two teens for his salvation.

"Thanks for letting me come with you this morning," he said.

"Our pleasure," said Lila.

As expected, Jack brought up the subject of traveling with them when they left for good.

"I can't stay here," he said. "It's so stifling. I need to get out."

"We've already talked about it," offered Lila. "You are welcome to join us."

He was grateful, and told them so. Since he didn't bring up the subject of his wife, neither did they.

They set off, rifles in hand, on their mission. They had mixed feelings about it all. Even if they had an abundant day, what would it really mean in the long run? These people were eventually going to die, thought Ben, and there was nothing they could do about it.

Strangely, they saw very little game that day. By noon, all they had were two rabbits. They sat under a tree and ate some granola bars they had brought. It was an unusually hot day, and they were exhausted. Lila had spells of dizziness.

"Are you okay?" asked Jack.

"I'm pretty sure I'm pregnant."

"Ah, and you have morning sickness. My wife had it. It passes."

"I hope so. I didn't know you had kids," said Lila.

"We don't. We did. We had a son. He died from leukemia when he was seven. That's when we gravitated to Reverend Wilson's church. It's also when my marriage died."

"I'm sorry," said Lila.

"It was a long time ago. Maybe it was for the best. He probably would have died from this anyway."

They started back mid-afternoon, with slim pickings. They managed only two quail in the afternoon.

As it turned out, it didn't matter at all. They walked out of the woods and into the camp, and stopped dead in their tracks. It was carnage. Jack immediately threw up.

Everyone was dead. They had all been shot, and were lying at unnatural angles all around the campground. Some of the women had been violated.

Lila dropped to her knees. "Noooo," she cried.

Ben just stood there, not knowing how to react. Finally he walked slowly into the camp and checked to see if anyone was left alive. He saw Reverend Wilson lying there, with a bullet hole in his head. He heard a moan and moved quickly over to a man he remembered as Raymond. He had been shot in the stomach and the chest. Blood was everywhere. Ben knew there was nothing he could do for him.

He knelt down. "Who did this?" he asked.

"Men," said Raymond, choking on his blood. "Prison uniforms…some had."

"How many men?" asked Ben.

"A few … don't know." And he died.

What had happened to the world? In disasters, weren't people supposed to come together and help each other? Was our society even more screwed up than I had thought? If the disaster hadn't happened, was this the future we were looking at anyway?

He walked back to where Lila was standing, tears streaming down her face. She was clenching and unclenching her fists. Her face had turned to stone. Her eyes reflected an anger he had never seen before. It scared him.

"I'm going after them," said Lila.

"I thought you were tired of all the death," answered Ben. "It would be better if we just headed for the Smokies and got lost in the forest."

"Do you realize how much killing they are going to do?" asked Lila. "This isn't like Wells and Sharp. These people live to kill and rape. They're machines. I don't care where we end up, we will never be safe with them out there. I'm going after them. I have to. You can come or not."

Lila's remarks stung. Ben had never heard her like this. He grabbed her arms and tried to look into her eyes. "Lila, calm down."

"Calm down?" she cried. She pulled away and smacked his chest in frustration. "Look around you. How can you tell me to calm down? Look at the women. Look at the children. How can you be calm? Who would do that to children? I have a child inside me. You think I want her to die like this? They have to be stopped. I've had enough of it. This world has gone to hell. I don't care what I said about the killing. I want to see their blood flowing like a river." She was talking nonstop. "We've wondered what our purpose is.

Maybe this is it. Maybe we're meant to stop anyone else from suffering the fate these people suffered. If you want to go on without me, that's fine, but I'm going after them."

Lila had snapped. She was shaking in her fury. Ben grabbed her and held her in a bear hug. She struggled at first, and then collapsed into a heap at his feet, tears flowing down her cheeks.

Ben sat down next to her and put his arm around her.

"Lila, listen to me. It's always been you and me. Always. What you do, I do. We'll go after these guys. We'll get them one by one, and when they're all gone, we'll head to the Smokies and live our quiet life. Don't ever think I would leave you."

She looked at him. He heard a quiet "I'm sorry." He continued to hold her.

Meanwhile, Jack was standing over his wife. He said nothing and shed no tears. But Ben knew he was grieving in his own way.

The night we had talked about the killing, and how it made us feel, seemed so long ago. We were sure then that it was over. But this was different. We were hunting now, hunting the worst type of vermin, the kind who killed just for the fun of it. I thought back to Nick's explanation of the mob mentality. This wasn't that. These weren't basically good people caught up in something exciting. These were hardcore murderers. Raymond had said some wore prison uniforms. If they were convicts, this wasn't going to be easy. At the same time, it made it even more urgent for us to do something about it. A group this violent would be a danger to everyone—ourselves included. How could we ever live a peaceful life, knowing that at any time these men could show up? Lila was pregnant. Could I really let my wife—did I really use that word?—and child be in danger from them? Our reputation would mean nothing. Not to this crew. No, it was time for one final act of violence on our part. An act that could very well save the lives of many. If we didn't do this, we would always wonder. We would always be looking over our shoulder. No, we really had no choice.

CHAPTER 18
(Lila)

I was seven. Thinking back, it was the last time I remember my parents smiling. I guess it was probably a year or two after my sister died, and I'm sure it was hard for them to put on the facade of happiness, much less even be able to function.

We were sitting at a picnic table next to a cabin my parents had rented on the shores of Lake Winnipesaukee. We had just come back from the beach and were having lunch. The whole thing is hazy, but I remember three men coming up to us. I couldn't tell you what they looked like, but I'll never forget the smell. It was a combination of cigarette smoke, alcohol, and unwashed bodies and clothes, and was so offensive, I had my hand over my nose. They were creepy, and I think my parents sensed it. They were nice to the men at first--they might have been asking directions ... I don't really know--but after a few minutes, my father became agitated. There was some arguing, and the next memory I have is all of us walking into the house. My mother was crying, and she told me to go into my room and lock the door.

I remember the yelling and the noise of things breaking and of feeling so scared. There was a tiny closet in the bedroom and I crawled in and curled up in a corner. The men must not have had interest in me, because the next thing I remember, it was late at night and my father came and got me. He looked bad. There was blood on his clothes and his face was all puffy and purple. He hustled me out to the car where my mom was covered in blankets in the front seat. I asked her if she was okay, but she didn't answer.

We drove back home to Newton that night and nothing was ever said about the incident again. Being seven, it eventually faded from my memory, but obviously my parents never forgot.

I realize now that all these years, it wasn't that my parents didn't trust me. That incident, combined with the death of my sister, had sapped them of all confidence. They were going through the motions. They felt an obligation to keep me safe, but no longer had the energy or enthusiasm to do it rationally. Limiting my activities protected me in their eyes. What I saw as controlling and overbearing behavior on their part was simply shame; shame at their inability to control the situation so many years earlier. The end of the world had brought an end to their suffering. They were dead now, and for the first time in years, I realized that I loved them. The picture I took with me from my house was lost in the tornado, so I no longer had any reminder of what they looked like. That made me sad.

Their life was ruined because of what those men did to them. And that's why I had to go after this group. I vowed to never have to feel the shame of being at someone else's mercy.

CHAPTER 19

Lila was still shaking. Ben knew that something about this incident affected her profoundly — much more than any of the other deaths they had encountered. All he could do was to continue to hold her. He saw Jack pick up his rifle and walk up the path.

"Jack," he called. "Where are you going?"

"I have to go after them," Jack replied. "I just have to go after them."

"Wait," said Ben. "We're going after them too. We'll have a better chance together."

Jack hesitated, stopped, then turned toward Ben. "We have to go soon then."

"We will. Let's come up with a plan. It'll be dark soon. I think we should go at night. There will be less chance of us being seen and more of a chance of us seeing them. They'll probably have a fire."

"Okay." Jack, like Lila, was trembling with anger. "I'll go to the top of the path and see which way they went on the trail."

Ben looked down at Lila in his arms. She was breathing easier. At one point she had begun to hyperventilate. He couldn't understand why he wasn't as affected by the massacre as the other two. It was obvious that losing his wife—no matter what their relationship was—could be devastating to Jack. As for Lila, he was sure it was the sight of the women and children that did it. But what about him? Was he unfeeling? He was shocked, to be sure, and sickened to a degree, but his lack of emotion bothered him.

Lila was moving. She slowly stood up and hugged Ben.

"I'm sorry I said those things to you," she told him. "You didn't deserve that." She kissed him.

"I know you didn't mean it," said Ben. "Let's talk about how we're going to get these guys."

Jack returned from the top of the path.

"They headed south down the trail," he announced.

"Okay, so they're going the way we were," said Ben. "They will be setting up camp somewhere for the night. Probably not too far down the trail. If we let it get dark enough, we'll see their fire from a good distance and can sneak in. Now I wish we had kept some of those M-16s. They would be more effective, and they hold more bullets. But we didn't, so we work with what we have."

Ben realized as he was talking that he was going to have to come up with the plan. Lila and Jack were anxious to get going, but they were too emotional to plan effectively.

"Wouldn't they be the kind to find an abandoned hotel or some building for the night?" asked Lila.

"I think they would, if there were any around. A little further north they would have run into some, but not here. Besides, if they're heading south on the trail, it means they are going to find even more wilderness than here, so they'll have to camp."

"It seems odd that they're even on the trail," said Lila. "I would've thought they'd stick to the cities."

"Yeah, except that probably most people left the cities for the coast or the mountains, like we did. Hard to kill and rape if there's no one there."

Jack and Lila both winced at that, and Ben was immediately sorry he'd said it.

He changed the subject by continuing with the planning.

"Them heading south is an advantage for us. Towns will be few and far between. I'm sure we're better equipped for dealing with the wilderness. The only way we can do this is guerrilla warfare. If it really is a group of convicts, I don't think they'll be expecting that. I say we go in for a quick attack, then take off and hide for a couple of days. Just when they think we're gone, we go in again. We could do some real damage."

"What's your plan?" asked Jack.

"I think you and I should go into the woods and shoot into the camp from different corners, driving them out. They're not going to camp too far off the trail—they have nothing to fear. As they run back onto the trail, Lila will be positioned to pick them off." He looked at Lila. "You're the best shot, so I think that's where you would be most effective. After we send in a barrage of bullets, we head for some spot we set up in advance. Then we hide, and do it all over again." He addressed them both. "This isn't foolproof. Anything could go wrong. But that's how I would do it."

Lila and Jack looked at each other, assessing the plan.

"Lila, this group will be different than any we've run across. Wells and Sharp were bad, but these guys are far worse. They live to destroy. If they decide to come after us ..." He left it hanging.

"And that's exactly why we have to do this," said Lila, matter-of-factly.

"I know. I just needed to say it." He changed the subject again.

He knew he was dealing with two people on the edge. "We'll need to travel light. I suggest we find a place to hide our backpacks. We should just take our canteens, some light food, and, of course, a lot of ammunition. Then we need to figure out a place to meet, because there's no doubt we will get separated. On our way down the trail, let's scout out some spots."

"Can we go?" asked Jack impatiently.

Ben got angry.

"Jack, listen to me. The only way this is going to work is if we have a plan and we stick to it. You're mad and you're out for blood. I can understand that." He walked over to Jack and got in his face. "However, if you decide not to follow the plan, you will get us all killed. It's dangerous enough as it is. We don't need that. So I'm telling you now. You will be patient and you will follow the plan."

Jack's face softened. "I'm sorry. You're right. I just want revenge for what the bastards did. Don't worry, you can count on me."

Ben held out his hand and they shook.

"Thank you. Then let's do this."

The sun had gone down, but Ben was cautious all the same. He was pretty sure they'd be camped somewhere, swapping their sordid stories of the day. Chances were they would be tired. He assumed a person couldn't do what they did without expending a tremendous amount of energy.

They walked slowly down the path, letting the little bit of moonlight that made it through the trees guide their way. When they had gone about a half an hour, Ben made out a narrow animal trail leading off to the left. He told the others to wait while he explored it. He followed the path about thirty yards and came upon a batch of large rocks. He quickly retraced his steps to the trail.

"There's a perfect place to use as our meeting place down that trail just a little way. There are rocks to hide behind or defend ourselves from if we are followed. We just need to find a way to recognize the path."

"There's a broken tree limb over here on the other side of the trail," said Lila. "The tricky part will be not passing it in the dark."

"If you do," suggested Ben, "keep going until you reach the reverend's camp, and then find a place to hide. We'll know that if worse comes to worst, that's where we'll meet. Let's leave our backpacks here."

They hid the backpacks amongst the rocks, then returned to the trail and walked along in silence for another half hour, when they saw a faint light in the distance and heard the sounds of laughing and swearing.

"This is it," whispered Ben. He was nervous. He knew it wasn't much of a plan. If they'd had a few more people to help with the attack, it could all be over quickly, but that wasn't the case.

They got down on their hands and knees and crawled, single-file, on the edge of the trail the rest of the way. The noise was getting louder. Ben motioned for them to stay there, while he moved ahead to get a look. There was a large fire in the center of a clearing. The men had pulled some logs from the woods and were sitting against them. Others were standing near the fire warming themselves. The evenings were becoming chilly, and most of the men weren't dressed for it. Weapons were scattered around, leaning against logs. Ben counted six men.

He quietly made his way back to where Lila and Jack were nervously waiting.

"There are six," he began. "They're around the fire. I think the sooner we go in, the better."

"Shouldn't we wait until they're asleep?" asked Jack.

"No," answered Ben. "The fire will have died out and it'll be harder for us to see. And right now they are looking into the fire. They won't be able to see a thing in the woods. Are we ready?"

"I guess so," said Jack.

"Where do you want me?" asked Lila.

Ben looked around. "Actually, right in the woods across the trail there. There's a good hiding place. Your job will be to pick off anyone we don't get."

They hugged and kissed each other.

"Be careful," she said. "I love you."

"I love you too. We'll all be okay."

He only wished he was as confident as he was trying to sound. He also knew that Lila could see right through his false confidence.

She moved off into the woods, and almost immediately was gone from sight. Ben and Jack headed into the woods on the other side of the trail so they could come up from behind the group. The other reason Ben wanted to do it now, rather than when they were asleep was the ability to sneak up while they were still making noise.

They approached the camp. Ben found a spot for Jack behind some fallen trees at the left back corner of the camp. Jack's rifle had a magazine that held nine rounds, so he wouldn't have to change them as often as Ben. Jack pulled out a couple of extra magazines and set them beside him. Ben patted him on the shoulder, then moved over to the right corner and found a place behind some rocks. The men in the camp weren't more than thirty feet away. The plan was that he was going to shoot first, and Jack would follow his lead.

It didn't happen that way.

Ben had barely gotten himself in position, and hadn't even pulled out his extra magazines, when Jack's gun went off. He heard Jack swear. He had fired it by accident.

The camp went quiet, then erupted in confused bedlam as the convicts went for their weapons. Ben pulled out a couple of extra magazines, then took aim and began shooting. Immediately after, he heard Jack firing. The men were close and Ben's skills with the rifle had improved immensely since the day with the coyotes. Jack wasn't very good at all, but at that distance, even he couldn't miss all the time. The convicts grabbed their weapons, then hit the ground and started firing. Most of them had automatic weapons, and the spray of bullets was overwhelming.

Then Ben realized that he had made a major tactical mistake. They weren't running to the trail. They were fighting back. Leaving Lila there had been a mistake. She had no one to shoot at. They had done all they could do. There was no more element of surprise.

"Jack, go!" he shouted. He backed out of his spot and ran further into the woods, keeping low, bullets hammering the trees around him. He felt one clip his neck. He stumbled, then regained his footing, and continued on. He could feel blood running down under his shirt. It was pitch black in the forest. The running was slow and dangerous. He stopped behind a tree for a moment to pull out his knife and cut a section off his shirt. He pressed it against his neck wound and held it there as he resumed his escape.

Gradually, the roar of the guns died down, then finally stopped. By now, though, he was deep in the forest. He came across some rocks and slid down behind them, gasping for air. He felt like his lungs were going to burst. Gradually, his breath returned to normal and he took stock of the situation.

Jack's gun going off was unfortunate, but in the long run,

probably didn't make a huge difference. They were more prepared than he had figured, and he hadn't planned on the automatic and semi-automatic weapons. He realized in hindsight that he hadn't planned on a lot of things.

Ben knew that he had taken down a couple, but he didn't think Jack had gotten any. That left four—still a formidable number. He hoped that Jack had made it away safely, and he wasn't too worried about Lila. They didn't even know about her.

He was safe for the moment. They wouldn't come after him this far into the forest. He just had to make sure he could find his way back up to the trail. If he got lost, he could wander out there for weeks. Suddenly he was scared of being separated once again from Lila. He hoped he had gone in a straight line from the trail, but suppose he hadn't? After all, he was running for his life in the dark of night. He didn't know if he had veered to the right or to the left. Frankly, he had absolutely no idea where he was.

The ground rumbled under his feet. It was a strong one, but it quickly subsided.

Oh great, he thought. Just what I need.

While the rocks he was behind were okay, he felt he needed something a bit safer, so he looked around. The tree cover was a little sparser here and the moon shed some light. Further into the forest he saw a small knoll, so he headed for it. It was about ten feet higher than where he had been, and it had a few more rocks on top for protection. While he knew they would never follow him, he still felt better with the added protection. He took off his rifle, his crossbow and quiver, and settled down to wait out the night.

I made a lot of mistakes that day. Overestimating my abilities was probably the biggest. I had let this folk hero thing go to my head. Granted, I hadn't even wanted to go after these guys in the first place, but once I had made the decision, I felt I was invincible. From ice cream scooper to Rambo in a couple of months. Who was I kidding? We had come a long way, but this time we had bitten off way more than we could chew. I was lost in the forest with no idea of what had happened to Lila or Jack. Could things get any worse?

Just before sunrise, Ben had to pee. He got up and moved over to a tree to relieve himself. He was halfway through the process when a bullet struck the tree inches from his head. He fell to the ground, wetting himself in the process. He quickly tucked himself in, zipped up, and crawled back to the rocks. He looked over the top to see four shadows moving in the woods.

He knew then that he had made yet one more critical mistake. They had followed him after all!

CHAPTER 20
(Lila)

Something had gone wrong. Lila could sense it almost immediately. The first shot had come from Jack's gun—she knew its sound from the hunting they had done. That wasn't the plan. Ben's first shot came next. Then all hell broke loose. The convicts were more heavily armed than they had figured. She waited for the first of the convicts to come up to the trail, but deep down, she knew that wouldn't happen.

After a few minutes, she no longer heard Ben or Jack's guns. But the other guns continued, and they were receding on the right side of the camp—the side Ben was on. Hopefully this meant that Ben was still alive and was eluding his pursuers. Had Jack escaped, or would she find him dead by the fire? She had to force herself to stay where she was. It would do no good to go after them now, not in this darkness. She'd have to wait until the sun came up. She found herself praying to … to what? ... the universe, she guessed, that Ben was okay.

The gunfire continued for a while before finally trailing off. She took that as a good sign. If it had stopped suddenly, she would have assumed the worst, that he had been found and killed.

She sat wide awake all night. There was no way she could sleep. The hours passed excruciatingly slowly. A half a dozen times she got up to go after them, and a half a dozen times she sat back down. She'd never find their trail in the dark. Meanwhile, the convicts' camp was silent. They hadn't returned from their hunting mission.

Finally, the first faint signs of morning appeared in the eastern sky, and she started to stand up. Suddenly, she heard the sounds of footsteps on the trail, and she knelt down, quietly cocking her rifle.

A ragtag group of five survivors furtively crept down the trail, not saying a word. The group was comprised of two teenaged boys, a younger boy, and two middle-aged women. Lila could tell that they weren't a family; events had probably thrown them together. They had some small backpacks, but no weapons.

Lila wasn't sure why she made the contact with them. She could have just as easily stayed hidden. But she knew she had to warn them about the convicts.

"Good morning," she said softly from her hiding place.

She would have thought a mortar had gone off. As one, the five jumped, with terrified expressions on their faces.

"Shh," she put her finger to her lips. "I'm friendly. C'mon off the trail for a minute. You could probably use the rest." She was anxious to get going, but besides being able to warn them, she was also curious about any news that might be passed on. Every bit of information could be helpful down the line.

The survivors looked at each other, then moved near to where Lila was hidden. They all sat down and were invisible from the trail. They seemed relieved for the break.

"My name's Lila."

"We've heard of you," said one of the teens. None of them

offered their names, so Lila didn't push it.

"Just wanted to get any news you might have. Don't see a lot of people out here."

"It's bad," said the same teen. "We're heading to Florida. We heard that a lot of people are, so we figured there might be some towns, or at least camps down there."

"There's a group of really bad men out there," said the youngest one. "We're trying to get away from them."

"They've killed a lot of people," offered one of the women.

Lila's worst fears were confirmed. They had left a long trail of death behind them.

She cocked her head and said, "I find it curious that you're going in the same direction that they are."

"We didn't know that. We weren't quite sure where they were going," answered the woman. "We were scared. They killed the rest of our group. We just started walking."

One of the teens dropped his eyes to the ground. It was obvious to Lila that he didn't want to admit in front of her that he was scared as well. The other one, however, the one who had spoken first, needed to impress.

"I wasn't scared."

"You should be."

He shrugged off her comment. "Why don't you come with us," he said. The way he was looking at her, Lila knew his hormones had kicked in.

'No thanks. I have things to do."

The fact was, every time I ran across other survivors—with a few exceptions, like Nick and Jason—I wanted to be sick. I didn't feel as if I belonged to the human race anymore. People were just getting in the way.

The thought of joining some group in Florida was worse than the thought of dying.

Lila was sorry she had made herself known. Now she just wanted to get rid of them.

"Their camp is right over there." She pointed across the trail. The five stiffened. "But they're not there. You can get ahead of them. If you're lucky, by the end of the day, there won't be any left to worry about."

No one bothered to ask her why.

"So I'd suggest you leave now and go fast."

Without another word they got up and filed out.

Lila just shook her head.

She moved from her hiding place and crossed the trail into the woods, skirting around the right side of the camp hoping to pick up Ben's trail. She looked into the clearing as she crept through the woods, and saw two downed convicts. One twitched, but didn't make a sound.

Two down, four to go, she thought. Now she was regretting the whole thing. Ben was right in wanting to avoid them, but being the loyal person he was, he did it for Lila, even if she wasn't being rational about it all. Her irrationality might have gotten Ben killed. And there was no sign of Jack.

She saw where Ben had chosen to shoot from, so she used that as a starting point. It was easy at first. The area was pretty trampled down from the group who had pursued him. She followed the shell casings and the broken branches into the forest, keeping her eyes and ears out for the return of the convicts. She came across blood splatter on some leaves and went cold with fear. Ben was wounded. She knew it was him because she hadn't heard him shooting back at his pursuers. She came across the tree Ben had hidden behind to fashion a bandage, and saw a blood stain on the trunk. She picked up her pace, her heart pounding.

The sun was rising. She had been on Ben's trail for almost an hour and was surprised at the perseverance the convicts were showing in their pursuit of him.

It didn't fit. These were men who were used to taking what they wanted. They had to work at very little. Why would they expend the effort to chase a man through the forest? I seriously doubted that they cared that much for their dead comrades. For that matter, I doubted that they cared for much of anything or anybody. And then it hit me, and I found the rage returning. It was a sport for them. They were after Ben, not out of anger, but out of amusement.

She heard a shot. It didn't come from Ben's gun. They weren't too far ahead of her. She ran for a short distance, then slowed down and carefully made her way through the trees.

Another shot. Much closer this time. And then a voice.

"Hey you up there. You know we've got you surrounded, right? You might want to think about using one of those bullets on yourself, 'cause when we get to you, we're gonna carve you up. Did you think you were going to be a hero and wipe us out?"

Automatic gunfire punctuated the speaker's point.

No sound came from Ben. Lila could see where he probably was—on a small hill with a ring of rocks at the top.

She looked around and, one by one, located the convicts. It was up to her to lessen the odds a little. The closest one to her was about forty feet away. He was nearly the same distance from the next one in line. They had spread out so that they had, in fact, formed a semi-circle in front of Ben. Lila took a deep breath. One more time. She vowed to herself that her child was only going to see the beauty in the world, and if she was going to ensure that happening, then she had to immerse herself in violence one more time. One last time.

When did I reach the point of no return? When did I change from Lila the incredibly average teenager to this? I thought of my friends in school, and some of my teachers—oddly, not my parents—and their reactions if they saw me now. What I was about to do went far beyond the limits of my former life. The transition was now complete. The person I once thought I was died along with millions of others. But it gave birth to a new version of me, and despite everything, I wasn't unhappy with the result.

She slipped her knife from its sheath and silently crept closer to her prey, all the while trying to decide how to dispose of him. She could see that he was a lot bigger than she was, so her first thought of grabbing him by the head and slashing his throat was risky. If he had fast reflexes, he could grab her before she had a chance to use the knife. She could use her rifle or her Sig, but that would alert the others quicker than she wanted. No, she had to kill him before he had a chance to react.

He picked up his rifle—an M-16—and fired a few shots at Ben. Lila moved closer with the sound of the gun masking her movements. She was within a couple of yards. He aimed his rifle again and shot a few more rounds. As he did, Lila moved in and swung her knife hand in an arc from right to left, embedding the knife to the hilt into his temple. He dropped his weapon and slumped over forward. Lila felt her stomach turn over and she thought she was going to throw up. She sat and let the wave pass. Now the hard part. She pulled the knife out to a slurping sound.

Blood and bits of brain-matter flowed out of the wound. Her stomach let loose and she vomited. She was able to do so somewhat quietly, and no one heard her. When she was done, she wiped the knife on the man's shirt. She didn't think she'd be able to do that a second time.

She wasn't given the opportunity. The man in the middle of the group quietly called out to his men that it was time to move in. It was now or never. She picked up the M-16 and aimed for the next man in line. As soon as he moved, she let go a burst. As she shot, the barrel raised and she missed her target. He turned to her in surprise and she shot again, this time catching him in the body and propelling him backwards. She swung the rifle toward the tree line and opened fire at the spots where the two others had been. She heard a scream, followed by shots from the top of the rise. Ben was alive and shooting!

She searched her first victim and found a couple more magazines. She figured out how to change the magazine and quickly did so, immediately continuing with her firing. She saw the man who had screamed on the far side limping into the woods. She aimed and fired a burst. The man dropped to the ground.

"I surrender!" The last of the four threw his weapon out into the clearing where it would be seen and came out of his hiding place with hands over his head. "I give u….." Ben shot a hole in the man's forehead.

Lila ran across the clearing to the knoll where Ben was hiding. He stood up. She saw a bloody piece of cloth stuck to his neck. They embraced and stood hugging each other.

*****

(Ben)

Once again, one of us saved the other. If Lila hadn't shown up, there was no doubt that I would've been killed. But it also brought up the fear of how dependent we were on one another. Sure, we had each developed a sureness in ourselves, and our skills were improving by the day. After all, for Lila to do what she did to rescue me required an ability that neither of us would have ever developed in our old life. Now it was becoming second nature. But we still needed each other. It was a strange dichotomy. As our skills increased, so did our dependence on each other. Maybe it had to do with fear after all. The more violent acts we committed, the more scared we were of what we were becoming. Our need for each other increased because it remained the only positive thing each of us still had. This wasn't the normal independence that we would have learned as we got older in our other life. That would have happened at a gradual rate of speed. It's why people looked forward to going out on their own. They could handle it. This was a whole different world. We realized that we weren't afraid of death, we were afraid of being alone.

Lila cleaned Ben's wound with water from her canteen, then wrapped a fresher piece of material around his neck and tied it off in a knot. The wound wasn't too bad, and Ben felt okay to keep going. They had to return to the convicts' camp and find Jack. They hurried back through the forest. Finding their way back to the camp wasn't as hard as they thought it would be. The convicts had left an easy trail to follow. As they approached the camp Jack emerged from behind a tree, rifle in hand.

"I didn't know if you had made it," he said as he hugged his friends. "I was on my way to the meeting spot, but realized that the job here wasn't done. If they had killed you, I had to do whatever I could to make sure they never killed again. So I came back to wait—for you or for them."

And like that, one of the scourges of the new world was gone. Lila told me about her encounter with the survivors who had said that this group had killed so many people. What a waste of life. If people were serious about starting a new society, how many of the good ones had died at the hands of this group's viciousness? Well, we were done. We did what we had to do with the convicts. Now it was time to do what we had to for ourselves. There was no society in our future. That, we'd leave to someone else. We needed to get on with our own dream.

"Funny," Jack said, when they had found the spot where they had left their backpacks. "You guys are less than half my age, but in some ways, I feel I've learned more from you than from anyone in my life. You've taught me the importance of survival. Not just existing, but really surviving. I'll miss what my wife and I once had, but I was missing that already. I won't miss my wife, though. She had changed into exactly what I didn't want to become. That whole group was something I hadn't wanted to become. Maybe nothing would have saved them from the killers, but with the right guidance, maybe we wouldn't have even been there in the first place. Reverend Wilson always talked about salvation. I don't think he had a clue as to what it was. I have experienced the real salvation. I feel alive for the first time in my life, and I'm going to make the most of it."

Ben and Lila offered to let him accompany them to the Smoky Mountains, but he politely declined.

"Your destiny is different from mine. The nice thing? I have no idea what mine is. I'm going to spend the rest of my life finding it.

Without the noise of the previous world, maybe I can really find who I am."

They all hugged. Jack had robbed the dead men in the camp of some of their weapons, including an M-16 and lots of ammunition—Ben finally allowed himself an M-16, as well—and various knives, so he was going off on his own, feeling safe. Most of all, feeling excited for what lay before him.

As they watched Jack head north on the trail, Ben and Lila turned south ... toward peace.

You would think that finding peace in a world devoid of people would be fairly simple. It had been anything but. We were exhausted. We had assumed from the very beginning of the journey that it would be dangerous. Never in our wildest dreams, however, could we have imagined all that we encountered. And sadly, it wasn't over yet. Not by a long shot. The next few months would be the happiest in our lives. But that bliss would be followed by our worst fear coming true ...

PART FOUR: SEPARATION

CHAPTER 21

Determined not to stop for anybody, Ben and Lila made their way south along the trail. Their focus was on themselves, and only themselves. There was no guilt in that. They had done more than their share of helping others. With each passing day, the country got more beautiful. Lila was sick a lot, but it didn't stop her determination in reaching their new home.

They were also in a hurry because the weather was turning colder. Nick had told them that the climate in the Smokies was fairly moderate at the low levels. But he also warned that the weather, already inconsistent over the previous few years, could play a lot of tricks on them, and that the sooner they got settled for the winter, the better.

They met no one in that last leg of their journey, which thrilled them. The silence of nature calmed them, helping them to put aside the events of the past many weeks. Ben made sure to camp early enough at night to allow Lila the longest rest possible. They were fortunate to find lakes or ponds almost every night to camp by. The only somber moment came when they passed the wreckage of an airliner. Despite the fact that every plane in the sky would have plummeted to the ground that day, this was the first one they had come across.

They passed it with a reverence. It was scattered in a thousand parts over a square mile, but much of the fuselage was still intact.

"Look how big it is," whispered Lila. "How terrifying it must've been for them."

"They were already dead, remember?" said Ben. "They would have died instantly in mid-air. They never experienced the crash."

"That actually makes me feel better," responded Lila.

One morning, they rounded a bend and there, sitting in front of them, was a large sign that read "Entering Great Smoky Mountains National Park." They stood in front of it, not uttering a word. Finally, hand in hand, they continued along the trail. At one point, they came across a visitors center and picked up some literature.

"Fontana Lake looks like a good place to head for," said Ben that night by the campfire. He pointed to the map. "But not the main lake. I think that's too close to the dam and the resort area. If we go up one of the tributaries off the main lake right here," he ran his finger along the map, "we'll probably run across some cabins, but it'll be away from everything."

"That sounds good," said Lila. "Ben, can you believe how far we've come?"

"And all that we've learned in the process," added Ben. "We should be very proud of ourselves. You know, my father tried so hard to make a man of me. I wonder what he'd think now."

"He'd be very proud of you," replied Lila. "I realize now that even though your dad and my parents had trouble showing it, they loved us. Your mom was the only one who could really show that love. But they'd all be proud."

A few days later, they reached Fontana Dam. The lake was enormous and beautiful. The morning sun created diamonds in the water, and they sat on the edge of the trail in the warmth of the sun, just soaking in the scene. Suddenly, Ben had an idea.

"I'm looking down at the water and I see boats of all sizes down there. We've done a lot of walking. How about we borrow a boat and find our new home by way of the water?"

As he said that, he looked into the parking area of the dam and saw an old beat-up pickup truck. He left his pack with Lila, told her he'd be right back, and ran down to the truck. It was unlocked, as he assumed it would be. He found the ignition key in the visor, inserted it in the ignition and turned it, crossing his fingers. The truck started with a rattle.

"Yes!" he shouted.

The gas tank was about half full, but Ben figured he could find more gas somewhere. He pocketed the key and ran back to Lila. She looked at him quizzically.

"If we're going to make this our home," started Ben, "we're going to need some things we can't find in the woods: cloth diapers, books on childbirth—all kinds of books, for that matter—a good supply of canned food, a good propane grill, an axe to chop wood, seeds for the spring, gardening equipment, a cradle … the list is endless. This truck can get us to a larger town so we can get all that."

They made their way down to a marina, where they found a small boat with an ancient outboard motor.

"If old cars work, then this should too," said Ben.

It did. They loaded their packs and Lila cast off. The sound of the outboard was almost out of place on the deserted lake, but the thought of rowing didn't appeal to either of them.

"I read in the literature that when they built the dam, they had to create the lake over a town. All the townspeople had to leave," said Lila. "So we're floating over a town that was dead decades before the rest of the country."

In a little while, they left the main body of water and traveled up one of the arms. Already it was more peaceful. All around them was forest. Many of the trees had lost their leaves for the winter, but there was still the sense of privacy. They passed the occasional vacation cabin, but nothing stood out.

Finally, they saw a little cabin nestled on the banks of the lake, and Ben knew immediately that they had found their home. It was important to Ben that Lila be comfortable with the choice—after all, she was the one having the baby, and comfort was going to be a big factor—and he could see the excitement in her face. The cabin wasn't large, but it was sunny, with oversized windows, and a deck around two-thirds of the house. They pulled the boat up to a small dock and walked up to their new home. The inside was very simple: A living room, a kitchen, and three small bedrooms. There was a wood stove in the living room, as well as a fireplace. An outhouse could be seen at the edge of the woods. No other cabins were close by.

It was rustic, but that was exactly what they were looking for. Anything too modern would have been uncomfortable. The cabin came with dishes, cooking utensils, beds, and chairs, but not much else. Lila suggested they raid the resort across the lake for amenities, while also raiding the kitchen there for institutional-size cans of food. There was so much they needed, even to lead a simple life, that Ben was happy he had seen the truck. It would come in handy.

It was exciting! The next month was spent setting up our home. As best we could figure as we counted back, it was probably late November, maybe early December. In one of our forays into town, we found a calendar for the next year at a bookstore. We decided then and there that it was December 1st. We wanted to establish a date so that we could keep track of Lila's pregnancy, when to start our garden, and to be able to give our son or daughter a birthday.

I scrounged for gasoline and did pretty well. We had very few choices for towns that were large enough to have the kind of stores we needed, but we settled on Waynesville as our source for everything. It was sixty miles away, but it was the best we could do. Bryson City was closer, but fire had destroyed much of the town. Waynesville, on the other hand, was surprisingly devoid of blackened buildings. We had gotten used to living in the woods, needing very little. But to survive a winter and plan for the future required a lot of things. I don't remember how many trips we made, but our little cabin was pretty crowded in no time. One of the bedrooms became our storage room.

Finally, we had everything we needed. Our child would be well taken care of, as would we. Two of my favorite "buys" were finding a large selection of seed starter kits left over from the spring—so we could get our garden started in the house—and boxes of beef jerky. You never knew when that could come in handy if it was a harsh winter and supplies ran low.

There was a good-sized clearing on the side of the cabin. While Lila organized the inside of the house, I prepared the soil so that, come spring, it would be easier to start the garden. I had picked up some rolls of wire fencing, and fenced in the future garden against the expected hungry animal. Being clueless teens, books became our resource for everything and we developed quite a library.

We made numerous trips to the resort on the main part of the lake. They had a large supply of wood for their fireplaces, and, while I also had to chop a lot of wood, having this source made things a bit easier. By the time the first snowflakes fell, we were fully ensconced in our little home.

On one of their trips to town, Ben pulled Lila into a jewelry shop.

"Lila, maybe you'll think this is stupid, but I'd like us to get married. We can have our own little ceremony at home and give each other rings."

Tears formed in Lila's eyes. "I don't think it's stupid at all. For a long time I've thought of us as married. I think a ceremony would be perfect. And who better to perform it than us? We know us better than anyone else in the world."

They spent the next hour picking out rings. Ben also found a beautiful onyx bracelet for Lila that he'd give her as a wedding present. Three days later, they held their ceremony. It was a bright sunny, warm day. They stood out on their deck, overlooking the lake.

Ben took Lila's hand. "Lila, when we were in the freezer so long ago, I knew you were special. You had an intelligence and a heart that you only find once in a lifetime. The last couple of months have proven that. But it has also uncovered your courage and your soul. I never imagined being so deeply in love." He placed the ring on her finger.

"Ben, there is so much to say, but I think you know it all, anyway. Your wisdom and your connection to the universe has kept me alive. When I think of where I came from, and what I now have in my life, I feel like crying. In a few months, I will give birth to a child … our child. The most beautiful symbol of the deep love we have between us. I am so proud to be your wife." She placed the ring on his finger, and they kissed. And then they sat on the deck holding each other, knowing that they were together for eternity.

*****

Winter came with a vengeance and caught them off-guard. Being from New England, they were used to winter storms, but from the safety and comfort of their warm homes. Snowplows made traveling accessible, and supermarkets were convenient if they ran out of milk and panicked.

This was a new world to them. Rather than lose its intensity, the violent weather picked up with a destructive fury. They were embarrassingly unprepared for what hit them. The snowstorms were ferocious and constant, and the cold relentless. By mid-January (by their calendar), they realized that they didn't have anywhere near enough wood to last the winter, and it had become impossible to hunt for fresh meat. The supplies in their storeroom were dwindling. They were trying not to panic, but it was hard to ignore the obvious.

"Food and wood," said Ben one evening, as they sat at the table. The latest storm was on its third day. "Water will be fine. We just keep melting the snow, like we've been doing. But we have to get fresh meat."

"Besides the fact that we're sick of canned food," said Lila, "I figured out that we only have about three weeks-worth left, and that's if we eat one meal a day."

"The wood is about the same," added Ben. "If it would just stop snowing, I could at least walk across the lake to the resort. They still have a lot there."

"And we could cut a hole in the ice and catch some fish," said Lila. "It's going to have to stop sometime, right?"

Neither of us wanted to admit it, but we were scared. This was totally unexpected. Nick was right about the crazy weather. But all this? I should have stocked more wood, but I figured that I could always boat across to the resort and get more. Now, all we could do was wait for the snow to end, and it didn't seem to have any intention of stopping soon.

They slept that night with the woodstove turned down lower than normal. They bundled up and held each other close. During these cold days and nights, they also discovered numerous cracks in the construction of the cabin that allowed the wind to blow through. They plugged them as best they could. But as it piled up, the snow itself started to act as insulation, and less and less wind made it into the cabin.

The storm abruptly died the next day. One minute the snow was falling, and the next the clouds had parted and the sun was coming out. As the day wore on, the wind began to die down. They looked outside at almost four feet of snow on the ground. A snow shovel hadn't been one of their priorities, but they did have a regular shovel for digging in the garden. The one positive was that the wind had been so strong, the lake was clear of snow. Perfect for ice fishing and to get wood from the resort.

Ben spent the rest of the day shoveling a path to the outhouse and a path to the beach. The next morning was cold, but the sun was out, so Ben decided to head over to the resort for wood and Lila was going to try her luck at fishing. They didn't have any hole borers or saws, so they took the ax and chopped a hole in the ice. It was about eight inches thick, so Ben was confident it was strong enough to bring a load of wood back. One of the boats was of a lightweight construction and had a flat bottom. His intention was to pull it over to the resort and, hopefully, drag it back filled with wood.

They opened a can of sardines to use as bait, and Lila dressed warmly and took her fishing rod out to the hole. Ben put a couple of blankets in the boat just to be safe, gave Lila a kiss, and started the long trip over to the other side. He figured it would take an hour to get there, an hour to fill up the boat, and another couple of hours to drag it back.

The trip over was relatively easy. The boat was light and it slid well over the ice. The sun gave a little warmth to an otherwise frigid day. It took him a bit more than an hour to reach the resort. He then went through the tedious process of carrying the wood from the resort building down to the boat. He filled it as high as he could. The fewer trips across the lake the better. He also found a few institutional-sized cans of soup and threw them in with the wood.

It was heavy! Ben couldn't get it to move. Finally, it budged, and then the natural slide of the ice took over. It wasn't easy, but he was able to pull it. He revised his time table. It would take him a good three hours to get back. Halfway across the lake, the wind picked up and the clouds rolled in. It was going to snow again. Ben had a choice, leave the boat where it was and make a run for it, or keep on and hope the snow didn't get too bad. Too late. He didn't even have time to make his decision before it started snowing.

He kept going. Finally, he could no longer see. It had become white-out conditions. The wind was blowing right through him. He knew that he had to act soon or he would freeze to death. He no longer knew which way to go.

Then it came to him. He began to unload the wood from the

boat, creating a small wall about two feet high encircling him and the boat. Then he laid one of the blankets on the ground inside the circle, thanking his stars that he added the blankets at the last minute. He then struggled against the wind to turn the boat over inside the circle. He won the battle and crawled under the upside down boat, covering himself with the second blanket. The wall of wood helped protect him from the wind. It was cold under there, but not terrible. Then he waited out the storm.

All night long, the wind howled and the boat vibrated. Eventually, he managed to fall asleep. He woke up at one point shivering. The blankets helped, but because he couldn't move, the cold was setting in. Now he was afraid of falling asleep. With this cold, he might not wake up. He did everything he could to stay awake—singing songs, naming baseball players (now all dead), and thinking of his favorite movies. It only worked for a short time. Sleep took over.

He awoke to a pounding on the boat and someone yelling his name. He was disoriented at first, then started to think clearly. It was Lila! Then he realized the wind had stopped. He pushed up on the boat. It wouldn't budge. It was stuck to the ice. He called out to Lila. She heard him.

Finally, they broke the seal of the boat to the ice, and Ben climbed out. They hugged, but then he realized he was shivering badly. Rather than try to refill the boat, they left it all there and planned to come back when Ben had thawed out.

Death had been close, but for some reason I wasn't meant to die right then. If Lila had come any later, I might not have made it. It turns out that Lila had caught a half a dozen good-sized fish. We ate a couple that night, then created a homemade freezer in the snow. For the rest of the winter, we made sure the freezer was packed with fish. Over the next several weeks, I made a half a dozen trips over to the resort—the weather didn't give me any more trouble on those days.

The winter continued to be harsh for the next month, and then it gradually turned warm, slowly melting the snow. The relief they felt at having made it through the winter alive was overwhelming. They had learned a valuable lesson on preparation, and vowed to be ready the next year.

All winter long they read how-to books at night under lamplight, always jotting notes for things to get or to make when springtime came. Occasionally they took a break and read a novel, although Lila still found novels a little strange in the current state of the world. They also read as much as they could on childbirth. They figured the baby wouldn't arrive until mid- to late-summer, but the more they knew, the better prepared they'd be.

And through it all, the ground rumbled constantly. Not a week went by without two or three tremors.

"What do you think would happen if the earthquake hit and the dam cracked?" asked Lila one night, after a powerful tremor shook the cabin.

"We're on the 'good' side of the dam," said Ben, "so I don't think we'd have to worry about a flood. The literature says it's the highest dam in the east, which means the valley below would be flooded. I think we might lose the lake though." He smiled. "I guess we cross that dam when we come to it."

As the winter wore on, Lila's pregnancy became apparent. Ben loved to rub his hand over her belly and feel its smoothness. The daily bout with morning sickness had passed, and so far, Lila wasn't dealing with any problems. Ben attributed that to her being in excellent physical condition from the long journey.

The snow finally melted. The violent weather subsided a bit with the warmer weather, but was never completely gone. Although the tremors were constant, the "big one" had yet to hit. Spring arrived, and Ben got the garden ready for planting while Lila started many of the seedlings in the cabin.

It was mid-May when Ben decided to make another trip to Waynesville. Lila had been tired a lot and decided the trip would be too much for her. It seemed strange for Ben to make the trip without her, but they were low on a number of items, so it was necessary.

He grabbed his M-16 and his Sig, leaving the Bushmaster and his crossbow behind, gave Lila a long and passionate kiss, and told her to hold the fort while he was gone.

He took one of the boats—they had accumulated two more motorboats and two kayaks—and headed for the dam parking lot. The old truck started right away.

"Ah, they don't make things like they used to," he said to himself. "Of course, they don't make anything anymore."

The trip to Waynesville was uneventful at first. He stopped at his favorite hardware store and picked up a couple of axe handles—he had shattered the one he had—and walked out to the truck, throwing them in the back. He laid his M-16 on the front seat and was about to get in, when an army truck with four soldiers rumbled out of nowhere and pulled up in front of him.

Images of Sharp's fake soldiers immediately came to mind.

"Hey there," said a captain sitting in the passenger seat. "We don't see too many people these days. You out scrounging for things?"

"No," Ben was trying to play it cool until he found out their agenda. "Broke an axe handle and was getting a couple of replacements. I don't see a lot of people either."

"You live around here?" asked the captain. "You have family?"

"I do. My wife and I live a bit west of here."

"Well, we can accompany you back to your house so you can pick up your wife. You've both been drafted."

"What?"

"Drafted. You can pick up a couple of things, but we've got to move."

"I don't understand," said Ben.

"The president needs to rebuild this country, and he's going to start with Washington, DC. We're gathering up everyone we can to help with the rebuilding."

"The real president?" asked Ben.

"The one and only," answered the captain. "You didn't think he'd let himself get killed with the rest of the world, did you? He was underground when all this happened. He had a couple thousand soldiers, along with trucks, Jeeps, and even a few jets, hidden in a series of deep man-made caves. That's where we were. So now we're recruiting for the rebuilding effort."

"Wait," said Ben. "So the president knew this was going to happen?"

"Hey, I'm only a captain. How would I know what the president knew?"

But Ben thought he knew a lot more than he was letting on.

"Well," said Ben, "I'm sorry I can't help you, but I have a pregnant wife who needs me a lot more."

"How far along is she?" asked the captain.

"A little more than six months," replied Ben.

"Shit, that won't do. I'm afraid we can't use her. I've got very specific guidelines I need to follow. She doesn't fit."

"Good luck with your search," said Ben, getting into the truck.

"No, you don't understand," said the captain. "We still need you. I'm afraid your wife can't come, though. You can still gather some things and say goodbye."

"You're joking, right?" Ben loosened the Sig on his hip.

The other soldiers, sensing something was up, pointed their weapons at Ben.

"My wife needs me. We live about sixty miles from here," continued Ben. "I can't leave her."

"The needs of the country come first," said the captain. "Sixty miles is too far. I'm afraid you won't be able to get your things. It's only a six-month hitch. You'll be back in no time. Please don't make this difficult. The president sympathizes, but it's important that we rebuild this country. You know the old saying, 'the needs of the many outweigh the needs of the few.'" Ben thought the saying had come from a Star Trek movie.

He got the feeling that this soldier had long ago chosen to compromise whatever beliefs he might have had, in order to retain his command. But Ben couldn't leave Lila, and repeated that to the captain.

"Sir. We are under martial law. You have no choice but to come with us. We are under orders to shoot resisters."

For the first time in a long time, Ben didn't know what to do. He was stuck. He had to go with them, but he was determined to escape at the first opportunity.

"Can I leave her a note in the truck?"

"A quick one." The captain reached down for a pad of paper and a pen. "You've got about thirty seconds. And please leave any weapons you've got."

Ben quickly scribbled, *Have been "drafted" into the Army to rebuild Washington, DC. Wait for me. I'll be home as soon as I can escape. I love you! Ben*

He took out his Sig and his knife and set them down on the paper on the seat, then put the keys under the visor. He walked over to the Army truck.

The captain motioned to one of the men, who went over to red truck, pulled the note out, and read it to the captain.

The captain shook his head. "We could shoot you for even saying the word 'escape,' but we won't, because we need you. However, you lost your chance to leave a note. Let's go!"

The soldier crumbled up the note and let it blow away in the wind. Then he pushed Ben into the back of the truck. As they drove away, Ben couldn't help the tears from flowing.

He looked up at the sky.

"Please keep Lila safe," he pleaded quietly.

CHAPTER 22

I remember the desperation I felt that day. My heart was pounding so hard, I thought it would explode. Life was finally good. We were so happy. We had suffered so much to get to where we were. Why did we have to go through more of it? I flashed onto Phil and his version of God. No God could be so cruel. Was it really just random happenings? I couldn't let myself believe that. There had to be some purpose to it all. But what? What possible reason could explain all this?

Meanwhile, I couldn't get Lila out of my head. When I didn't show up, I could only imagine her panic. And what could she do? The truck was in Waynesville. How was she going to get there? Walk? In her condition? She would be frantic. If I couldn't escape from this, she was going to have to have the baby alone. How frightening could that be? And how dangerous? I had to get home to her.

The old familiar anger was returning. What right did these people have to disrupt my life like this? Was the president really behind all this? I could believe it. He was an asshole. He was responsible for all of the "us" versus "them" crap in the first place. Not many people had liked him after they voted him in. Now I knew why. I suddenly wanted to kill again ... starting with these four in the truck. Someone was going to pay for this.

Ben watched his truck, then Waynesville, then his life, fade into the distance. He tried one last time to plead with them.

"Please, you have to listen to me. My wife is all alone. If I'm gone, she will have to give birth by herself. She could die. Does one more person really matter? Don't you have wives ... kids?"

"Actually, no," answered the captain. "None of us do. I can sympathize with you, but in times of national and world crisis, sacrifices have to be made. I'm sure you read about it all the time in your history books in school—the sacrifices people made over the centuries to secure the freedoms we all grew up with. Problem is, you were removed from it all. It was all history. You didn't have to experience it. You grew up having no idea what sacrifice meant. Now it's real. Someday, school kids will read about me, you, your wife, and what we all gave to be able to rebuild this country."

In theory, it made sense, thought Ben. In reality, there was something whacked-out about it. He was starting to get the impression that the holocaust the world had gone through wasn't an accident. If not, why was it allowed to happen? And why should he and Lila be expected to pay the ultimate price for it?

"If you don't have wives, I'm sure there are others in your unit who do. Could I talk to someone there who might better understand?"

"I think it's you who doesn't understand," answered the captain. "None of us who were in those caves have wives—or husbands—and kids. We were picked for that reason. Sure, most of us had parents and siblings, and we're sad over losing them, but there's something about a wife or husband and children that makes people irrational, and we can't afford that. We have a mission to rebuild the government, and we have to keep our eye on the goal."

Ben was almost dizzy. Was this real? Not only did they know it was coming, they had already planned for the aftermath. President Tillman would probably declare himself president for life. He'd get what he wanted. But wasn't this how politics in this country had always been? What was best for the politician? And if you have a couple of thousand troops—the only troops—loyal to you and your cause, there was nothing to stop you from doing what you wanted. Over time, this could become an even more dangerous country than the one they left behind.

They got onto Interstate 40 and headed east. While there was some highway between Fontana Lake and Waynesville, it had been so long since Ben had traveled on a major roadway, he had forgotten just how much it looked like the end of the world. The small towns he had been in were dead, sure, but there was something different about this image. Twenty miles west of Asheville, they came across a middle-aged couple trudging along the side of the road. Ben immediately thought of George and Bunny, then thought about how long ago that was.

The truck pulled up beside them. The couple looked at them with vacant stares.

"We're drafting people for the rebuilding of Washington," said the captain. Ben noticed that his uniform gave his last name as Stokes. "You'll get regular meals and a bed in return for your work. Hop in."

Without a word, the couple climbed into the back of the truck. And then it hit Ben that for most people, this was probably a good deal. Food, a bed, and safety, all in return for doing some work. And if they bought the "patriotic sacrifice" bullshit, then it was a bonus for the soldiers—fewer people to control. Ben had to remember that he and Lila were the exception, not the norm. Most people out there were desperate and were looking for something to latch onto. That's why the "citizens" at Wells's and Sharp's camp wanted Ben and Lila to stay. They needed some sort of structure and leadership. Knowing this, Ben realized that he might not have a lot of support in any attempt to escape that he made. He'd have to be careful.

They pulled into a rest area outside Asheville and met up with three other trucks like the one he was in, as well as a gasoline tanker truck, probably used to keep the others refilled. The other search parties had about the same luck as the one headed by Captain Stokes. One truck had three new "recruits," another had one, and the third had hit the jackpot with six.

A sergeant with a clipboard climbed into the back with Ben and the couple and asked them their names and birthdates. He was all business and Ben knew it would be useless to plead his case to him.

At that point I started with the "if onlys." If only I had waited another day before coming to Waynesville ... or even a few hours. If only I had immediately taken them out. I had the M-16. But I had to forget all that. I needed to think about the situation I was in and how I was going to escape. I have to admit that beyond my panic about leaving Lila was a curiosity. What was going on? Suddenly I thought, if the universe is guiding things (which I still wasn't convinced about), maybe I was being led here for a reason. Maybe this whole rebuilding of Washington thing was going to turn dangerous for us. Maybe I had to see what was going on to be better able to deal with it in the future. If we had no knowledge of any of this and were suddenly confronted one day by the new army of America, it could turn out badly for us. With the knowledge in hand, we could plan.

The sergeant passed out some C-rations to each of them, and

they were back on the road. Ben heard Stokes tell his men that they would check out a few of the towns along the way, including Roanoke, Lynchburg, and Charlottesville, for more draftees, before arriving in Washington.

They rounded up another four in Ben's truck in Charlottesville. But that's where they had their first confrontation. They ran across two university students who refused to come—they reminded Ben of Lila and himself. They said they were perfectly happy where they were and the government was so corrupt to begin with, they couldn't in all conscience become a part of it. The soldiers tried to force them into the truck, at which point they fought back. When the male student pulled a pistol from his belt, it was all over. The soldiers shot both of them and left them lying by the side of the road.

Ben felt sick. Here were two obviously intelligent, self-sufficient people who could contribute to a society, and they were shot down for no reason. They probably fought hard after the disaster to establish what they had, only for it all to end in an instant. All of a sudden, it wasn't enough for Ben just to escape. He had to put an end to some of this madness. But how? Go against the government? His overriding concern was to get back to Lila. But if this was the direction the country was heading, they were always going to be in danger. It was all too much to think about and, exhausted, he finally fell asleep in a corner of the truck.

He woke up to the feel of the truck slowing down. He yawned and stood up to stretch his back. They were in Washington. It was awful. He was used to seeing people reduced to hair and bones, but there were so many all around him. Fires had consumed much of the city, and as they drove through the poor areas of Washington, not a structure remained. They approached the mall area, where more buildings were standing, but the eight months since the disaster had left their mark. Rats were everywhere and the violent storms had flooded many of the buildings.

Ben could see the Capitol and the White House, both still intact, and a tent city had been established on the vast expanse of the mall. The soldiers' tents were at one end, and the draftees' tents were at the other. There were fewer draftees than Ben would have thought, based on the number of tents. They pulled up to a staging area and were told to line up in front of a table, where a sergeant once again took their names and dates of birth. They were then moved to another tent and given pillows, blankets, and a bag of personal items. Ben thought back to the stories Lila told him of her experience at the "citizens" camp. This was similar, except that it was more tightly run. A nice surprise was the lack of fencing around the mall. They weren't prisoners ... sort of. Ben knew that most of the draftees were happy to be there. For those like Ben, it was a different story.

"All you men are in tent 14," began the sergeant, when he had gathered all of the new draftees together. "You women will be in number 7. For right now, your job will be to collect all of the remains you find and put them in the wagon that will accompany you. At the end of the day, all of the remains will be burned. For now, we're cleaning up a three block radius of the mall, of the Capitol Building, of the White House, and of the major monuments. That's a lot of area. And that includes all of the buildings, as well. We don't have a lot of you—just sixty-seven at the moment—but we hope that number will increase soon."

"You have a lot of soldiers here," said Ben. "Are they helping?"

"They have other jobs." He looked at Ben, then down at his sheet. "You're Ben Jordan, right? I hope we're not going to have any trouble with you. I see you gave the captain a hard time. If you behave yourself, you can be part of the rebuilding of America. If you don't, you won't like the consequences."

"You won't have any trouble from me," replied Ben, knowing full well that his first act would be to try to escape.

A soldier led them to their tent. It was pretty bare bones, holding eight cots and nothing else. It housed all of the men from the trucks in Ben's convoy. He threw his blanket down on one of the cots and turned to find three filthy guys about his age standing in a semi-circle around him. He thought they had been in one of the other trucks.

"You're Ben, right?" asked one of them.

"I am."

"You don't recognize us, do you?"

"I'm sorry, I don't."

"You and your bitch robbed us of our weapons one night. You remember that?"

The three guys on the path to the reverend's camp that he and Lila had scared away. He remembered.

"You left us defenseless," said one of the others. "We were just trying to scrounge some food."

"You were going to rob them of everything they had," replied Ben. "We could have killed you, but we chose not to."

"We almost died because of you. We ran across a group of convicts. We had to hide like fucking women."

"Consider yourself lucky," said Ben. "They would have killed you if you'd tried to stand up to them. They all had M-16s. You would've been dead. That's twice we saved you."

"How do you know that about them?"

"Because we hunted them down and killed every last one of

them," answered Ben.

It stopped them for the moment. But only for a moment.

"You don't have any guns with you now. Wonder how tough you are without your guns and your bitch to back you up."

He was right. It occurred to Ben that all of his fighting had come from behind the trigger of a gun. At least Lila had used her knife on someone. He had filled out since the trip began, and he had muscles from a winter of chopping wood, but he had never been in a fist fight. He knew they were going to beat him, so his only recourse was to get in the first blows.

He kicked the first guy in the groin. He went down like a rock. He quickly lashed out with the same leg and got the second guy on the side of his knee. He screamed out in pain. However, by then the third one was on top of him, pounding him with his fists. Ben was trapped. Now the first two were helping.

"Break it up in here!" Two soldiers came running into the tent and pulled the three off Ben. "Shit! You're a mess," said the soldier. "What happened here?"

"This guy went ape shit and started pounding on us," said the first one, clutching his groin.

"Not true," mumbled Ben. He could feel the blood welling up in his mouth.

"Is that what happened?" asked the soldier to the other four draftees. They took one look at the three and all nodded their heads.

The guards pulled Ben up. He had trouble standing.

"We were warned to keep an eye on you. Okay, grab your things. You're moving to a new tent." They waited as he slowly followed. One of the three tripped him as he went by, and he sprawled on the grass floor of the tent. They laughed. The guards pulled him up and pushed him out the door.

I had been there less than an hour, and already I was in trouble. Running into those three had ruined my plans. I was going to be the "perfect" worker until I found the right moment to escape. Now, I had already been labeled a troublemaker and was going to the "special" tent. That would make escape a lot harder, and that much longer to get back to Lila.

They brought Ben over to a tent that had two guards out front.

"This is the tent for troublemakers," said the soldier, and pushed Ben inside.

Three of the eight beds were taken. Ben put his stuff down on an empty one and sat down. His face was really hurting. He felt his teeth. None were missing, but a couple seemed loose.

"Ben? Omigod, it's you."

Ben looked up to see Dan and Gordon staring down at him.

CHAPTER 23

"I can't believe you're here," said Dan. "What happened to you?"

"Most recently? An encounter with three people who are going to regret it," he answered. His face really hurt, and it was difficult to talk. Gordon came over with a towel to wipe away some of the blood.

As simply as he could, he told them about Lila being pregnant, their new home, and then being yanked away from his life by the soldiers. Dan followed with their story, about being approached by the soldiers to help rebuild Washington. They were at a point in their lives where it seemed to be a good idea. They also liked that there was some sort of real government in place. The thought of rebuilding the country felt like a worthy cause.

"So why are you in the troublemakers' tent?" asked Ben.

"I'm going out to the bathroom," Gordon said suddenly, and left the tent. Ben saw a guard accompany him to an area containing about a hundred port-o-potties.

"Did I say something wrong?" asked Ben.

"He just didn't want to be here when I explained it," said Dan.

"It didn't work out like we thought. I never liked President Tillman, but I was willing to put my political opposition to him aside if it would help the country come back together. Almost immediately we started hearing stories from the soldiers. Some of them are really good people. It's easy to lump them all in together, because there certainly are some bad ones, but there are others who actually have a head on their shoulders and some sensitivity. I thought you should know that. They also have a commander they are loyal to, Colonel Jeffries. He seems to be a decent sort."

He continued. "Anyway, we started to get the idea that this catastrophe wasn't some terrorist thing or accidental explosion, but that there was some planning behind it. Obviously, the plan didn't work and we were left with this horror show. But I began to realize that the president had seen this, or something like it, as a possibility, and had made plans."

"Yeah," put in Ben. "I realized that same thing in the truck talking to the captain who 'drafted'—Ben made quotation marks in the air—me."

"Yeah, well," continued Dan. "We lost our patriotism pretty fast when we heard that. I'll tell you what else we heard a bit later. At that point, we were ready to leave, but of course, they wouldn't let us. We figured we'd make a run for it when the time was right. That time never came. Melissa, Gordon's wife, was put to work serving food to the workers, which is exactly what she had to do at the camp you saved us from, so I imagine she was having some flashbacks. And then some idiot soldier put his hands on her. Nobody really knows why. He said it was all innocent, but I guess we'll never know. Her experience at the other camp had a profound negative effect on her. So she freaked and started throwing things and overturned the serving table. It might have been okay and they might have been able to calm her down until she picked up a knife and went after the soldier who touched her. They shot her. Right there, in front of everyone. We hadn't come back yet from our work, so we didn't see it, but Gordon arrived back to find his wife dead. He went crazy, and I'm afraid I kind of lost it too. So here we are, troublemakers."

Gordon came back and stopped in the doorway. Dan nodded to him and he entered the tent. Ben got up and gave him a hug.

"I'm so sorry," he said.

"Thank you. This whole experience, from the moment of that terrible day, has been hell. To be unable to do anything when my wife was being violated at the other camp, then to not be here for her when they shot her down like a rabid animal, it's just all too much. And then to find out that our president is probably responsible for the deaths of billions of people, and responsible for my life being hell, I ... I ... just don't know."

He sat down on the bed and began sobbing. Dan and Ben put their arms around him to comfort him.

"What a girl," came a voice from the other side of the room.

"What?" asked Ben.

"He should learn how to take it like a man. Look at him. Crying like a woman." The speaker was a man in his forties, a real hard case, with pale, almost yellowish skin that suggested a lot of time behind bars.

Dan held back an angry Gordon.

"Shut up, Jake," Dan yelled.

Ben stood up and walked over to the pale man.

"Long ago, I reached my limit with assholes like you. I've lost count of the people I've killed. Every single one of them deserved it. The last batch was a group of a half a dozen convicts just like you."

"Was that you?" asked Dan. "We kind of figured. The story going up and down the trail was that they found two bodies." Ben could tell that Dan was trying to add emphasis to the story Ben was telling Jake. It was working. A change had come over the man's face. It went from bravado to wariness in a matter of seconds.

Ben turned to Dan. "Well, me and Lila." At the mention of Lila's name, Jake put it together. The wariness turned to fear. "No one will ever find the other four," continued Ben. "Not unless they like the deep woods."

He said to Jake, "So, you have a choice. You can apologize to Gordon, or you can find yourself on my hit list. It's up to you."

Jake considered his options. He called over to Gordon. "Hey man, I'm sorry. I didn't mean anything by it."

"Good choice," Ben said quietly, as he passed by Jake.

Ben needed that. The beating he had taken by the three hoods in the other tent had shaken his confidence. If he was going to get out of there, he needed all the courage he could muster.

Ben walked over to Dan and Gordon. Looking over his shoulder at Jake, he said to them quietly, "We'll talk later."

At that, Jake hopped off his bunk and came over to Ben. "Look man," he said. "I'm sorry about the comment. If you're planning a way to get out of here, I want to help. I want out of here as much as you do. You can count on me. Seriously."

"You expect me to believe that?"

"Look at me. I'm an ex-con in the tent for troublemakers. I can't even take a piss without a guard looking over my shoulder. You think I want to stay here?"

"Why are you here?"

"I punched out some army sergeant. He was hassling me."

Ben looked at Dan.

"I saw it happen," said Dan. "It looked legit to me. I don't think he's a plant in here."

"Okay," sighed Ben. "I guess I'll have to trust you. Don't cross me, though."

"No way. So what's the plan?"

"How can I have a plan? I don't even know the routine yet. As anxious as I am to get out of here and back to Lila, I need to have time to figure it all out." He looked at Dan and Gordon. "What were you planning?"

Dan answered. "Before everything fell apart, we were just hoping to sneak away while working one day. That was before they transferred Melissa to the kitchen. We lost our chance then. Now it's hard because we have the guards on us all the time."

A guard stuck his head in the tent and told them that it was supper time. They followed him over to the mess tent. It was a large open tent with dozens of tables. Because there was such a small number of draftees, many of the tables were empty. The soldiers had their own mess tent further down the mall. They got their food and sat at a table designated by the guard, away from the other draftees. Ben saw the three who had beat him. They looked at him and snickered.

Ben said to Dan in a low voice, "So you were going to tell me some other things you found out."

Dan looked around. The guard was far enough away to have a conversation.

"The whole thing stinks," he began. "Okay, so this is how I heard it. This thing—the bomb, or whatever—was developed with the full knowledge of the president and his inner circle of whackos. They planned to use it on China. They felt that China was the biggest threat to us. Hell, everybody hated us. Who really knows who the biggest threat was. Anyway, the way it was explained to me was that they were going to shoot it or drop it over China and detonate it. Something like that. I don't really know the details. They figured that it would take out most of China—electricity and people. If it got a little of Russia too, no big deal. Then they were going to place the blame on some other country—probably Pakistan, or someplace like that—and it would divert the attention and hatred of the world onto another country. Then America would come offering help and President Tillman would be hailed as a savior. Of course, if he had presented it to Congress, he and his crew would have been laughed out of office, so they had to circumvent the legal channels, which they did. The problem was, it was much more powerful than they thought, and for whatever reason, it impacted the entire earth. The guards I talked to have no idea why, and I doubt if the president even does. But he must have suspected it was possible that something could go wrong because he planned for the possibility of disaster. Under his secret orders, the army had been culling out these soldiers for a year. They didn't know what they were being asked to do, only that it was important."

"Who exactly is the government right now?" asked Ben.

"To the best of my knowledge," replied Dan, "it's just the president. I know he's got a couple of staff members and three or four secret service agents. From what I hear, he almost didn't make it to the shelter. Minutes to spare is what I heard. Some of his White House cronies were right behind him and didn't make it. But the Joint Chiefs of Staff, the Congress, everybody ... they are all dead. So it's really only the president. I guess next in line would be Colonel Jeffries."

He continued with his story. "So now the word out there is that the president is bummed that more people didn't survive. He's hoping that by rebuilding Washington, it will attract whoever is left and he can have his own little nation again, with him as benevolent dictator. They are trying to figure out how to get power going in the city. For now, they've brought in hundreds of gasoline-powered generators."

"So," summed up Ben. "In a nutshell, this crazy-ass president destroyed the world and killed my family and everyone else's families just to look good?"

"Uh, I guess you could say that."

Ben just stared into space. He knew what he had to do.

There's an old saying that goes something like: "Revenge is a dish best served cold." Maybe it's not an old saying at all. Maybe that came from a Star Trek movie too. Whatever. The point is, I never understood it. It never made sense to me. Suddenly it did. I didn't care anymore about the three stooges who beat me up. Somewhere down the line someone else would take care of them. Not me. They weren't worth my time. President Tillman, on the other hand, was worth my fullest attention. My cold, calculating attention. I was planning to assassinate the President of the United States! Put like that, it seemed almost obscene, but when put in perspective, I was just eliminating another piece of garbage. It was no different from killing Tank and his crew, or even the convicts. I don't know how many people the convicts killed, but it didn't come close to the billions of deaths this man was responsible for. I could have just found a way to escape this place and return to Lila, but then I thought of the young couple in Charlottesville. That could've been us. And I realized that it could still be us. Once Tillman had control, nobody was safe from whatever plans he had. The country was a festering wound, and I was the maggot who had to clean that wound.

But here was the big question: Suppose I did away with the president? What then? What would the consequences be? Do I put the soldiers into a panic because they are now leaderless, creating mass hysteria and more deaths? Do I take away any hope the survivors might have had for the continuation of their old way of life under an actual government? It was a shitload of responsibility to be put on the shoulders of a kid just a few years out of puberty.

The next morning they were roused from their bunks early and escorted over to the mess tent. Ben hadn't had eggs in many months, and even though these were powdered, they weren't bad.

As expected, they were assigned an area to clean up. It was gruesome work. They had shovels and would scoop the hair, bones, and ragged clothes of the dead into a waiting wagon. In all this time, he had rarely had to touch any of the corpses, and even though these were lacking skin and bodily fluids, it was somehow worse. But he did it, day after day. There was no chance to escape. The guards were always there and were smart enough to keep far enough away so Ben couldn't rush them without getting shot. The days turned into weeks. The frustration of being away from Lila at a time she needed him so badly just ate away at him.

As for his plans for President Tillman, Ben never saw the man. He stayed locked up in the White House, far away from his subjects. Dan told him that that was much of the criticism of him even before the events of that day. He had been the least accessible president in history.

Time passed by slowly. Almost two months after arriving in Washington, Ben figured Lila had given birth. Was she okay? Was his child okay? Would he ever know? Then, out of the blue, a slight hope for escape was provided. They had just come back from another mindless day of clearing out remains, when four guards entered the tent carrying handcuffs and leg shackles. They approached Ben, who was lying on his bed, and ordered him to stand up. Ben looked at Dan, Gordon, and Jake, and lifted his eyebrows. Dan shrugged back in confusion. He stood up and let them put on the irons.

"Your presence has been requested," said one of the guards sarcastically. They brought him out of the tent and put him in the front seat of a Jeep. The guards then piled in around him and the Jeep pulled out.

"Where are we going?" Ben asked. No answer was forthcoming, so he sat back and tried to figure it out himself. In a minute he knew. Up ahead were the gates of the White House. He stayed silent as they drove pass the guard house, and up to the entrance. Ben heard the humming of a couple of dozen generators powering electricity into parts of the building. He was pulled from the Jeep and escorted through the doors, where he was searched by a secret service agent. The agent, accompanied by another, took him from the soldiers and headed down a hallway to a set of double doors. They knocked, and the doors were opened by a third agent. He was ushered through, and Ben found himself in the Oval Office, looking at President Tillman sitting behind his desk.

"Put him on the couch where he can be comfortable," said the president, who got up and came around the corner of his desk. He was a squat man in his sixties, completely bald, with a perpetual pained expression on his face. He came over to Ben and shook his hand, the chains rattling as he did so. Then he went over to the opposite couch and sat down.

He looked Ben over, then said, "So, I hear you're famous. I've got to say, you don't look like much."

Ben wanted to say, you don't either, but held his tongue.

"Throughout the camp," continued the president, "I have a few people here and there who keep me updated on happenings. I must say though, that they were slow about this one. I'm told you've been here two months."

"I have."

"Don't I rate a 'sir' or a 'Mr. President'?"

"From what I hear," answered Ben, "you might rate a firing squad."

The president smiled.

"I think maybe you have wrong information."

"I know that you're responsible for the deaths of billions of people."

"You have me confused with the Pakistan government," answered the president.

"Whatever."

"I'm here to offer you your freedom, so you might want to temper your answers a bit."

Ben let him talk.

"My sources tell me that you and a woman named Lila are quite the heroes in this part of the country. Although my guess is that some of this has been exaggerated a bit," he said, looking down at a clipboard. "No matter. It's probably better this way. I take it Lila is not among us here?"

"I was not allowed to go back for her when I was kidnapped."

"Drafted."

Ben looked at him and made a face of disgust.

"Where is Lila?" asked the president. "No one seems to know."

"That's because I never said," replied Ben.

"Well, let me tell you my proposal. As you can see, my soldiers haven't been very good at picking up volunteers to help rebuild this nation. The civilian population here only numbers a bit more than 130. That's pathetic, as we know that there are a lot more out there."

Ben noticed he said "my soldiers" and not "our soldiers" or "our country's soldiers." He thought that said a lot.

"We need a recruitment drive," continued the president. "We need someone they know and trust to go where my soldiers wouldn't know to go."

"I assume you've figured out that I don't like you," said Ben. "What makes you think I'd do this for you?"

"Not for me. For your country." Realizing he wasn't putting anything over on Ben, he stopped that line of thought and got back to his subject. "You haven't seen Lila in a couple of months. She must be frantic. I can guarantee her safety. We'll send off a group of soldiers and they can pick her up where you tell them. They will bring her back here, and we will find some nice quarters for her. You can go into the hills—by yourself—and talk to people. My men will drop you off and pick you up at certain spots so you don't have to walk from here." He smiled, as if he had just told a joke. "You can come back every few weeks to see Lila, then when the weather turns cold, you can come back for the winter."

"What about my friends in my tent?"

"We will release them back into the general population, so they can have the same privileges as everyone else.

Ben desperately wanted to see Lila, but this would put her in harm's way. And even if it didn't, she would be miserable. This would be no life for her. It certainly wasn't for him.

He had no idea what this man was capable of. He couldn't even string him along. The minute he steered them in the wrong direction for Lila, they would be on to him. He was trying to think fast as to what to do. The president could see his mind racing.

"It's a sweet offer," said Tillman.

"Not sweet enough," replied Ben finally. "Let's face it, you need people, and I'm the one who can get them for you. Lila would be unhappy here. Let the two of us recruit for you. We're a pair. They know us as Ben and Lila, not just Ben. That's our world out there. That's where we're comfortable. We will spread the word of the new government and check in here from time to time."

"You're joking, right?" answered the president. "Do you think I'm stupid?" He was raising his voice. "I know your opinion of me. I knew it before you even came in here, so if you had tried to bullshit me by telling me what I wanted to hear, I would have known it. At least you were honest about that."

His face turned red as he worked himself up. "Lila was my carrot on a stick. It was the only way I would be able to control you, knowing you could see her from time to time. But I was being honest when I said it was a sweet deal for you, because it was the only way you were ever going to see her. I take back the offer." He looked at the secret service agents behind Ben. "Take him away. Make sure he doesn't go back to the camp. Take him to a cell and lock him up. He's officially an enemy of the state."

And that was it. I'd blown my only chance to see Lila. Yeah, it wouldn't have been perfect, but we would have seen each other. Who was I kidding? One look at the soldiers and she would've split for the hills. And would I have been able to recruit for him? Of course not. I could never compromise myself in that way. Unless a miracle happened, I'd never see her again.

CHAPTER 24
(Lila)

It had been two days, and Ben hadn't returned. Lila was frantic. She took one of the boats over to the dam to look for the truck. It wasn't there. She tried the other cars in the lot, hoping to find one that worked, but to no avail. Most were locked, and the couple she found keys for were too recent and wouldn't start. If she weren't pregnant, she would have walked to Waynesville. A couple of months earlier, sixty miles would have been nothing, but now it was just too taxing. She had been more tired of late than normal, and she had read in her books that there were often problems with teenage pregnancies. She needed to take it easy.

She took the boat back home to wait. The days passed. She spent hours each day sitting on the deck, listening for the sound of the outboard or the sight of Ben coming around the bend. Nothing. When she wasn't waiting, she was tending to the plants in the starter kits. Two weeks went by. She had to force herself to spend less time each day looking for Ben. It was planting time, so she focused all of her energy on the garden, recognizing the importance of its success.

At night, the loneliness would set in.

More than once I considered suicide. Early in our journey, we knew that we needed each other in order to survive, and it was an unspoken assumption between us that if one of us did die, the other would take his or her own life. That was then. So much had happened since those early days. We were now able to survive without the other. We had learned so many skills and had worked so hard to gain our strength and independence. So I could survive. But did I want to? If I weren't pregnant, I honestly don't know what I would have done. I think I would have been afraid of the whole Romeo and Juliet thing—I kill myself, then he shows up. So I probably wouldn't have ... I guess. It was moot anyway. I did have something to live for. I was going to bring a child into this screwed up world. I had confused thoughts about that, too. On one hand, I was already fiercely protective of my child—and she wasn't even born yet—and thought we could live a good life together in the wilderness. On the other hand, what kind of life would she have in the remnants of our old civilization? Maybe the best. Maybe growing up in the thick of nature would give her something I never had as a child—an understanding of her real self. She might develop the kind of spirituality that I was only now beginning to see. One that had nothing to do with religion, nothing to do with rules and laws, but had to do with your heart and your connection with something greater. Would that be such a bad life? I had been thinking of all the things she would miss. All the "things" in life. How could she miss them? She would never have them. I went from being afraid to bring a child into this world to being excited to provide the opportunity for someone to grow up with a deep passion for nature and understanding of peace. No, suicide wasn't an option.

However, it didn't make me miss Ben any less. My heart broke every evening, when the darkness set in and there was nothing left for me to do to keep busy. I cried. I cried every single night, and pleaded for Ben to come back to me. I thought of every possible reason for his disappearance, but it didn't help. I didn't know if it was better to declare him dead in my mind—but never in my heart—and try to move on, or hope that someday he would come around that bend, with the sound of the putt-putting of the outboard signaling his return. It really didn't matter. He was gone from my life and the hole was enormous. And I had no control over whether he would ever return.

Two months passed. The garden was flourishing, and as long as Lila didn't overdo it, she could take care of it. She was forever grateful to Ben for preparing the garden. She wasn't sure she would have been able to do it otherwise. The space was large, and she had it packed to the gills with every vegetable she could think of. Up until a month earlier, she had hunted. Not knowing what the effect the sound of a rifle would have on her child, she had become proficient with Ben's crossbow, and was never lacking for meat. If things got really bad, she knew she always had the jerky. She smiled when she thought of the jerky, and how proud Ben was of his find. The last month she abandoned the hunting and just fished. The lake was abundant with life, and it never took her more than a few minutes to catch a meal or two.

Meanwhile, she read constantly about childbirth and how to have a child on her own. Most of the books stressed going to a hospital, but when she could get beyond that, there was information to be had—even little things such as massaging herself daily in that area to make it more flexible to help prevent a tear when the baby came out. The last thing she wanted to be doing after the birth was stitching herself. At first she was scared of the prospect of giving birth alone, but as time went on, a stubborn determination took over, and she knew that she could do it.

It was mid-summer when she knew the time had come. She was sweeping sand out of the cabin and she felt a warmth on her leg. She looked down to discover that her water had broken. There was a puddle under her on the floor. She had already sterilized some scissors for the cutting of the cord, and had accumulated blankets and towels. She laid down in bed on her side and talked to her child, assuring her that everything would be fine. She was nervous, but not scared. She had prepared for this for a long time. She wasn't sure what more could be accomplished by having Ben there—except for the love and support. This was between her and her child. The contractions came and went, but slowly the time between each one decreased and they became more powerful. When she felt the baby was ready to come, she slid off the bed into a squatting position over a soft pile of towels. She had decided early on that this was how she was going to give birth.

The pain was intense, and she cried out, all the while trying to remember to stay calm and breath. Finally, she felt the head crowning, and then suddenly the baby squirted out. Lila managed to catch her … barely—she was right, it was a girl!—then waited for the placenta to emerge. It came in a gush, and blood was everywhere. Later, when she was cleaning it up, she thought back to how much blood she'd seen over the last ten months. This was the first that made her happy.

She leaned back against the bed with her daughter against her chest. She had wet cloths all ready to wipe the baby off, and following the directions of the books she read, cut the umbilical cord. She put her finger in the baby's mouth, who immediately began to suck. A good sign. She then put her up to her nipple. At this point Lila began to cry. But it was a happy cry. All kinds of things could have gone wrong, but they didn't. She gave a silent thank you and sat back, basking in the moment. The only sadness was that Ben wasn't there to share in it. Was Ben even alive?

When she eventually got up, she was unsteady on her feet, but made it to the bed, where she slept with her daughter. Katie. That was the name she chose. She looked up all kinds of names in the baby names book—names that had to do with nature, with peace, or significant attributes. In the end, however, she just liked the name Katie.

The next two months were frantic times. It wasn't easy being a mother. And yet, she felt lucky. She had none of the distractions of mothers before the disaster. She had no job to go to, bills to pay, groceries to shop for. She had Katie. She and Ben had found a baby pack in their search, and she would take Katie out to the garden with her to pick vegetables and to weed. The garden had turned out better than she could have hoped for, and, following instructions from books, she was able to can many of the vegetables for the winter.

Even after only two months, Katie was enormous. She ate constantly and was strong and healthy. Lila was so in love with her. She read to her all the time, and told her stories about her dad. Since Katie was so healthy, Lila debated walking to Waynesville to see if she could find some clues to Ben's disappearance, but she hesitated. If she didn't find him, the questions would still persist. And if she found his body, she didn't know what she would do. No, for now, she would concentrate her attention on Katie.

It was mid-September by her calculations, and she suddenly realized that it had been about a year since their old world had ended, and four months since Ben had rounded the corner into the main part of the lake, and out of her life.

She was sitting on the deck one day when a kayak appeared in the distance. Ben? She was shaking with the hope that he had returned. She ran into the house for the binoculars. It wasn't him. It was a man, but not Ben. She was wearing a long simple cotton skirt, which was cool in the hot summer sun. She went into the cabin and strapped her knife to her leg under the skirt, put her Sig where she could get to it quickly, and emerged back out onto the deck with her Bushmaster. Then she waited.

The kayak finally arrived and the man stepped out. He was tall, in his late twenties, and had an intelligent look about him. He waved as he got out of the boat.

"Saw your smoke and thought I'd stop by. Hope that's okay." He saw the rifle in her hands. He smiled and said, "I come in peace. Seriously though, if you'd rather I leave, I will. I don't want to make you uncomfortable."

I made the decision to let him come up. Looking back, I don't know if it was the right decision or the wrong one—I think the right one—but the need for adult contact was strong inside me. I loved being a mother, but I also needed to go beyond that. Here was my chance for some real conversation. Maybe he had news about Ben, as well.

She welcomed him into the house and asked if he was hungry. He admitted to being famished. She prepared a large salad while they made their introductions. The garden was mostly gone now, but she was still able to pick a few things. He set his backpack down—a rifle was strapped to it—and accepted a glass of water.

"I'm Peter."

"I'm Lila."

"Of the famous Ben and Lila?"

"I guess that's me."

"Where's Ben?"

"Not here at the moment," she answered, not wanting to reveal too much information.

"All those stories true?"

"Yeah, especially the ones we weren't even there for."

Peter laughed, then said, "That's the problem with a reputation."

"One we never wanted in the first place," added Lila.

She finished making the salad and they moved onto the deck. Lila's first impressions of Peter were good. He seemed genuine.

"So where are you from?" she asked.

"New York," he said. "I was in the Lincoln tunnel when it all happened. How about you?"

"Outside of Boston. Ben and I were in a walk-in freezer."

"Do you ever wonder why you survived and so many others didn't?" he asked.

"All the time. I never seem to come up with an answer though."

From inside the house came a cry from Katie. Peter looked surprised.

"A baby?"

"Yes, her name is Katie. She's two months old."

"So that's why you two dropped off the face of the earth."

"That was our goal all the time. To find someplace quiet. We were never looking for any of that other stuff to happen," explained Lila.

"Can't imagine you were. I've been lucky. I've been able to avoid trouble. I've always been into camping and backpacking, so avoiding crowds is easy for me. I've spent much of the last year in the woods. I make occasional appearances just to catch up on news, then retreat again. But as much as I like solitude, talking to someone intelligent is a real treat for me. It gets lonely sometimes. Thank you for letting me come by."

"My pleasure. I know exactly what you're saying."

"But at least you have Ben."

Tears started flowing down Lila's cheeks.

"The truth is," she began. "Ben has been missing for four months. If I didn't have Katie, I would have gone over the edge."

"What happened?"

Lila told him the story.

"And you had Katie all by yourself. No help? No support? Lila, you are an amazing woman."

She gave a sad smile. "Thank you. The worst part is that I have no idea what happened to Ben. None at all."

"If he's alive, he'll make it back to you," said Peter. "It's obvious how strong the love is between you."

"Thank you." She remembered Dan saying the same thing months earlier when she was in the camp.

They spent the rest of the afternoon talking. Lila was thrilled to have his company. Katie finally woke up, and Lila very proudly showed her off. The sun started to go down and Lila invited Peter to set up his tent, or bring his sleeping bag into the living room. He gratefully accepted. Lila made a fish dinner from a catch earlier that morning, with some potatoes from the garden. After dinner, she put Katie down and came back out to the living room, where they continued their conversation.

They talked late into the evening. Finally, Peter suggested that she go to bed, as she would have to be up early with Katie. Lila agreed and stood up.

"I'm very grateful you saw the smoke from my cabin," she said.

"Not as grateful as I am," Peter answered.

She walked over to him and gave him a hug, then went to her bedroom while he spread out blankets that Lila provided.

She lay in bed for an hour, the ache in her heart pounding away at her very being. She missed Ben so desperately. She missed his touch ... his warmth. Was he really out of her life forever? Finally, unable to sleep, she slipped out of bed and made her way into the living room, where she heard Peter's steady breathing. She knelt over him, tears running down her cheeks, watching him sleep. Suddenly, aware of her presence, he opened his eyes.

"Could you just hold me?" she whispered, her voice breaking. "That's all. I just need to be held."

Without a word, he lifted the blanket and she slid in beside him. He put his arm around her, and she broke down, sobbing and shaking. Finally, exhaustion took over, and she slept.

The next day, she was up early making them breakfast. Peter offered to stay a few days and help her with chores she had been unable to do because of Katie's birth. She happily accepted. They worked tirelessly side by side, and by the end of the day were worn out.

That night, the loneliness in her heart finally gave way to the kind of intimacy she had only ever shared with Ben.

Lila woke up the next morning in Peter's arms. Despite their exhaustion, their night had been long and beautiful, but she found herself crying.

"What's wrong," asked Peter.

"Me. That's what. I had a wonderful night with you. I so needed you with me last night. But ..."

"But you feel guilty. You feel like you've betrayed Ben."

"I did betray him."

"Lila, I'm not here to take Ben's place. I'm not the kind of person who can settle down. I need to keep moving. So if Ben makes it back—and I hope with all my heart that he does—I won't be here. But if we can have some comfort with each other in the meantime, it can only be good for us."

"But how do I deal with the guilt?"

"Let me ask you this: If you had to kill to get by, would Ben approve?"

"Of course."

"Well, sometimes you have to love to get by. You don't think Ben would approve of that?"

The fact is, he loved me so much, of course he would approve, as I would for him. I still felt guilty, but knowing that Peter had no intention of staying was somehow comforting to me. I was able to see it a bit more clearly ... two people desperate for some love, no matter how fleeting.

I was kind of happy that Peter didn't stay long for another reason. It was time—for better or for worse—to find out what happened to Ben.

CHAPTER 25

The cell was 6x10, with a bunk, a sink, and a toilet, and it had been Ben's home for the last two months. It was in the basement of the J. Edgar Hoover building, just a short walk from the mall. He basically did nothing all day. He ate in his cell, and was only taken out for exercise once a day for an hour.

I was a mess. After all we had endured, to now be sitting in a cell alone, dreaming about Lila—sick about her and what she must've been going through—I was climbing the walls. I could understand why people went insane in places like that. All I could do was think. I couldn't act. Our six months together were months of action—granted, too much action most of the time—and our moments of reflection were moments we looked forward to. Now it was all reflection. The guards did bring in a few novels for me to read, a distraction I appreciated, but it took me a few weeks before I had the attention span to tackle them.

His only saving grace was that he had befriended the guards. As Dan had said, most of them were pretty good people. The soldiers had had no idea what was happening when they were assigned to the caves. And, as Dan had also said, they all lost family members. So they were sympathetic. Over time, he found himself immersed in philosophical and political discussions with them. When the legend of Ben and Lila was discovered, the guards sought him out for the stories of his adventures. There was a lot of discussion about President Tillman, and Ben was finding that there was much resentment toward their leader.

From what I could understand, the soldiers felt he was an idiot. They were fearful of life under him. There was too much secrecy. I spent a lot of time thinking about the civilization that had disappeared, and how it seemed almost destined that the catastrophe happened. I wasn't the best read guy in the world, but some things were obvious. It was obvious that large corporations and people with money ruled the earth. Everything was done for profit. I learned from the guards that Tillman had a lot of connections with these corporations—but didn't most of the politicians in some way have those connections? Many of these were the same companies that were killing the earth. Then you get the egos involved, and it was a recipe for disaster. I think the only reason the disaster happened when it did is because we didn't have the technology for it to happen earlier. Now that it happened, Lila and I had been thinking that the earth had a second chance to live. But if Tillman was allowed to refashion the holocaust into his own vision, it would be no different from what we had already experienced. Just more of the same, without any of the good parts of our old life.

The more I thought of Tillman—and all of the politicians in Washington—the angrier I got. But I felt that there was nothing I could do. So when a possible solution was finally presented to me, how could I refuse?

The rumblings of the earth were becoming more frequent and powerful. Ben knew it was only a matter of time.

Then one day, he had a visitor. The guards escorted a tall, well-built black man in military fatigues down to his cell. He had Colonel insignias on his collar and hat.

"Ben Jordan? I'm Colonel Jeffries. Wonder if you'd mind if I come in and talk for a bit."

"Not at all," replied Ben. The man was a professional, and Ben appreciated that. Although, if he was here just to repeat Tillman's offer, Ben would send him on his way. But something told him this visit was different.

Jeffries had the guard unlock the door and lock it again after he entered. Then he asked the guards to wait outside the door at the end of the hall until he called them. That impressed Ben.

"I'm going to ask that what we talk about stays between you and me," began the colonel.

Ben looked around him. "Not too many people I can tell."

Jeffries chuckled at the comment, then turned serious. "And I apologize for that. I'm going to do what I can to get you out of here. Believe it or not, I only found out about you a couple of weeks ago. I was never consulted on this.

"Can't you just let me out?" asked Ben. "I mean, you seem to be in charge."

"I am, up to a point. But you're the president's pet project here. If I let you out, it will screw up plans that I have."

Ben waited.

"From what I hear," said Jeffries, "you and this woman Lila have the status of, well, let's say, Robin Hood. I understand you've been separated from her for about four months."

"And she was due to give birth two months ago," said Ben,

with anger in his voice. "When I got picked up, your Captain Stokes wouldn't let me go back for her."

"I apologize for his behavior. That should never have happened. Captain Stokes is a problem. But that's for another time. I will get you out of here as soon as I can. But I need to ask you a favor. As I think you know, President Tillman was responsible for this obscenity. We're taught in the military to follow our president, as the Commander-in-Chief, without question. I can no longer do so. The man was an embarrassment before this all happened, and he's only gotten worse. His only good idea was trying to rebuild Washington. We need a government. Just not his kind of government."

Ben was liking him more and more.

"You know the mood of the people. If a takeover happened, would they approve? You're the only one I can ask this of without word spreading like wildfire. President Tillman would be after my head within minutes."

Ben thought before answering.

"The things I've seen done to people over the last year have been sickening. It was one thing to have this event blow their lives to pieces, but to then have to endure the violence and madness that they've had to put up with, has many of them ready to just call it quits. I was kept apart from most of the people here, since I was labeled a troublemaker, but I didn't see happiness around me. I didn't hear sighs of relief that they were now in a safe, stable place. Lila had to endure a concentration camp-like place for a week or so. There's not a lot of difference between that and this. There are two men in the troublemaker tent—at least they were there—Dan and Gordon. They're good men. They can help."

"If you were free, would you be willing to let people know that we are trying to rebuild our government?" asked the Colonel. "People seem to listen to you, from what I hear."

"I don't plan to see a lot of people, but yes, if my word means anything to people out there, then I would do what I could."

The Colonel smiled. "I have a feeling you wouldn't need to see too many people. From what I hear, once news began to spread along the trail, that's all that would count." He stood up. "I appreciate your comments. I'll try to get you out of here as soon as I can. Now it's up to me."

He called for the guards, shook hands with Ben, and left.

This was the first good news Ben had heard in a long time.

A week later, Colonel Jeffries was back, but this time with a worried expression. Once again he was let into Ben's cell and the guards left.

He got right to it. "I need your help. I'm in a difficult position. I need to take over the presidency quickly, but I need it to not look like a coup. Most of the soldiers here are loyal to me, but they are also loyal to the office of the president. I think the president knows how I feel, and I think he's about to relieve me of my command. If that happens, all hell will break loose. The troops loyal to me will fight back. There will be other troops caught in the middle who won't understand what's going on and will naturally try to protect the president. Too many people will die. That includes innocent civilians. And if I let him relieve me of my command, this country will have no hope of ever succeeding."

He took a breath and continued. "If I try a forceful takeover, it will also result in much bloodshed. It would be a bad way for this country to begin again."

"So what do you need?"

"I need you to take out the president. Tonight. Also his new commander, a friend of yours, Captain Stokes. Now Colonel Stokes."

Ben sat back and gave a little whistle. "Why me?"

"Because you're not one of my men and from what I hear, you are very capable of performing the task."

"But I will always be labeled as the person who assassinated the president."

"If we do it right," said the Colonel, "no one will know it's you. We'll say it was an unknown assassin. As far as anyone knows, you're still in here. I just don't want it connected to me. If, for some reason, you don't make it, I will do what I can to clear your name. It's not much, but it's the best I can offer. I have about five men who know about this. They've replaced your normal guards, so I can get you out of here right now."

"How do you know I won't run?"

"I don't. I can only hope that your vision for this country is enough to convince you to stay. Come tomorrow, if you're successful, I'll have one of my men drive you wherever you want to go."

A couple of months earlier, I wanted to find a way to assassinate the president. Now it was being laid out in front of me and I was hesitating. Despite what I had been thinking, despite the fact that he was responsible for all of the sorrow of the past year, and despite the fact that I had already killed countless people, this was assassination. It had a whole different meaning to it. And he was right. There was no way I would accept the assignment and then skip. And it had nothing to do with the vision for the country. It had to do with my word. On the other hand, he was also right that if Tillman stayed in office, it could lead to even more sorrow, for decades to come. I could be on my way back to Lila the very next day. I knew that this decision could affect my life forever, one way or another.

"Okay, I'll do it."

Jeffries sighed. "Thank you."

"One request. If something happens to me, can you get word to Lila and provide her with whatever help she might need? I can tell you where she is."

"I will, and that's a promise."

He asked Ben what he needed, and called one of his men in and gave him Ben's list. Then they discussed strategy. Two hours later, the man returned with Ben's items: a pistol with a holster—a Glock this time; an M-16, a large knife that he could strap to his leg; and a small flashlight. Ben had asked for a pistol crossbow, but was told one couldn't be found, so he was presented with a second pistol, this one with a silencer attached.

"You might find this more mobile than the crossbow," explained Jeffries. "It's a Walther P22. A .22 with a silencer is about as quiet as you'll find—probably not much different from the sound of your crossbow. I suggest you take this along."

Ben thanked him and slipped it under his belt. He put on the Glock and the knife and slipped the M-16 over his back by the strap. Then they took him out a secluded exit. Jeffries shook his hand and wished him good luck.

Ben was free!

The sun was going down. Using parked cars and trees for cover in the waning light, Ben moved to a side road. Reaching the corner, he looked down the street. As expected, he saw no one. He stayed close to the buildings as he hurriedly made his way down the road. Time was of the essence. He had to get into a good position to make his move.

Jeffries had given him a little information. Tillman had three Secret Service men and about fifteen soldiers guarding him inside the building, as well as Colonel Stokes. Another ten men patrolled the grounds. Although Ben was to try to avoid killing anyone other than Tillman and Stokes, Jeffries was also an experienced enough military man to know that collateral damage was unavoidable. There were no alarms, and outside light was provided by spotlights powered by generators. Inside the building, only the offices and hallways around the oval office were lighted. Jeffries indicated that while all the outside areas were lighted, setting up generators for all of the inside had been deemed unnecessary. Too much of it was unused. So Ben knew where he was going in.

He heard voices and ducked into a store doorway. Two soldiers walked down the intersecting street, not really paying attention to anything around them. Why should they, thought Ben. Anyone who is in Washington is on the mall. He was hoping that the White House guards had the same lackadaisical attitude.

The soldiers were gone, so he continued on his way. Two months in a prison cell had sapped some of his endurance. He took a break about halfway to his destination.

I still wasn't happy about this assignment, but was quickly falling into hunter mode. I realized how much I missed the trail with Lila. The experiences were horrendous at times, but I think there was a part of me that really got into being a hunter of men. In some perverse way, it was a wonderful time of our life. And now I found myself getting back into the thrill of it. Had I always had a violent aspect of myself just waiting to come out, or was I just adapting to the world?

It was mid-evening. Ben still had no way to keep time, but it no longer mattered to him. If it was dark, it was evening. That's all he had to know. He was standing outside the wall surrounding the White House, looking at a darkened East Wing of the building. He looked around and saw two guards walking along the inner part of the wall. He waited until they had passed, then he climbed the wall, took another look, and jumped down onto the White House grounds. He hugged the wall, making sure he was alone, then sprinted across the lawn to the building. He found an accessible window and tried to smash it with the butt of his knife. It bounced off. Of course! The window had bullet-proof glass. Ben felt so stupid for not thinking of that in advance.

Now he was stuck. Which way to go? He had never been to the White House before and had no idea where the entrances were. He felt his way along the side of the building. It was much larger than he thought and it took him forever to reach the end of the wall. He poked his head around the corner, saw no guards, and made the turn, again hugging the wall. Finally, he reached an area with more activity, and realized that he was near the main entrance. Two guards were starting their rounds along the perimeter of the wall to the left, and two others to the right. He could see two guards standing in the entrance.

Ben had an idea, not one he had a lot of faith in, but what he saw as his only choice. He crouched behind some bushes and waited until the two pairs of guards along the wall were out of sight, then aimed the Walther at one of the spotlights. He pulled the trigger. The gun emitted a sound not much louder than that of the hammer striking the firing pin. There was a loud pop and glass showered the ground as the light went out. The two guards shouted and ran out to investigate. Ben shot at the next light, with the same results, then quickly made his way through the entrance while the guards were still distracted. He was going to have to hurry now before the alarm was raised.

He held onto the Walther in his right hand and pulled the flashlight from his pocket with his left. The beam was tiny, but enough for him to see by. He ran through the building, getting lost a couple of times and needing to double back. Finally, he approached an area with lights. He put away the flashlight and took off the M-16, holding it in his left hand. He slowed down and peeked around a corner before proceeding. So far, he hadn't encountered any opposition. He came across a large open area, looked around, and quickly crossed it to the other side.

"I think you can stop right there." The voice came from his left. "I figured Jeffries would try something tonight. Turn around slowly and set your weapons down."

Ben half turned, setting down the M-16. He was looking at Captain—now Colonel—Stokes.

Stokes had a surprised look on his face. "Oh, it's you ..." He died with that look as a bullet penetrated his chest.

Ben had been holding the Walther by his right leg, and Stokes had been concentrating on the M-16 in his left hand. Turning and shooting quickly, Ben took his prey completely by surprise. As Stokes was going down, Ben fired the silenced gun a second time, and Stokes's lifeless body hit the floor.

They would be ready for him now. Ben had to be extra careful. He heard the sound of running feet and ducked into a closet, keeping the door open a crack. Six guards ran by. He opened the door and looked warily around. No one. He continued on his way. Suddenly, he was in front of the Oval Office. Taking a breath, he was about to open the door when he heard the distinctive "click" of rifles. Not one, but many. He set down his weapons and raised his hands, then turned to find five soldiers pointing rifles at him.

One of them yelled, "all clear," and the door to the office opened. President Tillman came through, accompanied by the three Secret Service agents.

It was over. He had played the hero once too often. After all he'd been through, and after all of the times he had come face to face with death, only to miraculously survive, it had come down to this moment. There were no more miracles.

And then the ground moved. Violently. Ben recognized at once that it had come. This wasn't a tremor. It was the big one.

CHAPTER 26
(Lila)

Peter stayed a week. His presence was a much needed remedy for Lila's months of loneliness. He helped her prepare the garden for the winter, do repair work in the cabin, and provide conversation and comfort. By the end of the week, however, they both knew it was time for him to go. It had only been a temporary respite for them, but that was the way they wanted it. Peter was anxious to get back on the road, and Lila was needing her space. She knew that the only adult she wanted to share her life with was Ben, and if that was destined never to happen, then so be it.

Their goodbye was without tears. They hugged and expressed their appreciation for what the other had provided, and then Peter was on his way, and Lila was once again on her own.

She picked up Katie, walked onto the deck, and looked out at the lake. In the distance, she could see Peter's kayak. Someday, maybe, she'd look out there and see Ben rounding the bend of the lake and coming back to her.

I had been preparing myself for a life without Ben. But it was hard to even think about, much less plan for. I think it was as I was watching

Peter paddle away that I knew I had to put closure to Ben in some way. I had to learn what had happened to him.

It was time. It had been over two months since Katie's birth, and Lila had regained her strength. She decided to walk to Waynesville and investigate. She knew that it wasn't the smartest of moves to make a journey like that with a two-month old. It could easily take her three days to cover the sixty miles. On the other hand, it would start to get cold and she would lose her chance until spring, at which time, she would be concentrating on her garden, and still wouldn't be able to look for Ben. No, she had to do it now.

"Well, little girl," she said to Katie, "there might be a lot of traveling in your future. You may as well get an early start."

On one of their trips to Waynesville, they had picked up a nice, state-of-the-art baby carriage. Lila decided it would be perfect for the journey. Her trip had to be postponed a week though when a bout of violent weather overtook the area, and she had to hunker down and ride it out. The weather still demonstrated its fury on a regular basis, although Lila felt that the storms weren't as consistent as they had been. The tremors, however, were rumbling much more frequently. Hardly a day went by without one.

She really had no idea what she was looking for with this trip. Maybe a clue from Ben? Hopefully not his body. Just something … anything. Anything was better than not knowing. It was approaching five months without him. A lifetime. She looked down at the ring on her finger and started to cry.

"Oh Ben, I miss you so much," she said through her tears. And then the guilt of her rendezvous with Peter surfaced, and she cried even harder. She knew that it had been a therapeutic experience, but despite that, she also knew that the guilt would never leave her.

By the end of the week of rain, Lila was climbing the walls. Once she decided to go look for signs of Ben, she didn't want anything to get in her way. A week was an eternity. Finally, the weather cleared. She loaded Katie into the carriage and picked up her backpack—long since packed—and started on her way. She left a note on the table inviting any visitor to spend the night if they liked, and letting Ben know that she would be back, should he show up.

The temperature was in the mid-60s as she started on her way, at first by boat, with the carriage folded up in the stern, and then by foot.

It felt good to be back on the road. It somehow made me feel closer to Ben. All of the violence we had encountered was starting to fade, and the happy moments we had on the road took its place. I made that trip having no idea what I would find. I just knew I had to do it. I had to do something. If Ben was really gone, I had to know. I would spend the rest of my life with a gigantic hole in my heart, but how could that be any worse than what I was living through every day, not knowing?

She walked along in the middle of the road. It was such a different feeling from those early days walking along the Mass Pike. Granted, there were a lot fewer people here, so the walking would have been better even then. But when she did run across vehicles now, the people had pretty much disappeared. She thought back to the bloated bodies and the swarms of flies, just happy that Katie hadn't been alive at that point.

The day wore on. Katie had been handling the trip well, and Lila made sure she stopped often enough to feed her. That night, she set up the tent and prepared a comfortable bed for Katie. They had passed a few houses along the way, but Lila still felt a little spooked by houses. They all seemed somehow haunted.

It was the early hours of the morning when Lila woke with a start. Something was moving along the side of the tent. She heard it breathing and felt the side of the tent move when it touched it. She quietly slipped her Sig out of its holster, then grabbed the flashlight. Katie was sound asleep. Carefully, she unzipped the tent flap. Whatever it was, was still on the side of the tent. Once it was unzipped, she jumped out of the tent, turning on the flashlight. She hit the ground rolling, pointed it at the animal, and cocked her weapon. The animal jumped back in fright.

It was a dog. Actually, a puppy. It looked terrified. Lila holstered her weapon and quietly called to the puppy, being aware the whole time to watch for signs of abnormal behavior. Then she remembered Jason's comments about animals born after the disaster, and realized that the dog was probably okay. It slowly approached her. It was very thin. Lila figured it must have gotten separated from its mother and hadn't had anything to eat. She pulled a small bowl from her backpack and poured water from her canteen into it. He drank it down, so she filled it again. She pulled out a can of beef stew and put it in the bowl. It lasted seconds, as he gulped it down. After he ate, she found a couple of pieces of Ben's beef jerky and let him gnaw on it.

The next morning, the dog was still sitting outside the tent. Lila couldn't tell what kind it was. Most likely a combination of breeds, but it seemed to be predominately a lab of some kind. Lila fed Katie, packed up the tent and started on her way, with the dog trailing. She knew she had made a new friend. She named him Ralph.

Around mid-day, she saw a lone figure off in the distance,

approaching from the direction of Waynesville. She felt a momentary thrill at the thought that it might be Ben, but that quickly disappeared when she saw the gait. Even from that distance, she knew the walk was wrong. She took her rifle off of her backpack, cocked it, and laid it down crossways on the carriage. Then she loosened her Sig in its holster. It could be a perfectly harmless person. On the other hand, she had seen too many who weren't harmless.

Lila thought it must've been strange for someone walking along to see her and her carriage—a surreal image of the past, when things were normal. The traveler was youngish, probably mid-twenties, and somewhat scruffy-looking. But who wasn't scruffy these days, thought Lila. But there was something else, and it raised goosebumps all over Lila's body as he approached. He had a strange look about him. He reminded her of one of the animals they had fought off. It was the eyes. Something about the eyes...

"Hey," she said in greeting as they passed on the road.

He stopped and stared. He licked his lips as he looked Lila over.

Oh gross, she thought. And then she saw something that made her shudder. She stopped and looked back at him.

"Where'd you get that?" she asked, pointing.

He was wearing Ben's Sig. Lila would know that holster anywhere.

"None business."

Something was definitely wrong with him. His speech was halting, like all the words weren't there in his brain.

"Please, it's important. It's my husband's."

"Mine."

"No, not yours." Lila was freaked out, but also angry now.

How did he get it? "Did you take it from him? Did you see my husband?"

"Found. Can't have."

Normally, Lila would have felt sorry for him, but not now. She was consumed with the fact that he had Ben's gun. She wanted it. It would have made sense to just let him keep it and move on, but she couldn't. It was a link to her husband. She had to have it.

"I'll give you some food for it," she offered.

"Take food ... baby."

Katie was making noise in the carriage and the man was looking at her. He licked his lips again.

"Baby ... eat."

Omigod, thought Lila. He thinks of Katie as food! She picked up her rifle and pointed it at the deranged man.

"Take off the holster and let it drop. Then walk away and I won't hurt you." She had no idea if the man even understood her, but she had to say it. She had to give him a warning.

He lunged at her and she shot, catching him in the stomach. But he came on, like someone crazed on drugs. The bullet hadn't even slowed him down. She got off one more shot, not knowing if it even connected, when he was on her.

Looking back, I have no idea what his intentions were. I don't even know if he had any intentions. It was almost as if his only instinct was to attack. He reminded me of a zombie from the movies, acting only out of the most basic cravings or faint memories. Was that the kind of person he was before? If he had been a kind and gentle person, would this new version also have been kind and gentle? Or had it changed his personality, like with the animals? Lots of questions. No answers. All I knew was that his brain had been scrambled and that I was going to die. In a matter of speaking, it was Ben who saved me.

His mouth was moving, as if he was eating, and he was drooling. His body odor and breath were sickening. At that moment, Lila had her first vivid memory of the coyote attack. It was the drool that unlocked the experience she had kept repressed for so long. She cried out in anger. She was on her back, trying to fight him off, but he was heavier and stronger. His mouth was moving, and his fingers were tearing at her clothes. In the background, Lila could hear Katie crying and Ralph barking. She knew that if she died, Katie would die a horrible death right along with her.

Then she felt it. Ben's Sig. She continued to barely hold him off with her right forearm, while unlatching his holster with her left. She yanked the gun out of the holster and put the barrel up to his chest and fired. The sound of the explosion was tremendous, and the shot was powerful enough to jolt him off her. He was still alive, though, so Lila sat up and shot him again, this time through the heart. He was dead.

She got up quickly and whipped off her clothes to rid herself of his smell, his various fluids, and his presence. She pulled new clothes from her pack and dressed, before seeing to Katie. She didn't want any memory of him to be on her body when she touched her daughter. As she held Katie, she cried, the impact of the experience finally hitting her.

When she had calmed Katie—and herself—she put her daughter back in the carriage. She petted Ralph, who had been cowering near the carriage, to let him know it was alright, then she took Ben's holster from the man and pulled it out from under him. She put the gun back in, and put it in the basket under the carriage.

Finally, she was back on her way, her legs still shaking and her ears ringing.

As anxious as she was to find clues to Ben's disappearance, she decided that rushing would do no good, so she took her time. She didn't want any of her own stress to be felt by Katie. Ralph, meanwhile, had found a home. He trotted along happily at Lila's side, enjoying his new family.

The smaller road through the hills eventually led to a highway, and on the fourth day, she entered Waynesville. Knowing that Ben would have gone first to the hardware store, she headed in that direction. The town was small and Lila found the truck almost immediately. It was a weird feeling looking at the old pickup. She hadn't seen it in months, but it brought back familiar memories ... happy memories of them setting up house. There was so much of Ben connected to that truck, she felt he was right there. And yet he wasn't.

She looked in the cab and found the M-16 and the knife. That was her first clue. Maybe the Sig had been on the seat, as well. Why hadn't the zombie taken those too? Ben wouldn't have taken off his pistol and knife unless he was forced to. She spent the next several hours searching the area, but she knew she wouldn't find Ben's body, because it wasn't there. No blood either. Someone had taken him. That gave her some momentary hope. He was alive when he was in Waynesville. Where was he now? Was he still alive?

Lila found the keys to the truck under the visor. Another sign that Ben had been alive at that point. Since she was there, Lila picked up a few items she needed, including dog food, and loaded them into the truck. She found a store that had a car seat and installed it next to her. Ralph, with some help from Lila, hopped onto the seat next to Katie, and stood looking out the window.

As she figured it would, the truck started immediately. There was no sense in going any further from Waynesville, since she would have no idea where "they" might have taken Ben, so she headed home. The truck had a clutch. Ben had tried to show her how to use it, but she had only partly mastered it. The truck jerked a lot in the beginning, but she eventually got the hang of it. What took her four days walking to get there, took her two hours to get home. At one point, she passed the zombie lying in the road, her pile of clothes nearby.

She got to the dam and parked in the parking lot, just as the ground started to shake. It was violent. It wasn't just a tremor. Lila knew Nick's prediction was coming true. Ralph yelped and dove under the seat, and Katie started screaming. There was a tremendous noise, and she looked over to see the resort buildings collapsing. And then it hit her. The dam! Would it hold?

CHAPTER 27

The building came down around them. Ben saw one of the soldiers crushed under a falling beam. The sounds of breaking windows were like gunshots. As he dove away from a section of the ceiling crashing down, he saw Tillman push one of his Secret Service agents out of the way, so that he could stand under the door frame. The agent was instantly buried under a pile of debris.

Ben ran toward one of the broken windows and leapt out just as a major part of the ceiling collapsed. A piece caught his foot and he screamed in pain. But he was out of the building. He crawled toward the open area of the lawn, then laid there, waiting for the quake to finish it's destruction. The earthquake lasted little more than fifteen seconds, but it felt like minutes.

The city was strangely quiet. If this had happened a year earlier, it would be a cacophony of sirens, alarms, and horns. The silence after the quake was somehow comforting to Ben, as if nature had done its thing, and was now resting. He got up to his knees and looked around, finding that the silence belied the reality—what had been left of Washington was now in shambles. Whole city blocks had been leveled and fires were breaking out everywhere. He could now see the J. Edgar Hoover building from where he knelt, across the sea of collapsed structures. It was still standing.

The Washington Monument was still there, as well. Ben thought it would have been one of the first things to fall. At that moment, he thought of Lila and the dam. She was in no danger if it collapsed, but it would certainly change the landscape, and the lake would be virtually gone. Would she move? How would he ever know?

He turned back to the White House. It no longer existed. The symbol of strength and power in the world was now a pile of rubble. He stood up. His foot was killing him, but he limped over to the former building. He had to know. He crawled over the fallen walls to the approximate location of the Oval Office. The door frame that Tillman had so cowardly sought refuge under was still standing, like a lonely skeleton. President Tillman was lying at the bottom of the doorway, still alive ... barely. His right arm and right leg were crushed under tons of debris, and Ben saw a puddle of blood next to the president's body.

Tillman turned his head and looked at Ben.

"You were coming to assassinate me," he said weakly.

Ben said nothing.

"I did it with the best of intentions, you know."

"No you didn't," said Ben. "I want you to lie here with the life flowing out of you, and know that you were responsible for the extinction of most of the human race. It was a decision made from greed and ego, not with the best intentions. When your name is mentioned in the future, it will be with disgust and hatred. My family died because of you. I'm separated from my wife and child because of you. I'm going to sit here and watch you fade away into the history books."

And that's exactly what I did. He died fifteen minutes later. While he laid there choking on his own blood, I thought about what he had done. For years, so much of our focus in America and elsewhere had been on terrorism. But at what point do you become just as bad as the terrorists? In President Tillman's case, his fight against terrorism (prompted by his own self-interests) ultimately made him the most dangerous of them all.

I was relieved, though. I had killed a lot of people over the last year, but always in self-defense or in defense of another when I had no other choice. I had never assassinated anyone. As much as I wanted him dead, I was glad that I wasn't the one who ultimately did it. That was a stigma I didn't want to live with. The irony is that in the end, Tillman was killed by his own creation. Nothing could have been more appropriate.

A Jeep approached from the direction of the mall and pulled up in front of the White House. Colonel Jeffries stepped out, followed by two other officers.

Jeffries looked at the collapsed building and just shook his head in disbelief.

"The president?" he said to Ben.

"Right here," Ben replied. "He died about five minutes ago. He was killed by the earthquake. You'll find Stokes under the rubble too."

Jeffries and his men stood around him and looked down at the president. It was obvious that he was crushed to death, not assassinated. One of the officers looked at Jeffries and said, "It looks like you're now in charge, Mr. President. We'll spread the word."

"We have a lot of work ahead of us," said Jeffries. He looked at Ben. "As for you, thank you for your willingness to serve. I won't forget it. Unfortunately, I have to go back on one of my promises.

I'm afraid I can't supply you with a car and driver to take you where you need to go. I apologize, but half of our vehicles were destroyed by the quake, and my scouts have come back to tell me that most of the roads are now impassable to vehicles. But you are certainly free to go."

"Thank you," replied Ben, disappointed at yet one more delay. "If you could do me one favor, I'd appreciate it. I've hurt my foot. I don't think it's broken, but if you have someone who can tape it up, that would help."

Jeffries and his men helped Ben to the Jeep, and they drove him back to the mall.

I was astounded at the damage the quake had caused. It was a city unprepared for an earthquake. Jeffries wasn't kidding about the roads. Big gaping holes and long cracks in the pavement forced us to take a route over rubble and alternating between road and sidewalk. The scene at the mall was no better. Craters had appeared that were the size of houses. At the end of the mall where the soldiers had their camp, a couple of hundred had been swallowed up by the earth in an instant.

As they parked, Ben saw Dan and Gordon. He felt a profound sense of relief seeing them unhurt, and he introduced them to the new president. Jeffries called over a medic, who checked out Ben's foot. It wasn't broken, but it was badly sprained, and he taped it up, recommending that Ben not walk on it for a while. Ben knew that wasn't an option. He had to get back to Lila, and walking seemed to be the only way.

He was anxious to get on his way, so he quickly said his goodbyes. He no longer had his rifle or Walther, but he hadn't yet surrendered his Glock to the White House guards when the quake hit, so he still had that, as well as his knife. The medic rounded up a crutch for him to use until his foot was healed. He wasn't worried about food and water, figuring he'd be in city and suburbia for quite a while and could pick up the things he needed as he walked. He found a convenience store and located a map, and was dismayed to learn that Lila was more than 500 miles away. Walking with a crutch over a devastated landscape could take him a couple of months. He wanted to cry. Wasn't anything ever going to be easy?

He had gone only a half a dozen blocks when he hit his first obstacle ... a human obstacle.

"Hey hero, you're looking good."

Ben turned to find himself confronted by the three who had beat him in the tent. He thought of them as Moe, Larry, and Curley, of the Three Stooges. They were each holding rifles.

"I see you're real buddy buddy with our new prez," said Moe. "Wonder if he'll miss you when you suddenly disappear."

I was tired. I desperately missed my wife and a child I had never seen. I was tired of dealing with scum. Tillman was evil. Stokes, if he wasn't already evil, was fast on his way to becoming it when I killed him. And now these three idiots ... again. I just wanted to go home. Lila and I had left the violent world behind and were making a beautiful life for ourselves when I was dragged back into it. I had had enough. These three weren't even worth my attention, and yet, if I wasn't careful, I could die at their hands. What a sad and useless ending that would be.

"Guys, you don't want to do this. We could have killed you that night, but we didn't want to. It would have been a waste of human life. You didn't deserve to die that night, and I don't deserve to die today."

"You pleading for your life?" asked Moe.

"No," answered Ben. "I'm trying to make you see that we don't have much of a world left. It's up to us to turn it into something. This is not the way to do it."

"You embarrassed us out there," said Larry. "You took our weapons. We could've died. We knew that when we finally saw you again, we'd make you pay for that."

"And we don't think the beating was enough," added Curley.

"You're not killers," said Ben. "Let it pass and let's all move on."

"I don't think so," said Curley. He raised the rifle and aimed at Ben.

A shot rang out and Curley let out a cry and fell to the ground. Behind the Three Stooges was a man with a rifle. He pointed it at the others, then gestured toward Curley.

"I don't think your friend is dead. Take him and get out of here. You have about ten seconds or you'll join him."

They moved quickly, picking up their friend and supporting him by his shoulders. Without another word they carried him away. Ben approached the stranger.

"Thank you. I don't know why you helped me, but I appreciate it."

"You don't recognize me, do you?" asked the man.

Ben shook his head. "I'm sorry, but I don't."

"My name is Brian. You gave me a chance to walk away once. You told me that if you ever saw me again, you'd kill me. Hopefully, I've changed your mind."

"The four guards and the convertible," said Ben, slowly remembering the incident on his way to find Lila the first time.

"I didn't want to be with those guys," said Brian. "I just got caught up in something that I couldn't get out of. That experience changed my life. I was actually able to do some good for people after that. I'm not the same person. I kinda hoped I would see you and be able to thank you—before you shot me, that is." He smiled and stuck out his hand. Ben shook it.

"Thank you," Ben said again.

"I saw you on the mall when you first arrived. I saw what these guys did to you, but then you disappeared. When you showed back up, I wanted to approach you, but you were already on your way. Then I saw them follow you, so I decided to tag along and see what they were planning."

"Well I appreciate that. I'm heading back home. You want to join me?"

"No thanks. I've got to get back to the city. There's a lot of work to do."

"Well, Lila and I live on Fontana Lake, in North Carolina. You're welcome there anytime. And I promise not to shoot you." It was his turn to smile.

We parted ways. It was a short incident, but a meaningful one for me. It showed me that sometimes the good things we do can come back to us. Maybe that sounds trite, but the fact is, something I put into motion many months ago—my decision to let him go—suddenly saved my life today. I never totally understood why I let him go that day. It just seemed like the right thing to do. I had to stop and think about that. Why do we make certain decisions? Is there something, somewhere that is guiding us? Because it's weird how one thing seems to lead to another. And every one of our experiences made Lila and me grow in some way. So is it part of some great cosmic plan? I don't know. I still don't know to this day, but

I'm certainly putting more thought into it, and more and more I've begun to see how all of our experiences really do seem to be connected.

The cities were depressing. Much of what hadn't burned in the original disaster had burned in the quake. What hadn't burned was leveled. But he found occasional stores still standing and slowly collected the items he needed for the journey back to Fontana Lake, but it no longer generated the excitement it had when he foraged with Lila. Now it was just tedious.

Caught up in his tedium a week later, Ben almost missed it. He was on a back road, trying to avoid quake damage. If he hadn't heard the whimpering coming from some bushes, he would have walked right past. He parted the bushes to find a young black girl sitting on the ground crying. When she saw him, she backed away in fear.

"It's okay," said Ben. "I'm not going to hurt you. Honest."

She calmed down a little, but still shrunk away from him.

"Do you have parents, or anyone to take care of you?"

"My daddy," she said in a small voice.

"Where is he?"

"The men have him."

"What men?"

"The mean men."

"Can you show me where they are?"

She shook her head no, but then pointed through the bushes toward a house.

"Are they in that house?" asked Ben.

"Behind," said the girl.

"Okay, you stay here." Ben headed to the house she had pointed at, and quietly circled around to the back. He was met with a sight that—even after everything he had seen over the past year—sickened him. Standing atop a rickety wooden ladder was a black man with a noose around his neck and his hands tied behind his back. Gathered around the ladder were three white men. They were shaking the ladder and taunting the black man.

"Don't fall now," shouted one. "We don't want to hear that neck snap."

"Not sure about this ladder," said another. "Looks pretty old." He shook it extra hard.

Ben looked at the man on the ladder. There was fear, of course. Who wouldn't be afraid? But there was a dignity about him, as if he had been dealing with this sort of thing his whole life, and refused to give them the satisfaction they were looking for.

Ben lifted his Glock out of its holster and cocked it. The unmistakable sound of the slide being pushed back stopped the men cold.

"Back away from the ladder or I swear I will shoot you down where you stand."

Slowly, they moved away from the ladder and turned to face Ben.

"This ain't none of your business," said one of them, warily eyeing the gun.

"Yeah, we caught this nigger living in this house. It's not his house."

It occurred to Ben that with all of the horror he had seen since that day so long ago, none of it had been racially motivated. He had seen people spurred on by power, by anger, by need, by sex, and by desperation, but never by race.

"You guys are living in the wrong world," said Ben. "Look around you. Do you see anything that belongs to anyone? We don't own anything anymore. The only way we can survive is by cooperation. As far as we know, there's almost no one left on this planet. Why do you want to reduce that number even further? There's no place for this shit anymore. You make me sick. Now cut him down."

"Make us."

"You notice who's holding the weapon?"

"You won't use it."

And right then it hit Ben that these three would never change. Even if they let the man down, they would go after him again, and maybe this time they would hurt his daughter. And if not this man, then who else? This was a different world, and these three would never be a part of it. They would keep dragging people back into the old world, and all the ugliness that was a part of that world. No, he didn't have the patience for that.

He took two steps closer, aimed his weapon at the first man, and shot him in the head. He turned the weapon on the second man and repeated the action. The third man was so stunned by Ben's actions, he couldn't even move. Ben shot him.

There, now I knew what it felt like to assassinate someone. They weren't a direct threat to me, and I could have freed the man on the ladder without killing them. But I chose not to. There was no remorse. None whatsoever. I did it without feeling a thing. And I was okay about it.

He climbed the ladder and cut the rope binding the man's hands. The man removed the noose and climbed down. He held out his hand and Ben shook it. The man's daughter had come out of her hiding place at the sound of the shots, and ran over and hugged her father.

"You just reduced our meager population by three," said the man, with a slight smile. Ben figured him for a college professor.

"No. They were just taking up space." And then he told them about the efforts in Washington. "It's a good man leading the rebuilding, and he could use other good men. It's not easy walking, but it's a place you might want to consider."

The man thanked him for the information and after shaking hands again, Ben continued on his way.

He walked and pushed himself to walk more. Over time, his foot healed and he was able to pile on the mileage everyday. However, the earthquake had totally rearranged the land, sometimes creating fissures many miles long. Ben never knew which way to go along the fissure. Which way would be the shortest? Some days he walked thirty miles, but only gained five, because of the cracks in the earth. It was hard going. In some places, a crack had formed, then closed, pushing the earth fifty or a hundred feet in the air. This would be for as far as he could see, so his only option was to go over it. It was frustrating to make such little progress. But he pushed on, his perseverance never faltering.

Then one day, Ben walked into Waynesville and a flood of memories poured in. He was close now. He was hoping the truck was still there. He arrived at the hardware store. The truck was gone! Ben felt deflated. He hoped though that it was Lila who took it, although he doubted that she would have made the trip with a young child. Ben was doing his best to envision Lila with a child, hoping that nothing bad had happened during the birth.

Getting over the disappointment of no truck, Ben continued on his way, stepping up his pace. He wasn't going to sleep. He vowed to take short breaks and then get right back on the road. He was too close to rest now.

The road was better than most he had run across on his trip and the traveling was fast. The next day he saw a large blood stain on the road. Whoever had bled had probably died, but there was no body. Most likely animals had dragged it off and disposed of it. In the bushes, however, were the tattered remains of a t-shirt. He recognized it as Lila's. His heart was pounding and he was sweating.

"Oh, God, please let Lila be alive."

He found himself running. When he was exhausted, he would walk a ways, and then start running again.

Finally, nearly two months after leaving Washington, and over six months after leaving Lila, he reached the dam. It was still there. Washington was flattened, but the dam held. He could see cracks in it, so it might not always hold, but for now it was doing its job.

He looked in the parking lot and saw the truck. That almost surely meant Lila was alive! He made his way down to the dock and picked out a boat. Ben pulled on the outboard rope and the motor started. He cast off and slowly started his way to the cabin. Too slowly! But he just had to be patient. It wouldn't go any faster. Finally, he rounded the bend and saw the cabin in the distance. Smoke was coming from the chimney. A few moments later he saw someone come onto the deck. It was Lila, and she was holding a child!

*****

(Lila)

She was chopping wood, with Katie on the porch watching. She was having trouble with a large piece and had stopped to pry the axe blade from the log when she heard a noise. The sound of a motor ... an outboard motor. She hesitated only a second longer to make sure, then she dropped the axe, grabbed Katie, and ran through the house to the deck. She looked out across the water at a small boat with one person. Could it be? She grabbed the binoculars and focused in. It was Ben! Omigod, she thought, It really was Ben! She jumped up and down with Katie in one arm, while waving with the other. Tears were streaming down her cheeks. She ran down the stairs to the dock and waited ...

EPILOGUE

I sometimes wonder what my life would have been like if the disaster had never happened. I know it's a futile thought, because I could do that with just about anything. What if I hadn't found the courage to get the gun away from Coke? What if Lila hadn't gotten pregnant? What if I'd wiped all the maggots off my leg wound and not let them do their job? What if ...?

"What if" is really stupid. What happens, happens. We had no control over the events of that day, but we had control over our lives after it. That's what kept us alive. I look at what we have—oh yeah, Lila's pregnant again—and realize that while certain things from our old life are missed, what we've found in our new life far eclipses any of that.

We had to grow up so quickly. When I think back to the two socially awkward kids we were, and what we became, it's mind-boggling. It's too bad there had to be so much violence and heartache involved, but maybe it was the only way we were able to find the strength we needed to survive.

But we've finally found the peace we were looking for, and the beauty we see every morning when we wake up never ceases to take our breath away. I know we'll do some more traveling at some point, but it's hard to think about leaving paradise. Do we really want to venture back into the cities? Do we want to take the chance on encountering more of the negativity that we fought our way through to get here? Maybe things have settled down now that the quake is history.

Sometimes we hop in the old truck and make a trip to one of the towns on the outskirts of the national park. Ralph always accompanies us on our trips. We've found the best routes around the cracks in the earth. We always go together now. We load up on books and certain essential items, but we're careful not to bring too much of our old life back to the cabin. I think it's the fear that we'll begin to incorporate that life in with our new one. Nothing would depress us more. In fact, we are becoming so self-sufficient, our trips to town are much less frequent. Following the directions from a book, I've constructed a smokehouse in back of the cabin. It will keep our meat from spoiling and carry us through the winter.

On one of our forays into town, we ran into Nick and Jason. You could've knocked us over with a feather. We hugged and cried. Jason called it a massive coincidence, but I knew better. There are no coincidences. But it was quite a shock. We brought them back to the cabin and they stayed a month. They were heading west to see how badly the earthquakes had affected the rest of the country. They had had their own adventures since leaving us on the trail, and had seen a lot of the worst of human nature, as we did. But they also encountered numerous examples of people helping people. So it does still exist. That's encouraging. They ran across Jack in their travels. When they all discovered their shared link with us, they spent a few days together. They said that Jack is doing well. He latched onto a woman with two kids, and they seem happy. Like Nick and Jason, Jack and his new family are traveling around the country. A lot of people seem to be doing that. Maybe many of them are feeling a freedom from the old way of life. Once people get over the shock and the mourning, in its own way, it's exciting to be part of a new world. Nick and Jason promised to stop by if they come back this way. I wonder if we'll be here? We're both itching to *see the ocean again. Someday.*

Colonel Jeffries has taken over the job of rebuilding the government. Good. He seemed like a competent leader. The soldiers that are left are loyal to him, and survivors are trickling into Washington with hope. I wish him well. It won't be easy, but it's a start. I've kept my promise to Jeffries to spread the news about the "new" Washington whenever I run across someone, which isn't often. Nick and Jason have promised to carry the news, as well.

Lila opened up one night and told me of her experience with Peter. What could I say? I admit that there was more than a twinge of jealousy, but it was two lonely people in a world turned upside down. Lila thought I was dead. How could I begrudge her a little happiness in her sorrow. As hard as it was for me to picture her with another man, deep down I was grateful to him. He may have saved her. Someday, I hope he comes by so I can meet him.

When I held Katie for the first time, my legs buckled and I had to sit. It was an overload of emotions. She was more beautiful than I could have imagined. The significance of her birth was overwhelming, as well. She was one of the first children born after the disaster. This is the only world she knows. She has nothing to compare it too, whereas, the rest of us will forever be comparing—for good or bad. She will be able to do with her life what she likes, because the world has been given a clean slate ... a do-over. She will have none of the prejudices we were all raised with, and a strength that very few of us had in that life. I was so proud of Lila for everything she had gone through and the mother she had become.

Katie is growing so fast. She looks a lot more like Lila than me (thank God!), with Lila's black hair. I put her in the backpack and take her with me hunting sometimes, and have taught her to fish, sort of, but we spend most of our time playing. Ralph guards over her, and they play a lot together. We finally remembered to pick up a ball and a couple of gloves, and Lila and I play catch. It's relaxing, and we spend that time talking and laughing.

We still don't miss people, although seeing Nick and Jason was a treat. We don't miss the pettiness, the egos, the anger, the selfishness, or the neediness. Nick said that the legend of Ben and Lila has taken on a life of its own. We're now responsible for heroic actions a thousand miles from where we ever were.

Good. They can have their stories. As for us, we have the life we wanted. And it was worth it all to get here.

The End

ABOUT THE AUTHOR

Andrew Cunningham was born in England, but has spent most of his life living in the U.S.—the last 25 years on Cape Cod. A former interpreter for the deaf and long-time independent bookseller, he has been a full-time freelance writer and copy editor since 2000, publishing over 90 articles for *Cape Cod Life* and *Cape Cod and Islands Home* magazines. A 4th-degree Master Blackbelt in Tang Soo Do, he finally retired from active training when his body said, "Enough already!" Married, with two grown children—both in the military—Andrew and his wife spend much of their time travelling, and are especially fond of cruising to warm Caribbean islands (is there a cold Caribbean island?). *Eden Rising* is his first published book. He has a mystery/thriller, *Wisdom Spring*, soon to be published. He also has a series of children's books that might see the light of day sometime in the future, and is currently working on a mystery. He can be contacted at info@arcnovels.com. Please visit his website at www.arcnovels.com.

Made in the USA
Charleston, SC
11 November 2013